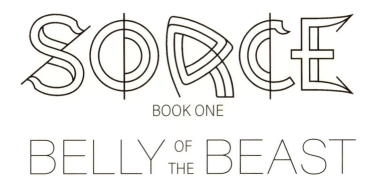

SORCE

BOOK ONE

BELLY OF THE BEAST

CHARLES ARMSTRONG

ILLUSTRATED BY KIRA NIGHT

Contents

For Sorce's original fans,

Nana & Ayumi

REAP

Amid a room full of young fauns, an elder sits with a puppet on each hand, bringing the story of a religious holiday to life. He is their educator, friend, and guardian.

Rap. Rap. A jarring knock interrupts the schoolhouse show. The old faun sets his puppets down and rises slowly. At the threshold, he slowly opens the door for a discreet chat with the school's visitors. The ensuing discussion lasts long enough that the little ones behind him lose interest.

In time, the elder steps back to fully open the door. Two robed figures with curling horns enter, each with a case in hand. These robed visitors don't seem menacing. As the elder explains to his pupils, today's the day they shall be inducted into OmniSync—a magickal connection that links the experiences of all fauns.

The robed guests have begun setting up stations from the contents of their boxes. Those who were paying attention seem excited. There's talk of how they'll soon be able to see what their brothers and sisters see. They form a line, unsolicited, that soon grows until all are queued.

A minute later, one of the visitors—the warmer, more approachable of the two—looks up and smiles. She beckons the first in line to approach.

A young child is seated and handed a device with several screens, triggers, and many rubbery nubs along its top. In every sensory way, this toy is remarkable. As the girl tinkers with her new prize, it makes delightful noises.

The other visitor proceeds to shave a small patch behind one of the child's ears. An ointment is applied. Then, without warning, the guest presses a metallic instrument against the newly shorn spot. From the instrument's tip, a deep, dull pop can be heard.

At once, the girl's eyes go wide. She looks up, and shudders. But just as she begins to wail, a colorful confectionery is laid on her tongue. One of the guests gently covers her mouth.

While the girl's chest tremors, it's clear she intends to keep the treat, that there will be no spectacular fuss. She's invited to hold onto the device as the next in line is beckoned.

This process is repeated until all of the little ones have been inducted into OmniSync.

The children are now seated in the middle of the room, new toys in hand. Amid a circus of zips, chirps, blips, and honks from their devices, a common virtual character is seen flashing about each of their screens: a beautiful, winged fairy the elder calls "the Coven's Herald." She's tall, packed with white feathers like a flower in bloom, and crowned with magnificent, golden horns.

The figure encourages and praises each child. Between their sugar highs, the delight of their new toys, and the warm approval of the winged figure, all are in a state of ecstasy.

Without announcement, the two guests disassemble their stations and step out, leaving their things momentarily behind.

They return a few minutes later with an exceptionally long, wooden crate, each gripping a handle on one of its ends. The two delicately maneuver it around the seated little ones into the center of the room. Then they prop it upright and open its top—now a door—to reveal a strange mannequin within. Not one child has paid them the slightest attention.

The ram facilitator retrieves a small vial from his case and returns to face the mannequin. He then pours the contents of the vial—a potion—into his hands and rubs them together as though cleansing them. Once done, he performs a triangular gesture with his arms and incants a spell:

"Animoto!"

Very slowly, the mannequin stirs. A rustling can be heard, prompting the spellbound children to look up. They may not have noticed before, but they are certainly seeing the figure now.

In its place, the tall, flowery fairy from their game now stands in real life. She is beaming down at the kids. Radiant joy fills the room as devices are dropped. In a state of awe, the entranced audience goes quiet. That is, all except one child.

A boy in the back is frozen with an expression of horror. He does not see this flowering, angelic entity. For him, the central figure is monstrous, dark, and unlike anything he's seen before. In place of awe, an engrossing fear immobilizes the boy. A shrill squeak escapes his mouth.

None of the other kids take notice, but his caregiver does. Quite alarmed, the elderly faun rushes over, followed in tow by the robed visitors. Something's very wrong with the boy.

The elder reaches him first. He embraces the child, then pulls back to look into his terror-stricken eyes. The visitors are rapidly approaching, zigzagging through the kids. Swiftly, the elder pulls from his vest a full vial—much like the one just used—and places it in the boy's own pocket.

Then, just as the approaching visitors descend, a blinding flash of light and an ear-splitting shriek erupt from the child's location. As this blast tears outward, it incapacitates everyone in its path. For a moment, pure white is all that can be seen, a deafening hum is all that can be heard.

As the smoke clears, the unfolding scene is one of chaos, coughing children scrambling over one another, over chairs and tables as they race to the opposite wall, fearful of whatever just caused the blast. Meanwhile, the elder remains at the epicenter, dazed as he turns circles. He's searching for something.… Nay, someone.

The boy has vanished—as have the facilitators—much to the dismay of the caregiver. At first, it's not clear what transpired, but as the unfazed fairy soon clarifies, the source of this extraordinary event was none other than the boy himself. With a look of delight, she explains in soothing tones that the boy has "ascended," that he's been accepted by the Grand Sorcerer to join him in the next plane. The blast was simply a sign of their friend's ascendance.

The front door opens. While no one saw them leave, the robed guests have just returned with their crate. They set it upright next to the winged figure. Then one of the visitors bids the fairy farewell. He encourages the kids to do the same.

A handful of frightened little ones apprehensively wave from the room's corners while the robed ram cleanses his hands with the contents of a new vial. He then repeats the triangular gesture and incants a single word:

"Inanimoto!"

As quickly as she had taken form, the fairy recedes back to her mannequin state. This time, everyone is watching.

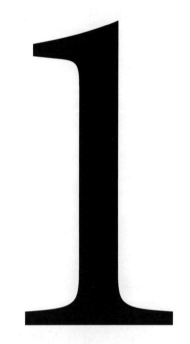

1

A MOTLEY ASSORTMENT
OF TROUBLE

Sera paused her walk to soak up the tranquil village before her. A sanguine sliver on the horizon was drawing new day from the darkness. In the fleeting moment, a slice of time free from other fauns, one could collect their thoughts. *Today's the day,* she asserted. Of course, it was hard to actually believe such a thing since she'd been repeating the same lie for months.

For any other coming-of-age faun, the dawn shift volunteering at a wild animal nursery would've quickly lost its appeal, but Sera was exceptionally motivated. She understood the death sentence awaiting babes untamed—a forced surrender to the surrounding Grimwoods—and it was this prospect that had driven her to rear all manner of rescued cubs and pups. As locals would oft comment, Sera showed a real knack for rearing feral beasts.

In fact, it wasn't until six months prior that she'd finally met her match with one particularly vexing varmint. Thanks to an aerie outlaw who had ditched his wagon of rare beasts on the outskirts of town, the nursery had inherited a motley assortment of trouble. Most notable among the aerie trader's keep was a baby deadringer —an undead, shapeshifting beast.

Deadringers were a thing of legend. Some said they were native to Mars. Others, the Underworld. "Once a deadringer finds somethin' interesting," Miss Florshem, the head of the nursery, had warned, "the beast copies it. Just don't expect it to stay that way; poor memory leads 'em to quickly decompose back into their grotesque, natural form: a decayed, boar-like thing with vestigial wings."

Miss Florshem had doubted anyone could tame such a volatile creature, one prone to spontaneous, dangerous transformations. But, after a great deal of pleading, Sera successfully negotiated a trial: three months to prove the beast could assimilate.

Early on, Sera managed to control his exposure to stimuli—which made care manageable. The real work came next: limiting his *response* to stimuli.

With a three-month reprieve long over, she knew she was on thin ice. Today, like every day, she would try to help "Pterus" maintain his true form as she exposed her true form to him. If she could prove he was capable of

not copying her, that would suffice.

Having made her way through the nursery's still-dark barn, Sera stopped at one of its stalls. On its door, a couple of bent nails suspended a metal pail and an old sheet. She grabbed a heap of dried squeeter beetles from the pail and threw the sheet over her head. Then she quietly unlatched the door, eased it open, and stepped inside.

Thanks to the low light, her bland appearance, and sedate movement, Pterus showed no interest. She shuffled forward. Then, quite deliberately, Sera dropped a dried beetle to the hay below. This the beast noticed, promptly turning to root through the dead grass until he'd found his prize.

With her reward system established, Sera slowly finessed the ragged, makeshift cloak upward. Pterus froze. It was difficult to see, but a new quiet implied she had his attention. Down plopped a second beetle to placate the boar. Thankfully, the sounds of messy eating suggested she was still on track.

Bit by painstaking bit, Sera carried on. But as her legs incrementally lost their veil, Pterus' pep and posture re-gained tense rigidity. *This isn't going to work,* she anguished. Another slow pull. Suddenly, a string of grotesque bone snaps could be heard as Pterus' natural skeletal form was supplanted by a much larger figure. The bottom half looked faun-like while the top half resembled what could only be described as a blob. The ghastly sight jarred Sera even though she'd seen it every day for months. In frustration, she whipped off the rest only to be treated to another *Pop Pop Crunch* as Pterus copied her full form.

And there it is: a second me, she observed dryly. A perfect replica gazed back, petite frame, silvery hair, and all. Sera studied her peculiar, mirrored expression. Hers was the look of a girl who gave the world everything while expecting everything in return. Of course, the world rarely showed Sera even the slightest reciprocity, which had inevitably paved the way to her current expression; a look of utter disappointment—not just with her circumstances, but with herself.

Why bother? If this beast can't be bothered, if my guild can't bother, then why in the world should I?

"Sera?" a strong voice called from outside the stall. Both Seras turned.

"Yes, Miss Florshem?"

"Hello, darlin'. I've been needin' to tell you; we're expectin' a litter of flits this mornin'. A full-term mother just delivered … so I'm sorry to say we're going to need to release your dead-ringer into the wild to make way." Sera looked wounded. *And there's my answer. How much clearer must this be? GIVE. UP.* But deep down, as was Sera's ultimate virtue and weakness, she remained defiant, determined.

"Pterus isn't tamable," the matron added. "Honestly, I don't know why we even bothered. But you did well. And he *is* strong. I think he's fierce enough to stand a real chance in the woods. I know you were thinkin' if you tamed 'im, you might keep 'im, but we're out of options." The matron studied her silent, heartbroken apprentice.

A moment later, she sighed. "Okay, let's just give 'im one more try, shall we? If he can give us any indication of progress—anything at all—well then, I won't stand between the two of you."

Sera pushed through the stall door and hugged the faun while fighting back tears of frustration. The grand lady met her with a warm embrace.

As the two reentered the stall, Miss Florshem found a spot behind a trellis in the corner. This gave her the opportunity to observe without being observed. Sera donned the sheet again and waited for Pterus to decay. Soon, he was back to his native form, ready for more training.

Over the next hour, Sera brushed off frustration and despair as Pterus repeatedly returned to the same half-faun form. Given the sheer number of beetles consumed, she'd begun to worry the next violent rupture might take place inside Pterus as his finite gut called to account his limitless appetite.

All of a sudden, the caged animals at the front of the nursery broke into a commotion of screeching and clicks. A visitor had arrived. Sera and Miss Florshem were out of time, yet they stayed put. Soon, these sounds were accompanied by squawking, whooping, and squealing as other beasts joined in. The nursery's entire keep was in an uproar as a visitor clumsily zigzagged through its many cages and

pens. Pterus, who'd just regained his native form once again, stayed put for additional treats as Sera gave their trial one last go.

A few seconds later, the loud bashing and calls of "Hello?" reached their crescendo as a metal container banged into Pterus' stall. An elder buck was struggling to maneuver a cage full of crimson birds into the stall, having apparently determined Miss Florshem's whereabouts.

Their time was up. Sera dropped the remaining beetles and threw off her disguise. Then she moped to the stall door. But just as she began to open it, a pronounced gasp pulled her attention back.

It took her a moment to understand; everything was exactly as it had been. Pterus was feverishly rooting through the hay for any remaining squeeter beetles, and Miss Florshem was still sitting behind her trellis—except that her mouth was agape.

Why? What is it?

Then the answer dawned on Sera. Pterus *hadn't* transformed. Perhaps

all of the sounds had distracted him. Perhaps the pile of scrumptious beetles had. All the same, the nursery's special swine was finally offering the anticlimactic performance Sera had always hoped for, gobbling up treats —and occasionally glancing in her direction—without changing state.

"I'd say you two passed the test!" Miss Florshem cheered from behind her cover.

Absentmindedly, Sera shut the door on their visitor and returned to Pterus. As she watched the oblivious creature, her worn-down expression, a thousand worries and curses molted away.

In the end, Miss Florshem did witness a transformation: the one that mattered most. Her apprentice, a girl who'd poured herself into a particularly grueling, nigh-impossible task, was finally able to enjoy the satisfaction that comes from hard-won success.

An hour later, Sera was still beaming with newfound pride and restored hope as she ventured back through Haveroh's sunny streets. Only now, she wasn't alone.

2

ALTERED EGO

"Okay buddy, now it's *my* turn for daily studies. Just keep quiet while you wait. I'll be back for you." Sera patted Pterus' head reassuringly, knowing full well he couldn't understand her. Then she rose up, rather riduculously, from an otherwise unremarkable thicket of shrubs.

After making their way to the bunker, she'd concealed her leashed companion in such a spot so that she could join her mother, little brother, Bram, and another family's kids in a nearby, underground study space.

The bunker wasn't much, but it served their assembly well enough. A tall, underground chamber, long-ago engineered from giant, timber retaining walls, the facility found light from a small, glass dome at its top that peaked just above the outside grass. It was inside this strange chamber that Sera's mother, acting as a governess, diligently taught the Vintallo children —and her own—the rules of science, language, arithmetic, and magick.

In magick today, they were returning to "OmniSync." Earth's planetary neighbors, the aeries, claimed the magickal network had been entrusted to them by the Grand Sorcerer to share with devout worshipers across the galaxy.

Here on Earth, OmniSync induction was a sacramental rite—one expected of children before they turned six. Like Sera, Enry (who was the eldest Vintallo kid) and his younger sister, Fay, had each been inducted. And with that distinction, each could join OmniSync anytime by incanting a simple spell:

"As above, so below."

Reciting aloud was easy; today's task wasn't. Today, they were practicing the art of silent incantations, reciting spells strictly in one's head. "Only in your mind," Mother repeated. "You *picture* the words without saying 'em."

"I am, … but it still isn't working," Enry smugly complained. The boy had been born into exceptional privilege and good looks—which, together, had begotten an infuriating sense of entitled lenience for his own bad behavior. The world bent for Enry in ways it never bent for Sera. It's not that Sera was unattractive—Mother oft noted her beauty, and she knew her words to be true—but without equal privilege, without an innate, utterly undeserved sense of superiority, Sera had never risen to Enry's ranks of expectation. And the world knew it, giving her less in return.

Patiently, the governess repeated her instruction. Sera scrutinized Enry's distant expression. *Why can't she spot his shenanigans?* Sera knew he was already in, enjoying OmniSync's vast library of fanciful games or endless catalog of live and recorded events. Eventually, Mother shifted her attention to Fay. But just as Fay was getting comfortable with the technique, Enry dragged her attention back. "Miss, why do we make sacrifices to the Sorcerer?"

Mother paused. "Well, because his Righteousness does so much for us, for everyone on Earth. But we're so minuscule compared to him. Only an act of great personal sacrifice, allowing some of our own to join him, stands to register the magnitude of our appreciation. I understand our offerings aren't easy to stomach. Believe me." Mother looked exposed, vulnerable. "Sometimes, what is right and what we're able to comprehend just aren't

aligned. It's important that you trust the wisdom of your peers, the Grand Sorcerer's will, and the natural order of magick."

Sera had always been reluctant to trust others, so for her, this exchange was too much to bear.

What if he goads her into a more candid admission? I have to intervene.

A second later, she exploded with laughter. "Oh, my god, this is gross! You have GOT to see 'Basil Butters Blows His Britches'!"

"That sounds utterly inappropriate!" Mother cried out. "Sera, you're the oldest; let's not set a bad example!"

But she was too late. In the blink of an eye, Fay had accessed the log. A moment later, she'd succumbed to its crude charm, bellowing an unrestrained, feral laugh. Begrudgingly, Enry shifted his attention, too.

The diversion proved successful. The hysterics eventually subsided, leaving a slate cleansed of any "sacrificial offering" business—except that neither Sera nor Enry had forgotten.

…

As their school day ended, Enry was careful to leave when Sera did. This

wasn't his first time trying to snag a private moment with Sera; the incorrigible boy had tried many times—a feat that would've been easy with any other girl—always to no avail. "Hey, what kind of animal you have there?" Enry was pointing at her leashed and blindfolded companion.

Sera shrugged as she walked on, the way only she could deny him. "I saw what you were doing," he continued, "your stunt to sidetrack my Grand Sorcerer questions. You know we have to get to the bottom of this sacrificial offering stuff." Enry leaned in closer than was necessary. "Do you remember that Berryweather girl, my friend a few years back? She ascended. At the time, I didn't really know what that meant. But I looked it up recently; Haveroh has contributed quite the offering to the Grand Sorcerer over the years. We're averaging something like one kid every Soliday. Just poof, you know, gone!"

Sera certainly did remember the girl. She also remembered a boy who had vanished under similar circumstances years prior. Such disappearances indeed troubled her, even when the

rest of the guild seemed little moved. Like their apathy toward defenseless babes, Haverohnians had shown, time and again, that they were all too willing to brush off matters of gravity.

Still, discussing such matters with Enry was a recipe for trouble. Unlike Sera, he lacked the tact, the will, and possibly the wit to carefully approach sensitive topics. Where Sera would plot and wait, seeking just the right moment to pull from the guild's elders answers normally bated, Enry would enter the room with arms flailing if so inspired. And somehow, whenever that room contained Sera, it was she who wound up having to make apologies. *Not today, you wily brat.*

"Did you see the Berryweather girl's ascension? Heck, have you ever seen a single sacrifice?" she retorted.

"No, but I found a discussion of 'em in an old exchange record."

"Hmm. I'm impressed," Sera lied.

"If it's true the aeries are nabbin' kids each time they visit, then I—" Better judgment would have left the remainder unsaid. "Then I think we ought to learn how to take up arms."

And there it is. "Because you're ready

to take on the aerie army?"

"I'm not afraid," Enry scoffed. Then he noticed Sera's dull expression. "I'm not! All these secrets, these rules, and traditions. It's a bunch of malarkey!"

"It's there to keep you safe," Sera countered, again not entirely believing her own words.

"Look," Enry pointed to the Grimwoods tree line to their left: a wall of foliage, trunks, and shadows. "Do you really think there are dangerous spirits lurking among the trees? You think some stupid ogre's watching us, waiting for us to edge a bit too close? Nah, they're controlling us with fear."

"I don't know what's out there," Sera confessed, "though I expect the lore's a mix of truth and lies."

Enry had lost interest in the debate. Without explanation, he turned from the road, bound for the clearing that separated Haveroh from the woods. "What are you doing?!" Sera shouted.

Everyone knew the Grimwoods was off-limits, that it was a vile and dangerous place not to be trifled with. Yet with each emboldened stride through the grassy clearing, the boy seemed to claim new confidence—and speed.

After a second, Enry's intentions were clear; he was sprinting toward the cursed thicket. "Don't be a pawn in someone else's game!" he called back. "Get out 'n see the world—"

But as Enry approached the edge of the clearing, something in the trees brought a sharp end to his arrogance. Sera witnessed in dismay and horror as a shadow between trees defied imagination by shifting outward. Like a bolt of dark lightning, a giant, shifting mass of branches hurtled across the field. Its tenebrous, twisted body was littered with the remains of prior victims. More upsetting, its cry was somehow a cacophony of screams—as though a broken chorus of tortured voices were wailing in unison.

Enry turned to Sera with terror in his eyes. As he swung around, his leg twisted unnaturally, and he tumbled. *He's not going to make it!* Sera grabbed her beast and sprinted toward the boy. *I'm sorry, Pterus. I hope you're ready to take on the Grimwoods.* As she neared Enry—and the ravenous spirit—she tore Pterus' blindfold off and dropped him to the ground.

Her beast performed as expected.

To witness the explosive burgeoning of his frame was truly a spectacle. A second later, he'd contorted to match his adversary. The real spirit's cries turned to shrieks as it faced its clone. But Sera's impostor held his ground, countering with his own fit of rage.

Sera rushed to Enry's side and thrust her head under one of his arms. The two wasted no time darting back toward the road. They'd only gained a couple of seconds' lead, but the extra distance would prove just enough. Sera and Enry ended their mad dash at the road's edge. Enry was in pain, but Sera suspected his pride had suffered the greatest injury. As she turned to take stock of the turmoil behind them, Sera found the wicked spirit recoiling back from whence it came.

After a minute lacking stimulus, Pterus started receding, too—back to his true form. While he steadily withered into the surrounding grass, Sera cautiously returned to the middle of the field. She found Pterus tending a modest leg wound, but all in all, the deadringer was okay. She picked him up and hugged him. Then she gingerly re-tied his blindfold, re-leashed him,

and guided him back to the road.

"*That's* the beast you've been taming?" Enry was utterly stunned. "Sera, I have so many questions.... Are those wings?"

"Yeah, but they don't do anything; they're vestigial. He's a 'deadringer.'"

While Enry accompanied Sera on her walk home, she filled him in on the lore of deadringers and her breakthrough with Pterus that morning. "The thing is, my parents don't even *know* about him yet. When I get home, I'm going to have to hide him —at least until I've figured out how to break the news that I've committed to taking him."

"Sera, I don't know whether I'm more impressed you managed to tame a deadringer or that you're planning on springing this surprise companion on your parents. You're supposed to be the play-it-safe, *good* girl."

"Mm. And you're supposed to play the perpetual jokester, yet here we are having a real exchange for once."

"Perpetual jokester." Enry let the sour label sizzle on his tongue.

"Listen, I know my actions today were foolish," the boy admitted. "I

knew it even before I stepped off the road. I'm not sure why I gravitate toward these stunts, these petty tricks. It's not for attention."

As they walked on in silence, the boy considered his own provocation.

After a league's walk—and as much soul-searching—he exhaled sharply. "I suppose I'm just frustrated. I feel trapped. We're surrounded by demons, many of our own making. But I can't accept such a life. I have to face these evils with open eyes. I need to know which are real. If something's coming for me, I need to know what it is. Maybe not by taunting it—that was stupid—but I refuse to idly accept a life where ancient shadows—or invented

ones—are free to stalk us."

Sera nodded in silent agreement. Guarded as she was, she could no longer shrug off Enry's words—not when they spoke to her as these did.

"I want to be honest. From here on out," he continued. "I want to see the world clearly, and I want it to see me clearly. If *I'm* the one giving chase," he turned to Sera, "I want my intentions known."

Like a chain reaction, Enry's newfound vulnerability triggered a hitherto unseen one in Sera. For the first time in as long as she could remember, the unflappable girl blushed.

"Your intentions are known."

3

FIRE FAIRIES, SPACE PIRATES, AND THE MEN O' TAUR

"Bram! ... It's dinner time!" Sera paused at the stoop to scan her yard. With each passing second, her stomach soured with contempt. Her family's grounds were in utter disarray —and had been since she'd traded volunteering as groundskeeper for her post at the animal nursery.

Sera couldn't understand why her parents lacked the will to keep up. *Surely, something must have caused this,* she often pondered. Everywhere they went, every moment of the day, her parents carried themselves with the same abandon, donning forlorn, haggard expressions. From sun-up to sun-down, they dressed shabbily, their hooves dragged, and their shoulders sagged. Inside their home, the shades were ever drawn, and beyond, their yard—the overgrown mess presently taunting her—was forever in ruin.

Sera breathed deeply, trading her home's stale air for the evening's rich summer breeze. Then she hopped off the stoop, descending into the dense vegetation in search of her brother. Past broken trellises and pails of maggot-laden rainwater, she zigzagged. Here and there, old toys and tools shimmered through the vegetation with a defiant metallic gleam or bright flourish of color.

Though Sera wasn't ready to admit it, nature, in its own chaotic way, was busy bringing new beauty to the grounds. The old trellises that had collapsed were nonetheless bearing a massive, blossoming sasquatch vine. All around, the out-of-control grass was full of fragrant wildflowers too, budding with pollen that attracted vibrant, red-and-black bramblebees. And on top of it all, a choir of flits filled the air, likely drawn by the rich ecosystem of insect life.

After a lengthy search—and a quick check-in on Pterus—Sera found Bram making a mess of a patch they might have once called a garden. He'd been difficult to spot because he was lying in the soil, with his top half hanging downward into a comically deep hole.

"So, *this* is what you've been up to?"

"I'm huntin' earfworms," he replied with absolute solemnity. Without questioning why he needed them, Sera joined in to help collect a few more. Once her brother had a proper fistful, she tousled the dirt from his wooly coat and threw the wriggling boy under one of her arms. Sera marveled at his hearty build. At four, he was already stout and tough to the bone.

Back at the stoop, Mother was waiting. "Opa's come for dinner."

It's story night! Sera's grandpa told the best stories. They weren't at all like others' dry tales; Opa's were epic, mysterious, often frightening, sometimes funny, and generally laden with just enough truth that it was hard to discern his embellishments from the real account.

Like all un-inducted fauns who reach old age, Opa was succumbing to "ruminoid deviation," which was a fancy way of saying he was taking the form of the elders. His elbows had lost considerable range of motion, his wrists had hardened, and his knuckles had formed callused pads that he sometimes used to walk as a quadruped. While his full-sized horns had dulled with age, his mind had not.

As she entered her home, Sera found Opa reared up on his hind quarters, catching up with her parents in the kitchen. Father was dryly recounting recent family happenings that end-

lessly tickled their guest. Opa squealed in delight reading Sera's latest poetry and laughed heartily as Father mentioned Bram getting his head stuck in the neighbor's fence.

At dinner, everyone squeezed in around the Skohlidon family table, a surface sized for three bodies, at best —not five. A delicious, smoky aroma filled the air as their home's biggest cauldron hung over the fire, slowly stewing spiced vegetables.

"Magnanimitus."

Father incanted the supper summoning. As was true every night before feasting, he, Mother, and Sera paid witness to a surreal phenomenon: from the middle of their table emerged a scintillating, three-dimensional projection of the Coven's crest.

In its magickal, shimmering form, accompanied by a prayer that could only be heard by the inducted, the

Coven's crest was very much the inescapable center of attention. Sera had long wondered what its diamond represented and whether the cauldron shape that wrapped it was intentionally suggestive of a crowned head.

While some unseen chorus thanked the Grand Sorcerer for the bounty before them, Sera studied the gathered faces. Father looked spellbound, as usual. Mother seemed forlorn. But Opa and Bram looked exhausted by the ritual. Bram had not yet been inducted, and Opa had long since rejected the procedure. So, for them, the weird, ten-second silence before dinner was always an annoyance.

After dinner, Opa settled by the fire with his old satchel and a topped-off ale. Sera joined him, followed, piecemeal, by the rest of the family. She ached to tell her grandfather about Pterus, about the beast's spectacular afternoon battle with a Grimwoods spirit. But she also knew that if her parents caught wind of the scary tale, no manner of assurance would sway them into letting the beast stay.

In time, Mother started filling Opa in on the latest, harrowing world news, courtesy of OmniSync. While nodding along to the second-hand broadcast, the old buck had started rummaging through his satchel. Soon, he drew forth a stitched canvas doll for Bram and a book for Sera. Ignoring Mother, he called Sera and Bram to come take their gifts. Sera reviewed hers. It was not like the books she was used to. For one thing, it had no title on its cover. For another, its pages were brittle and yellow. "What's this?" she asked.

"That's a right ol' book. It'll edify you on some things not popular these days. Back before there was immortal relics, before us fauns recanized the 'appropriateness' of great offerings, 'n long before that blasted network." Opa shot a glance at Mother who'd finally dropped her relay of the news.

Mother may not have noticed, but Father did. "Like most fiction," Father clarified, "there may be some good lessons to be learned from that book's fables, but Sera, it's important not to be confusing fiction for fact."

Opa shifted in his seat as the outrageous warning hit him like a jab before muttering: "A generation in denial is doomed to repeat its elders' mistakes."

…

As the evening bled on, Opa told splendid stories of fire fairies, space pirates, and the men o' Taur. Sera longed for adventure, to be like the brave crusaders of Opa's time—or, at least, like those of his imagination. Growing up captive to her guild's sad confines, she often found her mind inventing fantasies, worlds and ways unconcerned with Haveroh's drab existence. In Sera's guarded, imaginative core, fauns rejected the Coven, their magick, and the questionable trades being made in exchange for it.

In time, the fire dwindled. Bram moved from idly gnawing on Opa's callused knuckles to curled up with his newly-received doll by the fire. Opa stretched his legs, collected his things, and rose. "I mus' be gettin' a move on."

As he got up, he held out the old book for Sera. Unfortunately, Father had just returned to carry Bram off to bed. Jack turned to Opa with a disappointed expression and shook his hands in polite refusal. "Let's leave the stories for story time."

Opa looked wounded but he didn't argue. Instead, he returned the book to his satchel and embraced Sera in an all-enveloping hug. Then he once again muttered the last word: "I'll teach you what the book would've. Come visit." With that, he stepped out into the cold.

Sera was still standing by the fire when she noticed something peculiar. She retrieved Bram's doll from the floor and found "P.S." embroidered onto its belly. *Whose initials are those? Our familial name is "Skohlidon," but Bram's given name doesn't start with "P"—nor does any other in this family.*

Eventually, she concluded either the letter had been stitched in error or else Opa had bartered with someone in the guild for it and not noticed the monogram. *Either way, I'll ask him.*

Tenderly, she crept into the room she shared with Bram, tucked the doll under one of his chubby arms, and slipped into her own bed.

As she too drifted from consciousness, Sera's mind found its way back to a particular intrigue from the day. In a day filled with spectacle, Sera naturally returned to the boy whose inner voice echoed her own. *Where have you wandered, Enry? Are you off confronting our town's secrets? … Or, perhaps, are you listening for mine?*

SORCE

POSTSCRIPT

Who is the Grand Sorcerer?

"The Grand Sorcerer is a supreme magickal being from another plane. He is omniscient, omnipresent, and omnipotent—knowing all, being in all places, and having all power."

So why are sacrificial offerings made to him? Sera asked OmniSync, her words unspoken but just as real.

"An offering is an appropriate way to show gratitude to the Grand Sorcerer for his boundless generosity. If he accepts a soul's offering, the deferent being ascends. Given the significance of such an act, this is most likely to occur on the holiest of Earth holidays, the once-in-every-four-years 'Soliday.'"

Gratitude for what?

"The Grand Sorcerer has provided the lattice of your existence, the miracle of life itself, and the channel for your shared enjoyment of it: OmniSync."

What if no one's willing to sacrifice their soul for the Grand Sorcerer?

"Magickal gifts such as OmniSync embody his eminence. Without reciprocal endowment from the fruit of your plane, it would be impossible for the Grand Sorcerer to continue offering his divine essence to you."

If OmniSync embodies the Grand Sorcerer, does that mean you *are the Grand Sorcerer?*

… No answer was given.… *Who am I speaking with?*

… Still nothing. Sera found it odd that an all-knowing, universally-present being would go dark when posed such a simple question. She also found OmniSync's earlier answer preposterous: that an all-powerful being would need ongoing sacrifices to sustain the magick of their plane.

So, she decided to search for clues among old, obscure records that a censoring body might've overlooked, just as Enry had done. Of course, such logs are, by their very nature, not particularly easy to locate. *Let's see if Enry left me any clues: Replay the moment Enry mentioned sacrificial offerings on our walk home last week.*

Bizarrely, as she replayed the event before her mind's eyes, Sera's OmniSync-endowed hearing and sight both dulled at the moment Enry mentioned finding the relevant exchange record. It was as though she'd been abruptly submerged in murky water —a new and surreal phenomenon.

Again and again, she tried, each time experiencing the same effect. Eventually, she logged out with the requisite spell:

"Terminus."

The world in front of Sera was serenely lit in an early-hours pink hue. It was impossible to feel frustrated surrounded by such beauty. She was sitting on a ranch fence in front of her home—a structure one could reasonably call a cluster of shacks, or at best, a very modest, oddly shaped cabin. The sun had not yet risen, and she could still faintly make out the stars above.

For a moment, Sera marveled at the vast expanse. Everything she'd experienced had taken place in Haveroh, one of a near-countless number of guilds spanning Earth's lands. It tickled her to imagine Earth as just one spec of debris swirling around a white dot or to consider the Sun itself as similarly insignificant, just one in a soup of hundreds of billions.

In time, Sera's mind transited her planet's nearest neighboring spec; she wondered whether Mars could truly be Pterus' home world. In the week since she'd brought him home, she'd carefully introduced the beast to her parents. Mother and Father had been remarkably accommodating of their new cohabitant—a credit to Sera's distorted truth. Whereas he was actually exceptional in every way, she'd made him out to be nothing more than a sickly swine in need of care.

"Those are his occludo lenses," she had explained using a term she'd invented. Pterus had been outfitted with swim goggles painted black on the inside. They made it impossible for him to see anything—and thus impossible to shapeshift. She'd also wrapped his torso in bandages to hide his wings and exposed ribs.

Sera had mixed feelings about her newfound rebelliousness. Though a penchant for social craft was inescapable, she had never held much interest in dishonesty. She prized the truth more than most kids, and, considering the dishonest denial required to accept aerie religion, more highly than most adults too. But she had recently come to accept the fact that a twisted tongue was sometimes necessary just to survive a twisted existence.

"So many injuries," Mother had marveled. "It's a miracle he's alive at all. Just—just don't get too attached, Sera. It looks like he's on his way out."

With her newfound acceptance for a bent truth, Sera had had to bite the insides of her cheeks while considering Pterus as her gullible parents had. The idea that he was just a pig who'd been dealt a very bad hand was utterly ridiculous—and yet Sera's parents, who'd never known her to be anything but honest, had bought the story.

After reflecting on the experience, Sera rose from her perch atop their ranch fence and ambled to the stable. Pterus was very happy to see his friend —and to find his empty trough replenished with sasquash slop.

She adored him too. It had taken tremendous dedication to get him to accept her natural form, but the resulting bond they shared was iron-clad. On a planet full of stimulants, Sera was Pterus' only companion—one he could literally be himself around. For Sera, Pterus was a key reminder that the universe was full of splendor and secrets she hoped to one day know.

Once Pterus had sucked down his slop, Sera showered him with attention—and a handful of dried beetles for good measure. Then she patted his head, locked up the shed, and turned her attention to the road.

Were it not for Sera's direction, one could have been excused for thinking she was bound for Haveroh's animal nursery.

…

Situated at the tail end of Haveroh's Hollow, Opa's plot was separated from the rest of the guild by a thin, serpentine stream that wound its way out of the Grimwoods. Sera found her grandfather tending to his garden. "Hi, Opa! How are you?"

"My darlin'! I'm good. Nothing new, just as I like it." A soft smile resurrected weathered lines in his lively face. "And you?"

"Plenty new, just as I like it. Do you remember that deadringer I've been tending to?"

"The magickal fella?"

"Yes." Sera smiled back. "He lives with us now. Seems he's taken to me."

"I imagine a pet is one form them beasts don' take. But for you, Sera, anything's possible."

Sera's smile brightened. Opa's praise meant more to her than others' because she knew it was utterly sincere. He had long since rejected the world's strange practices, renouncing its old traditions, denouncing its new religion, and as such, freed himself of any need to mislead.

"I've also been researching Omni-Sync, offerings, and the Grand Sorcerer—or at least trying to," she confessed. "I was hoping you might have some answers for me."

Opa looked unexpectedly serious. "Perhaps it's best to find a moment of serenity first. How 'bout you take a break with a calmin' experience in OmniSync?" Sera was about to ask why when Opa placed his hand up as if to caution against inquiry. *Fine. Here we go.* She accessed a public log of a moonlit walk.

"Can you still hear me?"

For Sera, as was true of anyone immersed in an OmniSync experience, simultaneously conversing with a faun in the present world was quite difficult. Like patting your head and rubbing your stomach at the same time, dual presence required great concentration.

"Yes, I can still hear you. But I still don't *understand* you."

"This is an ol' trick I learned from some friends before they passed. When you're lost in OmniSync, you can't be found in the present—'n with the questions you're askin', that's for the best." Sera's distant expression was giving way to one of concern—a change Opa clearly noticed: "But don't you worry, this stunt ain't for me, Sera. We're doin' this for you. I'm old 'n stubborn. I don' give a swolerat's rump what some self-righteous aerie witch thinks o' me. But you have the world ahead of you—that's a mass more pliant if it don' know you're comin.'"

A mass more pliant. Even if no one else did, Sera appreciated Opa's odd eloquence. Slowly, she bowed her head in acceptance of their communion.

"So, you've come here for some answers, and you ain't worried about parsin' fact from fiction?" Opa didn't wait for a response. "For eons, us fauns have been at peace with our world, with the other beins that call Earth 'home.' It wasn't 'til a few centuries ago that we even knew about Mars' aeries. For a long time, their visits

were sporadic. Then, 'round the time *my* grandpa was a boy, they started showin' up every four years, bringin' gifts in the form o' new craft. They told us stories about the universe 'n how some mystical entity was behind it all: 'the Grand Sorcerer.' They said he had entrusted 'em to bestow his gifts on a holy day: 'Soliday.' Most folks didn't object. They was just happy for the gifts. In time, that's how our worship here was born.

"Problem is, 'round this time, some spooky stuff started happenin'. Fauns started doin' things we knew was unnatural: movin' like involuntary puppets or twistin' into pretzels when they challenged the new religion. I seen it. Wish I hadn't; hard thing to unsee. Some started speakin' up. Others just hid whenever the aeries landed. Them aeries weren't fond o' the insolence. Over the years, most of them resistant folks—many, my friends—got weeded out, ostercized not jus' by our neighbors, but by they own kin. I didn't give 'em the satisfaction though. Never got myself inducted, moved out here, 'n I stayed happy ever since. The clergy sweep my place each time they drop

down, but they have yet to discover my cellar lab—makes for a good hideaway.

"Meanwhile, the rest of the world's gone crazy, acceptin' more 'n more transgressions, like that ascendance nonsense. They're makin' our little ones—makin' them disappear." Sera couldn't see her grandfather, but his asphyxiating sorrow painted a vivid picture. Before her, his trembling nostrils were struggling to serve him, his barreled chest shaking as past offenses raged within, threatening to snuff the old buck out. "They got us acceptin' them atrocities as some self-sacrifice our kids are makin' to the Sorcerer. You show me a four-year-old, 'n I'll show you a child that don' know nothin' about swearin' away their soul to a sorcerer from—from another plane."

Sera could tell she was closer than ever to the truth. "How can everyone be okay with this? And why? Why take our kids? If the Grand Sorcerer has grievances or truly needs help, why turn to the most innocent and fragile among us? And … what do aeries have to do with the Sorcerer?"

"Our kind went along 'cause they were afraid—of consequence and the thought of losin' out on the Sorcerer's gifts. That fear helped 'em turn a blind eye. In time, it gave way to new truths, it rewired their minds. These days, I doubt they know they're in denial. But you do, my girl. You're special. You question when others don't. You look up when others look down. I don't know how I got so lucky as to have you for my granddaughter, but I'm thankful for it.

"As for them crafty usurpers, I don' know why the aeries do it. Never been much good at decipherin' motives. I suppose if anyone knew the truth, it'd be the relics—poor souls."

"Relics? I thought they were just lore. The Crimson Core is *real?*"

"You betcher britches, relics are real. But don' you go tryin' to visit 'em now, you hear?"

"Are they really immortal?"

"They are. But listen, dear, that's no group you want to visit."

Sera's mind was reeling. "Do they really live in a mineshaft in the middle of the Grimwoods? And why would you expect them to know what's really going on?"

"Sera," Opa sighed, "how much you really know about them woods?"

"I know they're as dangerous as we're led to believe."

"They're *more* dangerous than you're led to believe." Opa paused. "I want you to have answers. This trust we have is important.… But it's got to go both ways; if you're going to rely on me to tell you about the darkness, I got to count on you havin' the sense to avoid it."

Sera exhaled sharply with a terse "Terminus." It would've been easy to lie to anyone else, to placate with a promise that she would abandon her pursuit, but she couldn't lie to Opa —which meant her hush-hush history lesson had run its course.

She emerged from Omni-consciousness with an irked look that betrayed her silence. *I have sense. If I lacked it, I'd have long since accepted the world as offered. It's this sense driving my hunt for truth untold. I know you want the best; for me to see the danger plainly so I can avoid it. Well, that may've worked for you, but it doesn't work for me. I can't avoid the truth, and I refuse to hide.*

After gazing at her grandfather for a few seconds, Sera's intensity gave way

to a look of disappointment. "I wish we had more time; I need to get to the bunker for my studies." Opa nodded glumly. He knew minutes of their prized time had just evaporated, seared from Sera's visit by his good intent.

But just as she turned to leave, she pivoted back. "Actually, I do have one more question for you: Did you barter for Bram's doll? He loves it, and it doesn't make a difference. It's just—"

"It's just you saw them letters on it?"

"Well, yeah."

Once again, Opa seemed to carefully select his words. "Best you learn the answer yourself. I know you don' have any other reason to be there, but next time you're out near the ol' school-house, search for logs from 17 years ago. You'll want to listen for the name 'Theo.'"

"Who's Theo?!"

"Ain't my place to say. Just remember, you'll need to be *at* the school when you search." Then Opa reared up for a hug—a signal he wouldn't be pushed any further. Sera met him for a heartfelt embrace before turning back in the direction of town. She still had to get to the bunker for studies, but with her grandfather's mystery tantalizingly close to unraveling, she was intent on making another stop first. Sera followed the hollow's stream back into town, bound for her guild's communal schoolhouse.

THEO

*S*era reached the schoolhouse out of breath. Before her, a steady stream of parents were dropping off their children. "Roe, be a good boy today." … "Good luck on your test, Elaina." From a position opposite the drop-off, Sera returned to OmniSync. *Show me logs from this spot 17 years ago.*

In a surreal shift, the schoolhouse reappeared before Sera—only this representation was subtly different. Here, grass occupied much more of the land beneath her hooves, the sky was overcast, and a different stream of families was approaching. Sera entertained the urge to step forward. As she did so, she was treated to a matching, stepped-forward view of the preserved spacetime. She approached the front of the school.

"Watch where you're going!" The voice of an unseen faun outside of OmniSync demanded Sera's attention, reminding her that she wasn't simply navigating a log, she was also quite literally walking through space—and families—in the present. Sera muttered an apology while keeping her focus on the reprojected space before her. All around, unfamiliar parents and children were arriving. And while the experience was certainly a delight, she couldn't help but feel a bit hopeless. She had no idea what she was looking for, who she was looking for.

But just as Sera was about to call it quits and race to the bunker, a voice she recognized called out from nearby: "Have a blessed day." *That sounds like Father.* Sera spun around to find the faun before her wasn't at all the form she'd expected. This buck was considerably younger. He also wasn't the gaunt, nigh-skeletal figure she had grown up with. Sera was stunned. *What business does he have here? Is this child— Am I to believe I have an older sibling?*

Sera turned to study the child. He was about Bram's age and build, if not a bit lankier. The boy waved at his father—at *her* father—and then turned his attention to the school beyond. As he ran off, another boy raced to catch up. "Hey, Theo!"

THEO. The name shook Sera. The doll, the tip to search this place and time, Opa had wanted Sera to find out about her brother—despite what had been an extraordinary coverup on the part of her parents. *But why?*

And where's Theo today?

With a head full of questions, Sera withdrew from OmniSync. On any other day, she probably would've seen the humor in her current circumstances. She had been standing in front of a school, staring vacantly at bodies not presently there as bodies that were there tried to keep their distance. But even as she returned to the present, the bodies before Sera drew little of her attention; she couldn't get the image of Theo out of her mind.

As she made her way to the bunker, a lingering sadness and frustration born from this image simmered in her belly. She had never known Theo, but his similarities to Bram were enough to force gut-wrenching comparisons. *He existed. His life mattered. Whatever happened, our guild and my parents were able to pretend otherwise. No amount of sacrosanct rationale can make that alright.*

…

Mother was miffed when Sera finally showed up at the bunker, late from her stop at the schoolhouse, but Sera remained unapologetic. She spent much of the day fuming and plotting

how she would confront her parents. Then, with just an hour left in the school day, Mother assigned the kids a self-study block. Sera had already been eager to understand more about the location-tied log Opa had pointed her to, so she spent her time researching how OmniSync logs work.

In the course of her investigation, she learned about three log classes.

First, there were personal logs. They were the ones that could be replayed by their originators—in full fidelity—anytime, from anywhere. They could also be replayed by anyone else who visited the site of the original experience and knew the right time to search for. When accessed this way, as Sera had experienced in front of the school, they were commonly called "local logs."

Next, there were public logs: ones that had been made available to everyone, everywhere. They were the bread and butter of OmniSync, with experiences ranging from the mundane to the remarkable.

Finally, Sera strengthened her understanding of private logs—ones that'd been intentionally hidden from local access. Only the clergy could see them.

…

As their school day came to an end, Mother left with Bram, but Sera hung back. She and Enry had agreed to meet under a giant tree outside the bunker.

"Access any sort of serene scene in OmniSync," Sera advised. She waited for Enry's expression to morph from confused to distant. Then she did the same before explaining herself.

After a few minutes, Enry was up to speed on the notion of "cloaked conversations." Already, the afternoon was blowing his mind, and Sera was just getting started. Over the next hour, she filled him in on what she had learned from Opa and her visit to the schoolhouse, what she'd learned about logs, the peculiar responses she had gotten when she posed questions to OmniSync, and the dulled senses she had experienced while trying to replay their discussion.

"Seriously?" Enry's sudden quiet suggested he was already validating the claim. Sera waited. "Surreal! So what're we going to do?" Like Sera, it hadn't occurred to Enry that doing nothing was an option. This brought a slight smile to her face—one that she knew he couldn't see.

"Soliday's right around the corner," she explained. "This is the year Bram and Gordy are supposed to be inducted. I just can't take the risk. I refuse to sit by as another child is taken. I've decided to visit the relics before the festivities kick off. It sounds like they may be the only ones with a clue as to what's really happening here. I figure if I can get back in time, we can be better prepared."

"Great! That's what I was thinking. We just need a way through the Grim—"

"Um, sorry, Enry, but this has to be a solo expedition." Sera didn't really want to explain herself, but she also didn't want Enry to get the wrong idea. Secretly, she had wanted him to join. She'd already imagined Enry braving the thicket with her. But the risk was too great. "I can't be the reason you don't come back. If anything happens to me, I alone am to blame. But if anything happens to *you,* then my family—who works for yours—would also be responsible." Enry's absolute quiet invited more conciliation. "Don't worry," she added. "I'll have Pterus."

"Now you're going to tell me where I can and can't go?!"

"No, you can go wherever you want. You just can't venture to the mine *with me.* I have a lot of planning to get through this afternoon; I'm sorry I don't have time to tiptoe around your feelings." Sera's frustration from the day was now boiling over. She knew it was wrong to direct her scalding angst at Enry, but she felt out of control. "I thought I could trust you with my plan, but that doesn't mean I intend to see you wrapped up in the execution of it. I thought you would be willing to help me prepare, you know, figure out the best way of reaching the mine."

Sera took a deep breath. She and Enry were still cloaking the exchange, so they couldn't see one another. The extra distance made empathy difficult. "You're versatile in OmniSync," she added. "I figured we could make short work of this."

"Always on your terms, huh? I spend my days thinking of you, a girl who couldn't be more bored of me. But the minute you need a sounding board, we're friends."

"Enry, I don't know what we are … or what we might become, but I am coming to you because I'm *not* bored of you. Anyway, I'm going to log out now. Feel free to do the same."

A few seconds later, Sera regained local awareness. Enry had apparently beaten her to it, stealing a moment to study her, unrequited. For a fleeting second, she looked back into his wistful eyes. If she weren't careful, if she lingered too long there, the boy would come for her, to steal an afternoon or a kiss. Hurriedly, she retrieved a piece of parchment from her pocket. Then Sera closed her eyes to collect herself. "I—I made a checklist. I have most of this stuff. It's the list of spells and map of the Grimwoods I have yet to find."

Gear & Provisions

tent, sleeping bag, rope and hook, harness, list of spells, kettle, flint, oat bars, greens, map of the Grimwoods, kerosene, lantern, knife, squeeter beetles for Pterus

"We know, firsthand, that hulking spirits roam the thicket. Animals are pretty good at carving paths through underbrush, so I expect there are trails. Whatever you can find to make those trails discernible would be helpful."

Enry nodded as his focus drifted again. At once, Sera eased.

But after a couple of hours, the two accepted, in frustration, that they were facing defeat. Either the woods held nothing noteworthy or else whatever was worth noting had been concealed from view. The imagery OmniSync offered wasn't useful: no trails, clearings, or bodies of water. Nothing was discernible. And Sera had also turned up empty-handed: the only spells she'd found were so common, Bram himself could recite them. There was no need to speculate as to why.

The two had just opted for a break when Sera's mind wandered to the dense tree cover high overhead. "I've always felt secure under the protection of our ancient trees." She studied the natural canopy, imagining all it'd weathered, the thousand lives the trees had sheltered.

"A roof for the indigent," Enry noted.

Hmmm. "A veil for the vulnerable," Sera quipped.

"Wait! Hyperspectral imagery!" Enry had gone wide-eyed, as though his lips had just erupted a preposterous, cataclysmic idea. "I think I may have figured out a workaround." He sat up and turned to Sera. "Remember our studies a month ago; we learned about the electromagnetic spectrum? It spans more than just visible light. We learned about wavelengths like shortwave infrared, and microwaves. OmniSync's imagery *isn't* limited to what our eyes can see. Your mother had shown us sample images made from radio waves. My point is, whatever censoring is happening, they may have overlooked wavelengths *outside* of visible light. Different wavelengths pass through surfaces differently. I suspect it would be easy to see through the leaves of this tree,"—Enry looked up again—"well enough to distinguish a dirt patch from something more substantial like thick undergrowth.

"Let's request a view of the Grimwoods," he suggested, "except with a visible color like red replaced by microwave or shortwave infrared."

You were listening. For a second, Sera lay stunned. Then she nodded and submerged herself in OmniSync.

A moment later, still in the network, the girl sighed. "Shortwave infrared is a dead end. Nothing's standing out."

"That's okay," Enry reported back. "I started with microwaves. Just studying all these trails." Now Enry was smiling though Sera couldn't see it. "I wonder what the triangles are."

Hurriedly, Sera requested overhead imagery of the Grimwoods, specifying red be replaced by microwave. The results were staggering. There, in the middle of solid tree cover, emerged an intricate web of trails, spiraling from a clearing at the center. Just as Enry had said, there were some quite out-of-place triangles between the trails.

Sera laid her parchment in the dirt.

Better to have a map and not need it than need a map and not have it. Lacking ability to see her parchment, she did her best to scribble a copy of OmniSync's composite. It took quite a few attempts, jumping into and out of the network, but in time, Sera was able to reproduce the map.

Upon her final return to the present, she found Enry too had been studying features—hers. Shyly, she turned away, even as her mind lingered.

Tell me, Enry, are you a wolf? I hear you skulk among the logs. And here, you study your prey with silent, wanting eyes. Where's the cavalier boy spurring spectacle, chasing girls with the same blindness?

Sera turned back to Enry as her eyes continued speaking for her. *I've decided I prefer this newfound restraint. It suits you … and I think it suits me too.*

SORCE

THE GRIMWOODS

6

KNIVES AND FIRE

At home, Sera found her father finishing post-dinner cleanup. "Hey there. I figured you'd be home with your mother. You alright?"

"I um—" Sera had spent a chunk of her early afternoon preparing for the exchange, yet now that the moment was upon her, she felt rushed and ill-prepared. "I'm struggling with the fact that we are all so sheltered from the truth in the face of danger." A look of concern replaced Father's tired expression as Sera continued: "Do you ever question the magickal gifts brought to us or the price we pay for them?"

"Listen, you're a bright kid, but sometimes even the brightest among us see more in circumstances than are there."

Sera stared at her father with great intensity. "So, Theo wasn't there?"

After a moment, Jack cleared his throat, ready to fire back. But then he paused. A minute later, he tried again: "Listen, knives are real. Fire is real. But we don't let our kids handle knives and fire. Sometimes the truth is more dangerous than either. Just like parents gradually expose their kids to dangerous instruments, matters of ascension require gradual acclimation."

Theo's … "ascension." Father's words knocked the wind out of Sera. Deep down, she'd long suspected a matter of such gravity, some dark truth that could explain their broken home. She had hoped, of course, that she was wrong. Even after her visit to the old schoolhouse, Sera told herself Theo had simply run away, that he had likely taken up early studies in the Royal Guild. But now there was no room for denial. And with the crushing weight of this revelation, no room to breathe either. Sera could feel herself losing control, succumbing to the same bestial impulses she loathed in others. "So, things were going according to the gradual-reveal plan when your first-born opted to give his life to an entity neither of you had ever met?"

Father staggered, as though his daughter had just physically stabbed him. "Sera, you have *NO* idea how hard it is to cobble together a sense of normalcy in the face of factors beyond your control! Real strength isn't having the power to tackle any adversity. Real strength is having the resolve to carry forward in the face of forces you can't influence.

"Whatever you think you understand about ascendance, you don't have a clue. The Grand Sorcerer is Earth's ultimate provider. He gives us identity, he endows us with community, he sends information from the clouds, and occasionally, he allows a soul to join him there. If you look for evil in every corner, you'll find it. But ours is, and always has been, a house of love." Father's temple was throbbing in sync with Sera's racing heart as he turned to leave.

…

Sera was still sitting in the kitchen an hour later, replaying their conversation, when Mother approached. Like a haunting spirit of the Underworld, she shuffled her cadaverous body into the room. The doe's bones seemed to rattle as she clattered into a chair of her own.

Sera wasted no time confronting her mother. "You always tell me how mature I am. But if I'm as mature as you say, then why carry on with such a substantial lie? I know *you know* I could've handled the truth."

Unkempt hair matted to her face, Mother's head teetered back. "I think you're right," she croaked, "but in this case, our silence—at least mine—was more for my well-being than yours.

"I'm deeply ashamed of how we handled ourselves, burying secrets under the floorboards while seeking absolution. What sort of mother am I? How broken I must be to accept my child's ascension." Mother trembled in misery.

"Sometimes I imagine how you'd have enjoyed an older sibling, how he would have enjoyed you and Bram. Theo was such an intelligent child … like you. A sweet boy too, through and through." Clementine gave way to fresh tears as Sera swept to her side.

"One day—a day of 'divine' endowment—he just disappeared. In a flash, our baby was gone." Mother's pitiful sobs were now shredding each word into huffed syllables. "At first, we barely noticed. *No one* showed concern. Our friends merely revered his offering. The guild praised us for rearing such 'a worthy child.' And like dumb, unfeeling beasts, we accepted the change.

"But as our bedtime routines found new form, as drawings left the mantle 'n our child's beloved toys were tossed, something ugly crept into the void

SORCE

Theo had left behind: horror. Some terrible, unknown hex was peeling away." Clementine labored to breathe. "By the time we'd regained our wits, by the time the dull tinge of some foggy loss had become a heart-rending acknowledgement of our own parental failure, there was no going back." Mother threw her head forward and bawled uncontrollably.

For Sera, there was, at that moment, no matter more important than her mother's trembling body. She finally understood what had robbed her parents of their vitality, their will and joy: It was shame. "I'm so sorry, Mother. For your loss. For all of it."

Sera thrust her cheek to her mother's bosom and hugged tight. Mother had said everything she needed to. And while Sera disapproved of her parents' actions—or their lack of actions—she could at least sympathize with their belief that they'd done the right thing.

In time, Mother stood up, kissed the top of Sera's head, and left for bed. Once again left alone, Sera replayed parts of her exchange, this time with Mother, attempting to process more than she'd been able to in the moment.

For one thing, she realized Mother's chosen role of governess was likely by design as it allowed her to keep her kids close—and specifically not under the watch of the system that'd allowed her child to ascend to another plane.

But it was something else that stood out the most, something Mother had said: "I am deeply ashamed of how we handled things, burying secrets under floorboards while seeking absolution." At the time, Sera hadn't noticed, but Mother had glanced to their living room. *Peculiar.* What had seemed a mere metaphor was perhaps more.

"Decluma."

Sera used a darkness spell before creeping to the middle of the room. Very quietly, she rolled up the large twill rug that spanned its floor. Then she knelt to inspect the exposed floorboards for even the subtlest suspicious detail. That's when she found what she had been looking for: one of the floorboards was loose.

When she hooked her fingertips into opposite ends of it, the board moved as though it lacked nails to hold it down. Gingerly, she worked the board upward until it was free. Then she reached her arm down, into the rectangle of darkness, and felt dirt. *Not sure what I was expecting.* Sera swirled her arm around for confirmation.

To her great surprise, her fingers brushed past something. She could just barely touch whatever it was, but one thing was certain: the object was out of place. Sera pushed her shoulder into floor's cavity for a little extra reach. Working through her fingertips was painstaking, but after a few seconds, she managed drag the mysterious object closer. Then, with a proper grasp, she finessed it up, through the opening and into their living space.

It was an old, wooden box with a broken hinge. Inside, she found an assortment of things. At the top, there were a few drawings she surmised to have been Theo's. They were similar to Bram's, but more detailed. Beneath the drawings, Sera found a thick piece of old cloth parchment with handwriting she recognized to be Father's:

We gave you life to show you love, but love alone was not enough to hold you here on Earth with us. As below, then so above, we'll love you always, Prometheus.

...

As she finished reading, Sera realized her tears were defacing the artifact of her father's pain. *"Theo" was short for "Prometheus."* She did her best to dry the card. Beneath it, she found another surprise: a half-full vial. The bottle had a label attached.

Disenchantment Helixir
For those who seek the truth, "Beguile"

Did Mother mean for me to find this? Was it used on Theo? If so, why? Sera decided to hang onto the helixir. Her mind was racing through questions as she put everything back and resealed the tomb beneath their living room. It was still racing as she crept off to bed.

The girl's day had demanded too much. With a heavy head cratered into her pillow, Sera descended from her real-life adventure to an invented one; a terrible dream involving the Grand Sorcerer and an apocalyptic storm.

In the end, she wound up sleeping poorly and rising early. *Good riddance,* she fumed. The sooner she could shake free from guarded family secrets and bad dreams, the sooner her mind, at least, might rest.

Sera left her house once again at sunrise. Donning a loaded rucksack and guiding a goggled beast, her quite-remarkable appearance was *too* conspicuous. If she were spotted, she would surely be asked where she was headed.

So, Sera moved briskly on her way to the Grimwoods. She was bound for a particularly convenient break in the thicket—one that would serve as her point of entry.

But as she approached, she discovered the one thing she'd been fearing: a faun was waiting—surely for her. Sera froze, her heart in her throat as she considered whether to turn back, walk by, or defiantly advance.

After a few seconds, her confident inner self seized control. *I've come this far; I shan't avoid you.* Sera resumed her forward march.

A dozen paces onward, she finally recognized who she and Pterus were approaching. There, in the same field where he'd been attacked days earlier, stood Enry. He was smiling, and this time, even though he could see it, Sera was smiling back.

7

BROOK OF SHADOWS

As Sera stepped past the first few trees, her eyes adjusted to the world within. The last time she'd neared the thicket, a spirit had entered her world as a shadow out of place. This time, she was entering its dark domain like an emissary from the light.

The first thing she noticed were intense beams of sunlight punching through the canopy. Each was creating a near-blinding spotlight on the underbrush. Strangely, in this place, Sera couldn't help but feel that the light was the enemy.

While pondering the absurd notion, she spotted something else: pockets of smaller lights were also crackling up from the ground, some far away, others, much closer. Only once she had approached one of the nearby pockets did she understand what they were. "Firefleas," she explained with hushed enthusiasm. "We found one on a sick naught once. I managed to pry the one I encountered from its prey, but then it went for *my* arm instead. They deliver a nasty bite. I ended up having to slap it to death. Anyway, its light lingered on my arm for the rest of the night. That part made the lesson worthwhile."

"Slick." Enry observed as he wrestled his way deeper into the thicket. It was hard work making headway through underbrush, but given the sort of monsters the kids knew to be lurking, both were motivated to find a trail as soon as possible.

After ten minutes of scrapes, bites, and pricks from all manner of nasty flora and fauna, the group reached their target: a spot that should have hosted one of the hidden trails. What they found instead was a stream. "I think this *is* the trail we were planning to follow," Sera remarked. Their new path wasn't as nice as she had hoped, but it was easier to venture through than the underbrush. With fewer hazards, the kids wasted no time picking up the pace. But with Pterus' top speed still holding them back, Enry picked him up as well.

The next hour's jog drained what little energy the kids had left. As they tired, their pace slowed, eventually spurring a break.

In time, Sera reignited conversation. "The helixir I found—it doesn't specify whether its effect is the temporary or permanent sort. A world stripped of enchantments will be cool, but what if it's permanent? That almost sounds like its own form of disability. I mean, there will surely be times when I just need to see the world the way others do, enchanted as it may be."

"I never thought about it like that, but listen,"—Enry lowered his voice and leaned close—"we may have an issue: I think we're being followed. Pterus keeps looking in that direction." Enry motioned to the left with his head. "And just now, I'm pretty sure I heard it too." Indeed, despite his goggles and Enry's restraining hold, Pterus was focused intently on something at the edge of the brook.

Sera stopped to study the area. She scanned the bank, its muddy edge, and the dense vegetation beyond. Nothing immediately stood out, but she was sure Enry and Pterus were right. "You're a fool if you think we can't see you!" she shouted. Then she leaned close to Enry to explain herself. "If something's tracking us, it has more restraint than an angry spirit would." Sera lifted her head to shout again. "You think you're sneaky, but we have enhanced vision," she bluffed.

"I can plainly see you."

Sera endured a tense second waiting. A second second. A third. Then, very slowly, something in the brush started moving. A concealed being was choosing to be seen, revealing a reserved strength in its slow, measured response. It was a real-life aerie. This wasn't the first time Sera had encountered one of her Martian neighbors —she'd seen them, on occasion, at Soliday celebrations—but they were most definitely a rare sight to behold.

The ram maintained a dry—if not marginally annoyed—expression as he slowly rose and stepped forward. "I wasn't hiding—not from you two."

"Whatever. You were *creeping* in the shadows," Sera quipped. "State your purpose."

The aerie continued his approach, bending to fit his large, curling horns under branches. The kids stood fast. Only after he'd stepped out, into the brook's edge, did he respond. "You have to understand, it's rare for me to encounter others here—'n young ones at that. You lost? What's your story?

"What's *your* story?" Sera shot back. "Where are *you* headed?"

"Right," the aerie sighed. "Let's start over. My name's Willy. Well, that's what my friends call me. My real name's Wilford. I got left behind last Soliday. Seems many folks in your village still don' take kindly to aeries. Bein' solo, I thought it best to hide where most o' your kind ain't likely to venture."

"You seriously thought the spirits in these woods would make for better company?" Enry scoffed.

"They aren't so scary once you know how to exploit their weakness."

Sera studied Wilford. He was tall, much taller than any adult faun. He was thin. His dull brown hair was matted in many spots, while in others, patches seemed to be missing. And though he had already emerged from the low-lying branches, his head had remained cowered. "Well, excuse us for the less-than-cordial welcome, *Wilford*, but we've been raised not to engage strangers, let alone *aerie* strangers, and certainly not aerie strangers who stalk from the shadows. It's fine you chose not to approach us, but now please be on your way and leave us to ours."

"Sure, but uh, aren't you afraid o' the kindread spirits?"

"The *what?*" Enry asked. Behind him, Sera shook her head. *Come on, Enry.*

"That's just what we call 'em. You know, them wicked, branchy things that storm through the woods. I heard you say you have enhanced vision. Whatever you have, I don't expect it will be much use when you come up against a kindread spirit. They're too fast to anticipate, and they ain't hiding any secrets your 'enhanced vision' can help with." Wilford had gestured air quotes for "enhanced vision" as if the term were clearly fabricated. "Kindread spirits have only one weakness. But don't mind me. Do as you please. I have no business with you."

Sera was cautious not to lower her guard. "So, what are you suggesting?"

"I ain't suggestin' nothin'. My existence here is simple—'n I'd prefer to keep it that way. In a few days, my kind are returnin' for Soliday. When they do, I'll be hoppin' a ride home." Sera could feel her defensive shell softening. "I don't exactly know what you're tryin' to accomplish—'n I ain't particularly sure I wanna know. But if you wanna avoid bein' consumed by a spirit, I'd think about makin' some

changes. 'N if you were to seek some pointers, I'd think about bein' more cordial-like."

Sera kept her eyes on the aerie. "Give us a minute, please." Wilford raised his hands dismissively before turning back toward the thicket. Sera leaned in close to Enry again. "I'm not sure we can trust him."

"True, but he clearly knows how to get along in here. What if we have a rule that he has to run out ahead of us —you know, so that we can keep an eye on him?"

"Wouldn't hurt to ask," Sera offered.

"Okay," she projected, "we would appreciate some pointers—but seeing as we don't know you, we'd need to ask you to jog out front. Just being safe, you know. You be up for that?"

Wilford stopped, turned back, and offered an ugly smile. "Alright then."

…

Wilford proved his value early on by showing the kids a better way to follow the brook. By jogging through its shallow waters—rather than its muddy edges—they actually made less noise and were able to move faster. The ram ran a few paces ahead, still

close enough to be heard as they advanced upstream.

"You mentioned kindred spirits having a weakness," Enry prompted. "What's that?"

"Fire. But you have to go about it real careful-like. I set traps for 'em. Them 'n the relics. Nobody has my back, you know, so I been doin' what I can to survive. If I hear a thunderous racket, first thing I do is make my way to the nearest pit (I've dug a bunch out here). Then I secure my net over it, throw a bunch o' dried leaves overtop, 'n start makin' a whole lot o' noise from an overhead perch. If I'm lucky, my pursuer falls in, becomin' my bait. When that happens, I pour fuel down 'n wait for their squealin' to attract others. It's just a waitin' game at that point." Wilford paused to hack phlegm from his throat.

"Once my bait's lured other beasts, I toss in a lit torch, 'n … WHOOM!" Wilford craned his head back again to flash a gross, proud smile, "I've taken down six kindread spirits that way. Only one relic, 'n when that happened, it was 'cause I had help. A kindread spirit ripped my relic to bits before thrashin' its way out o' the trap. Should 'ave seen that thing though. HOO BOY, it screamed off into the forest like a ter-nado o' fire!"

Enry laughed. "Assuming relics have ghastly, gaunt heads, I think I've encountered that particular spirit. The head of your ripped-apart relic was still tangled in the spirit as it chased me."

Enry and Wilford may have found humor in the stories, but Sera was disgusted. "What makes relics so bad? I've heard they're super-old fauns, but that doesn't make them evil. Not sure why they'd be out to get you or anyone else."

"Oh, they're quite vicious," Wilford explained. "I'd say they're worse than the spirits. At least with them spirits, you're dealin' with a simple, predictable foe. Relics are demented—yes, likely 'cause they've been around for so long.

"You see, a couple hundred years ago, they were minin' the land alongside an aerie fleet to find 'n destroy the prophesied Yantra."

"What's a Yantra?" Enry interrupted.

For a moment, Wilford stared as though surprised by the boy's question. "The Grand Sorcer's Yantra is an

unholy object—the most unholy item ever to exist, in fact; it possesses the power to end the Grand Sorcerer."

"I sure hope there's no such thing as an 'Enry Yantra,'" the boy teased.

"'An Enry Yantra,'" Wilford repeated the preposterous term with a chortle.

"As I was sayin', the Royal Coven were convinced it was buried here, in the middle o' these very woods. Them relics—who, back then were just normal fauns—never found the Yantra o' course, but they *did* steal an immortality helixir from the Coven. So, the Coven just left 'em to rot in the mine. 'N with each passing year in solitude, they discovered new depths o' madness. Their bodies too," Wilford added, "they jus' keep gettin' bigger 'n uglier. These days, they call themselves 'the Crimson Core' or some nonsense."

"Aren't the Coven immortal too?" Enry poked. "Do they suffer from the same madness? How are they looking these days?"

"Tsk-tsk. Yes, they too are immortal, but our royalty are sound o' mind. It's them crafty relics you have to watch. They're holdin' a grudge though they're too old to remember why."

"That's terrible," Sera commented. "I suppose I understand your current position, the need to defend yourself, but the relics' story still seems a tragedy in my book."

Wilford slowed to a stop. On the right, the stream's edge was opening up to a larger bank. In the middle of it, a ring of massive stones had been arranged on the ground. He turned to face Sera and Enry. "Looks like a good spot for a lunch break if you ask me."

"Was this your doing?" Sera asked.

"Goodness, no. If I bothered to arrange a seat—which I wouldn't—I'd only need one, 'n even moving one o' them rocks would be a challenge. No, this is the work of the original aerie expedition I was tellin' you about —from a couple hundred years ago. We're gettin' close to one of their old encampments. The closer you get, the more you encounter stuff like this."

Sera realized she hadn't checked for an overhead view in a while. *Time to see how well were tracking.* "Alright" she agreed, "let's take a breather."

Enry rejoiced as he set Pterus down and unloaded his rucksack. Sera dropped her pack too before slipping into OmniSync. To her surprise, she was no longer able to see any hyperspectral imagery. After several failed attempts, she resurfaced from the depths of Omni-consciousness. "Good thing we have the map," she commented before discreetly unrolling her sketch.

"Weird, I didn't realize anyone *drew* maps anymore." Wilford leaned in as Sera regretted her inadequate discretion. "What're them triangles?"

"You tell me."

"Hmmm." Wilford leaned further over Sera's shoulder. "I think those are the old aerie encampments. Impressive. I'm not sure how you managed to get a map of 'em when they were supposed to be a secret." He pointed to a spot on the map. "We're here. You can see we're on a good path to come across one in six or seven hours.... You know, it might actually be a smart place to set up camp for the night. Better than sleepin' outside anyway."

"What're the encampments like?" Enry asked. "All we know about them is that they're triangular."

"Their *bases* are triangular. The full shape is called a 'tetrahedron.' It's a very logical shape, in fact. Common

to Mars. These buildings are massive, made o' native timber to last centuries."

Sera wanted to listen, but a growing storm of huffs and snorts was denying her the focus. *That's Pterus, but where is he, and WHAT is he eating?*

She found answers behind one of the boulders. Her beast was neck-deep in her rucksack, frantically devouring something. *Oh no!* Sera leapt forward to pull him from her bag. In the brief moment he'd stolen, Pterus had eaten nearly all of her provisions. Oats—at least what was left of them—had been strewn from her bag to the ground beyond. His dried beetles were entirely gone too. "Not good," Sera cried. "That was all of our food."

"That's okay, I brought some too." Enry looked pensive as he considered the implications. "If we ration it, we ought to have enough to get where we're headed."

Wilford had been quietly watching. "There's plenty o' food out here. Foraging ain't hard. I know your kind is long past simply grazin' on greens, but there are safe mushrooms, some stomach-friendly plants, acorns. You'll be fine." Forlorn, Sera faced Wilford

and nodded. "You guys take a break," Wilford continued, "you need it. I'll find some things to make up for the loss." Then he stepped away, crossed the brook, and disappeared into the trees beyond.

"What do you think, Enry? Should we see if he wants to join us to the encampment?"

"Yeah, I think so. Let's ask him."

Soon, Wilford returned. Cupped in his dirty hands was a bundle of roots he swore were edible. Before waiting for the kids to distrust him, he rinsed one of the roots off and began chewing it. Sera and Enry followed suit, awkwardly gnawing at "food" that looked more like a sapling than sustenance.

Once replenished, the group packed up and resumed their jog. Wilford had returned to his vanguard position when Sera called out, "Hey, don't worry about that. You don't need to stay ahead of us." She waited for their guide to briefly glance back. "Sorry, you know, it's just that we have to be careful with strangers."

"No sweat," the ram replied. "You're wise not to trust."

Sera forced a smile between huffs.

"You suggested stopping at the old aerie encampment. Let's say we were bound for the mineshaft in the central clearing. Wouldn't it be better to simply power through, get to the mineshaft before resting for the night? It looks like the encampment and the mine are pretty close to each other."

"They are, but the mine's where real danger awaits. Best to rest in a place where you can actually *rest*."

"Okay." Sera had claimed a new spot jogging next to Wilford. "So, listen, would you be up for guiding us there?"

Wilford weighed the invitation for a moment. "Sure. You mind if I rest there too? There's enough space," he added. "We'd each have our own room."

Sera shot an appreciative nod to their new guide. "Sounds like a plan, Willy."

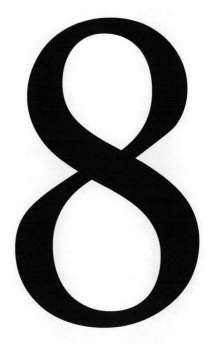

8

LONG SHADOWS

The group's afternoon journey was mostly without incident. There'd come a point when a spirit could be heard thrashing through the woods, but Wilford quickly proved his worth as he led the group to a shadowy cliff hidden off to one side of the creek's bank.

In time, as the intensity of canopy-piercing spotlights dulled, Sera noticed additional fireflea blazes cropping up. "That's their nighttime ritual," Wilford explained as he again slowed his pace. "During the day, they're more dangerous 'cause they're a lot less visible." He rubbed one of the bald patches on his forearms.

The group had recently strayed from the brook to cut over toward the base. In the distance, flat surfaces of its pyramidal shape were briefly coming into view. And from the little Sera could see, the building was truly massive —at least by faun standards. *Its top must nearly pierce the canopy!*

Soon, the exhausted group found themselves at its entrance. Though overgrown with vegetation, the structure was intact. With some muscle, Wilford was able to swing one of its enormous front doors open.

Inside, the main room was nearly pitch black. "Oh…right. Be right back." Wilford promptly retreated from the building and approached the nearest pocket of firefleas. To Sera's dismay, the aerie briefly stuck his arm into the frenzy. As he withdrew it, he slapped and squashed the many glowing specs that had latched onto his arm. Then he rubbed his skin as though applying lotion. By the time Wilford had returned to the doorway, his entire arm was aglow.

"Nice!" Enry praised.

"Like I said, you learn to make do out here." By the light of his arm, Wilford guided Sera, Enry, and Pterus through the building and up a central staircase to the sleeping quarters. The rooms were quite like Sera imagined soldiers' barracks to be. There were many of them spanning the upper floors, each identical to the others, mostly square, and entirely devoid of amenities. "Take your pick," Wilford offered. He waited as the kids chose adjacent rooms, for Sera to unpack and light her lantern.

"Alright you two, I'm wiped out," Wilford confessed. "I'll see you troublemakers in the mornin.'"

Wilford turned to the staircase and headed up, presumably for a floor that could afford him total peace and quiet. Sera removed Pterus' goggles before continuing to unpack her bag.

"I wonder what our parents have pieced together by now," Enry called out from next door.

"Yeah, they must be worried sick. Did you tell them you were leaving?"

"I just said I was going camping with friends." Enry peeked around the corner into Sera's illuminated room. "I'm sure they'll be mad when they find out where I *really* went, but at least they aren't gonna worry in the meantime."

"Nice move. I didn't even leave a note," Sera lamented. "I wish I'd said goodbye to Bram at least. The poor boy. He's never been apart from me."

As she looked up, she realized Enry had been getting along without a lantern of his own. "Let's share the light." Sera grabbed her lantern, and headed to the hall. As she moved, long shadows shifted all around. Pterus' shadow was particularly scary, growing and twisting until it resembled a demonic beast. "This place gives me the creeps. I can't imagine living here," she ad-

mitted. "Wait, who needs to imagine?! There should be local logs!" Once she'd reached the hallway, Sera plopped herself to the floor and started a search.

A minute later, she returned to the present with an audible sigh: "I don't know why I even bother. Clearly there should be logs. I checked a broad span of time but still was unable to locate a single log."

"I don't like it," Enry muttered. "I think you should be ready to use that helixir on a moment's notice. I wish we knew whether it's temporary or permanent though n' whether you have to drink it or anoint yourself with it."

"Mhmm. There's so much we don't know about it. I've also been wondering whether I have to perform the sacred gesture when I use it or just say

'Deguile.'"

Pop. Pop. Pop. A string of gruesome sounds erupted from Sera's room. For a few seconds, she sat frozen. With her pulse echoing in her ears, Sera slowly rose to her hooves. Lantern extended, she then ventured forward. As her light reached the center of the room, Sera gasped. a gurney had just appeared.

With buckled straps at both ends and its middle, the bed looked as though it had been designed to restrain a small patient. "Oh my god," Enry muttered as he too entered the room. Cautiously, he approached the bed to study it.

Suddenly, there was another explosion of sounds as the gurney contorted itself into Enry's likeness. Sera, real Enry, and the new clone of Enry all stood motionless. Then *real* Enry started laughing. "It's Pterus! It's just Pterus! … Yeesh, keep goggles on him, would you? Nearly gave me a heart attack!" But as he turned to Sera, he found her none the calmer. "What? What is it?"

"Where's the gurney?!"

Enry's face abruptly went pale. "Oh. Oh no. What—what does that mean?"

"I don't know yet. Stand back." Sera ushered Enry to the door. Then, very slowly, she waved her lantern before her as though painting the room's barren walls in light. As she reached the far corner of her room, she was met with another bout of bone-crunching pops. At once, Enry's copy imploded. In his place sat a pristine teddy bear. Sera shook her head. "Can you check my bag for the helixir?"

Enry was quick to oblige. Behind Sera, he hurriedly fished through her rucksack for the vial. After a moment, he stopped. "You want the good news or the bad news?"

"The good news." Sera kept her eyes on the stuffed animal.

"I found your bottle…. Now the bad news—"

"It's empty," Sera interrupted.

"Um, yeah. Just a few cork pieces left. How did you know?"

"Pterus is seeing this room as it really is—not the enchanted form we're seeing," Sera explained. "In its disenchanted form, this room apparently hosts a gurney, and some sort of doll to comfort children. The only explanation for why Pterus can see these things is because he must've worked the cork off my disenchantment helixir while eating through the provisions."

"So, your shapeshifting pet used the helixir?" No part of the question tickled Enry. Pale-faced, he scanned the empty room, imagining the many horrors it harbored. "That's—that's not good."

"No, not good at all." Sera continued studying the stuffed animal. "The bear's not that old. Not centuries old."

Feeling at her limit, she plopped herself and her lantern back down. After a couple of minutes sitting in silence, she and Enry watched the unnerving bear in the corner morph back into Pterus' natural form.

That's enough for one day, little fella. Just as Sera had re-bound and goggled her beast, another terrible crack rang out behind her. Then the room shook.

To her side, Enry's body lay limp, his face pointing straight into the floor.

Frantically, Sera grabbed and lifted her lantern to make sense of things. In the split-second that followed, she caught the briefest blurry glimpse of Wilford's glowing arm as it landed a blunt instrument into the side of her head.

9

BADUMBADUM,
BADUMBADUM

As Sera came to, a wave of nause-ating dizziness washed over her. From the light seeping through a cobwebbed window, she could tell she was still in her enchanted room. But knowing she hadn't been the one to close its door, the room was no longer a place to rest. It was a cell.

"Rise and shine," Enry croaked from across the room.

"Mmmphhh." Sera tried to sit up, but her limbs had shackles on them. She held up her hands to see them more clearly. "Seriously, Wilford?"

"Wilford?" Enry exclaimed. "Good grief! I wish I'd seen that coming."

In the dim light, the boy mulled over their betrayal. "This place was part of his plan," he eventually noted. "Before you came to, I was combing over the logs. We weren't looking at the right time. You mentioned that teddy bear looking new. The stretcher didn't look old either. So, I got to thinking: 'What if this whole facility (including its con-tents) is much newer and we just can't see its true form?'"

"And?" Sera asked. The discussion was distracting her from a throbbing headache.

"This place is no good. It's a child internment camp. They don't simply ascend to the Sorcerer's plane as we're told. They're brought out here by the wagonload, wearing these shackles, and then they're thrown into these rooms. I can't find any logs from the kids' perspectives, but I did find a couple from some grown-ups' logs. Really terrible. Seems to be highly organized. From what I've made out, they process the kids here for a few hours. Then they shuttle 'em out, and I lose local logs access."

The sound of a sliding deadbolt an-nounced a visitor. As the door swung open and Wilford stepped through, Sera noticed his head, for the first time, wasn't hunched over. His eyes landed on her first. "Oh good, so I *didn't* kill you."

"All that talk of danger in the woods; *you* were the real danger!" Sera spat.

"I said you were wise not to trust. Then you went 'n showed yourself *un*-wise. Seems you've caught the eye o' the Coven. The Queens Corps have access to reporting you don't. As soon as you entered the woods, you became a 'faun of interest.'

"Now, let's get a move on. I'll fill you both in as we resume our hike."

"'Resume?'"

"We've got the same destination. The central clearing also serves as a landing site. Now, come on!" Wilford noticed Sera searching for her belongings. "Your stuff? You won't be needin' it."

The girl shook her head. "Where's Pterus at least?"

"I threw your bandaged critter outside with the rest of your stuff. Might still be there, but to check, you'll have to GET UP." Neither kid made the slightest effort to rise. "Maybe I ain't bein' clear. This…" Wilford pointed to their shackles, "is me being nice. Get up, or you'll see what *not nice* looks like." Slowly, the two kids obeyed.

As the group made their way downstairs, they finally entered enough light to see clearly. The encampment's doors were open, and tree-canopy-defying light was shining through. Sera found her gear—plus Enry's—strewn everywhere. Pterus was indeed there, busily rooting through Enry's bag for any remaining provisions.

"You weren't kiddin' about havin' enhanced vision," Wilford remarked.

"Not sure how you got your hands on a disenchantment helixir. But it don' matter; it obviously ain't workin' for you, else you'd have seen this place's true form."

Sera ignored the ploy for answers as she grabbed Pterus' leash. "I'm bringing him."

"Long as he can keep quiet, I don' really care." Wilford's attention was elsewhere as he carefully secured a chain to both of Sera's and Enry's shackles. Only once he had finished daisy-chaining the kids to one another did he resume the exchange: "Don't yank my chain today, 'n I won't yank yours." Wilford hastily snatched several strewn-about items from the ground and shoved them into Sera's emptied rucksack. Then he donned the bag himself—which looked utterly ridiculous given how comparatively small it was. "Time to head out!"

In a reversal of the prior morning's order, the kids were in front while Wilford guided them from the tail of their chained procession, as though mushing dogs. For a long while, Sera marched forward in silence, stewing over Wilford's betrayal, boiling at her

own failure to see past it. *You're naïve. You're reckless and weak. Opa warned you out of love, but you scoffed at his concern. Your piddly effort to spare Enry was a bust. Your commitment to avoiding strangers was a bust. A day after your grandfather pled for your safety, you marched into the darkness and threw your body to the jackals. But it's not just you who pays the price for your stupidity. So much for Enry, for defenseless siblings back home, for parents who'll grieve again! So much for Opa's joy of sharing stories with you, for the Skohlidon story! So much for happily ever after!*

With two sets of clenched fist thumps to her chest, Sera summoned her life meter. *Let's see just how much trouble I've caused.* Every inducted faun had such a meter. A form of clairvoyance, a life meter would tell you how many months you had left to live based on your choices and actions up until that point. Many in the guild obsessed over theirs, tuning diets and habits to painstakingly optimize for longevity. Opa had once warned that life meters were fallible, at best a probability based on very biased aerie

assumptions, but all the same, Sera had never been able to resist tracking hers. And, as it turned out, hers had just taken a turn for the worse—a very bad turn. *I SERIOUSLY HAVE ZERO MONTHS LEFT TO LIVE? SERA, YOU FOOL!*

Eventually, Wilford pushed through the kids' bitter silence. "Last Soliday, I was brought out to retrieve a lost artifact from the mineshaft. But two piddly days on the ground wasn't nearly enough time. As Soliday ended and the rest of our fleet prepared to depart, I was still no closer to accomplishing my mission. Them ruthless relics had made mineshaft entry 'n exploration impossible. My superiors were most, uh … let's say, *displeased.* They informed me I'd be stayin' here 'til their NEXT Soliday return (by which time they assumed I'd have reclaimed the device). I tried to explain what I was up against, but it didn't matter. So here I am, day after day, working to whittle away the relics' numbers 'til I can actually make my way into the depths of the mine. It's a suicide mission to enter when it's full o' them things."

"What was so important?" Enry seethed. "And why in the world would your superiors pick *you* for a critical mission? You're a dope. Everyone can see that."

"Watch your tongue!" Wilford jerked the chain backward, causing both kids to stumble. "It's called a 'Horroscope,' boy. That's the common aerie name for it anyway. We made a few of 'em to pinpoint the location of the Grand Sorcerer's Yantra. When our search expedition concluded this spot was a dead end a couple centuries ago, they left behind one o' them Horroscopes —which is a big no-no. That thing coulda fallen into the wrong hands, helpin' heretics locate the Yantra."

"Why? What's the scope supposed to do?" Sera pressed.

"Its design was inspired by the prophecy. If you spin it to a particular day and time—in the past or the future— it reveals the closest points between Earth and Mars at that time. One o' them sites—if you select the right point in time—hides the long-prophesied Yantra. Needless to say, no one —not the aeries nor most o' your simple kind—want to see our common

god meet his end. So, the Coven's greatest mission is to find the Yantra before an ill-intentioned party does."

Sera turned back to make eye contact with Enry. Without a word spoken, he nodded solemnly. It was as though he'd somehow read her mind. More than that—that he agreed with her absurd supposition: *WE may be the ill-intentioned party.*

As the group neared an immense tree set apart from the rest of the thicket, Wilford ordered the kids to stop. Without explanation, he then approached Enry. Using a string-tied key pulled from his pocket, Wilford unlocked the boy's portion of the daisy-chain. Once he'd done so, he secured the balance of the chain, and Sera with it, around the base of the tree. Then he tucked the string-tied key back into his pocket.

"I need to make one last go o' the mines for that Horroscope. Before I do, you, Enry, are gonna help me improve my odds. The reports are talkin' about Sera, but they haven't mentioned *you* by name. Far as I'm concerned, that makes you fair game to help me with my mission."

Sera sensed foul play. Pterus seemed to as well; since the group had stopped, he'd started grunting and squirming to escape Sera's hold. But before either could discern the nature of this evil, Wilford abruptly lowered his horns and launched forward, charging into Enry with all his might. The boy was thrown backward. But he didn't merely fall to the ground. Rather, Enry kept falling, plummeting to some depth beneath the surrounding vegetation.

From her vantage point, it was hard to make out details, but Sera didn't need to; she perfectly recognized Wilford's dastardly plan to use Enry as bait. "STOP!" she screamed.

As she futilely wrestled with her restraints, Wilford showed no restraint of his own. Unhurried, he plopped her rucksack on the ground, removed her lantern, and proceeded to unscrew its bottom. Even at her present distance, Sera recognized the pungent smell of kerosene. Then the ram leaned forward and poured its contents into the void that had consumed Enry.

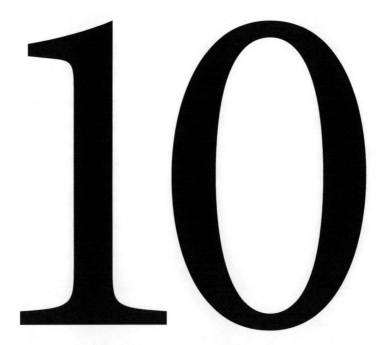

10

OOGADEBOOGADEBOO!

Sera thrashed against the chain binding her to the tree. With every violent jerk, she etched new marks into her skin to claim the most miniscule slack. But her struggle was more than physical; she found herself rejecting her senses too, denouncing harrowing cries now invading her ears. If her hearing was to be trusted, high overhead where Wilford sat perched, a captive child was in excruciating pain. *But it's not real,* she rebuked. *It can't be. I saw no such child because there IS no such child!* Sera suspected dark craft, a wicked ruse on the aerie's part. But without proof, the pitiful sobs had become a debilitating weapon.

At wit's end, she switched to a new plan. It wasn't easy maneuvering one-handed, but after a minute fumbling with the beast under her arm, Sera managed to remove Pterus' goggles. Then she dropped him to the ground. "Enry," she projected in a low tone, "call Pterus to you."

The boy obliged. A second later, as Pterus peered down at him from the edge of the pit, Sera heard the string of grotesque pops she'd anticipated. Pterus—now in the form of Enry—

was standing as though aimless, at the edge of the pit. "Thanks," she said in a hush. "Now Enry, hide, stay quiet, and ignore everything I'm about to say."

Enry couldn't know what Sera had in store, but he could be heard burying himself under the pungent leaves. Sera then waited a breath before projecting a phony exchange upward for Wilford: "Great work, Enry! Now free me too!"

Branches overhead snapped as their captor repositioned himself for a better view. The two didn't have to wait long for confirmation Wilford had taken the bait. "What the heck?!" he exclaimed.

The irate aerie's return to the ground was much less graceful than his prior climb after plowing Enry into the pit. This time, he seemed to snag every single branch the tree had to offer. While he clambered and cursed, Sera tracked the loop of string hanging from his pocket with myopic focus.

"What's wrong with you, boy? You hit your head on a rock? Why you just standin' there?" As Wilford reached the front of false Enry, the boy's frame fractured, burgeoning out at once.

The sight was predictably horrific. In a second's time, the figure standing before Wilford had transformed into a mirror image of himself—one that waved its arms just as aggressively while speaking angry gibberish back.

Shocked, the real Wilford stumbled to the ground. "That—that thing's a deadringer! But that's impossible!" He struggled to get up without taking his eyes off the replica. "They got no place here!" As he regained composure, he sneered at Sera. "I thought they were bigger … 'n meaner."

"Only when I need him to be," she shot back. She could see his mind still reeling.

"The goggles 'n the bandages," he muttered to himself as he processed having spent a day with a deadringer —and not knowing it. Wilford approached the edge of the pit to see whether real Enry was still there but found no sign of the boy.

Frustrated, he shifted to scouring the ground in search of something. His eyes landed close to Sera's hooves as he spotted a long branch. At once, he huffed over, grabbed it, and turned back to the pit. But as he stomped past the base of the tree, Sera intercepted him, frantically grabbing at one of the

stick's small, branched ends. Wilford grunted as he yanked his new weapon back. Still, Sera's little end of the stick broke free. "Stupid girl!" he spat. Then he elbowed her in the stomach.

Wilford returned to the pit's edge to stab the stick downward. After a few good jabs, he heard what he was after: a cry of pain from real Enry. "Good," he observed. "Now, do your job, boy! YOU. ARE. THE. BAIT! Act like the bait, or I'll just light the—" Wilford fell abruptly silent, even as his replica continued to yell like a lunatic. Sera realized another monstrous cry was reaching the same excessive volume —and it was still growing louder. In the distance, she could see the tree canopy shaking as a beast—surely a kindread spirit—raced toward them.

Wilford darted to the base of the tree. As he scrambled to its lowest major limb, Sera was ready. Very carefully, she thrust her slightly-hooked stick into his leg. It snagged the loop still dangling from his pocket such that, as he continued his climb, it pried his key free.

That's when she heard it: a vicious, guttural voice. "FREE THE CHILD!"

Sera didn't bother to scan—she didn't have the time. Frantically, she used the key to unlock her shackles and sprinted to the pit. Wilford's stick—which she could have extended to Enry—was gone from sight. Without time for a better plan, she pulled Pterus—who still looked like Wilford—to her side, eased him down to the ground, face down, and pushed the bottom half of his body into the pit. "Climb up!"

Enry was ready. He jumped up, grabbed Pterus' Wilford-like ankles, and scaled his body to the top of the pit.

But Sera's attention was elsewhere as Enry escaped. She could now see the terrifying relic closing in on them —and in the distance, a kindread spirit too. Sera knew she had mere seconds to act before Wilford launched his torch down into the pit, engulfing everyone in flames to end the relic. "Get back!" she shouted.

But it was too late. Just as she had delivered her warning, a torch pelted down from above. In an instant, the pit erupted in savage fire. Enry was already out, but Pterus—as Wilford— was still dangling into the void. Frantically enduring a lack of air and an abundance of heat, Sera and Enry pulled their friend from the fire. As they labored, Sera finally noticed the brutish relic. He had suddenly stopped his fierce advance with a look of utter confusion. A second later, he whipped around, turning his attention to the descending spirit.

Sera and Enry feverishly rolled their companion on the ground to extinguish the flames consuming his legs. Deafening roars and ear-splitting cries abounded. Death seemed certain. But the two stuck with Pterus.

By the time the fire spanning his legs was out, the conflict seemed to have moved on. Neither the spirit nor the relic were within view, though their loud brawl raged unabated nearby.

As *real* Wilford descended again, the kids and a still-Wilford-like Pterus rose to their hooves. Once up, it took no time for the thunderous noise to coax Pterus into the thicket.

"You two cost me a spirit! I may have to hand YOU in, but your friend here," Wilford pointed down at Enry, "is gonna pay the piper! Any last words?"

Enry's attention, however, was elsewhere, focused in wide-eyed terror on

some horrifying surprise apparently just behind Wilford. The ram turned for a quick glance. Indeed, it *looked* like the spirit was back, closing in on them. Impulsively, he jumped toward the big tree's base like Enry and Sera.

But after his lurch, Wilford stopped. He realized what he was actually facing—and he wasn't about to be made a fool again. "Deadringers are only as dangerous as you allow 'em to be! Watch how easy it is to disarm your pet." A second from being devoured by the supposed spirit, Wilford scoffed in the face of danger, waving his arms and shouting "Oogadeboogadeboo!" He knew the show would get Pterus' attention, and in so doing, disarm him.

It worked.

Wilford did get Pterus' attention, … just not as expected: from the trees behind him, he heard Pterus' effort to copy him. "Oo–ba–doo–ba–gee–boo."

As the gravity of Wilford's mistake crashed down on him, so too did the authentic spirit. In a flash, its mass of densely twisted branches opened wide and consumed him whole.

A moment later, Pterus stepped from the thicket, drawn by the grisly sounds of Wilford's demise. For him, the sight was plenty stimulating, triggering yet another transformation, this time to match the spirit.

Sera and Enry craned to watch from behind the tree as the monsters hissed and reared at one another for the second time in a week. Like colliding freight trains, they struck one another with impossible force. Wreckage was raining in all directions. Pterus was at his terrifying best. But this time, his adversary was in its native domain, and it wasn't backing down.

Then, amid the pandemonium, Sera spotted the relic. He had returned and was sizing up the fray. At once, she burst forth from her cover. "That's the *REAL* spirit!" she shouted.

With the slightest nod, he turned and charged the authentic spirit. The force he brought to bear shocked Sera, nearly rivaling that of the spirits. Suddenly, one of the two spirits imploded. Pterus had discovered the relic. As he cracked and popped his way down to a smaller form, the real relic continued to push his target ever closer to the raging fire.

A few forceful paces later, the aggressive spirit flailed. It had been pushed

so far that it was now falling backward into the blazing pit. As it caught fire, Sera found the sight shamefully exhilarating—but its horrible cries were too much. At once, she covered her ears.

After a few breaths, Sera spotted a detail she would've otherwise missed: a severed relic head was caught in the blazing spirit. But more appalling, its bloodshot eyes were moving.

There was no choice to be made as to whether she should intervene; Sera knew she must. With only the most nascent plan in place, she grabbed one end of the chain that had previously bound her to the tree and sprinted for the pit.

At the pit's edge, she could see for certain that the head was indeed animated, somehow alive. Sera had never lassoed anything before—and the chain was too heavy to throw with any precision—but she was without options; she had to loop it over the head's only exposed horn.

Just as she attempted the impossible task, the whole-bodied relic boomed an order. "GIVE IT TO ME!"

Every instinct told Sera to flee. Her body demanded it. But so too did her conscience loathe cowardice. A heartbeat later, after wrestling her fears into submission, she faced the monster and heaved her chain to him.

For a few seconds, there was nothing to do but watch in awe as the relic leaned into the flaming pit and grabbed ahold of an engulfed branch. With his body braced, he looped Sera's chain over one of the severed head's exposed horns. Then he pushed himself free of the fire and yanked backward with all his might.

The once-entangled head ripped free from its hellish cage, hitting the ground many paces away with a quick succession of thuds. As it rolled to a stop, Sera skidded next to it.

The head was a sad sight to behold. Instinctively, Sera reached out to wipe the muck from its pitiful face.

"MOVE ASIDE." The once-fearless relic was now kneeling next to her. He embraced the severed and burnt head as fresh tears wicked clean stripes from his ash-coated skin. "She can't die," he huffed, "but she *can* feel pain."

Then the headless one gasped and blinked. After a few raspy wheezes, she looked up. "Let me … see … the girl."

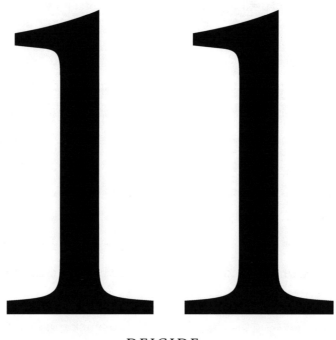

11

DEICIDE

"Thank you, lass." The disembodied head spoke in slow, labored parts, her voice nearly as gritty and deep as the other relic's. "What's your name?"

"It's Sera, ma'am. I can't imagine what you've been through." Sera found herself choking up.

"Don't fret, you did well." The head forced a smile. "I'm Adelaide, and this is Thomas." Adelaide gazed up fondly. "He just witnessed what I observed a year ago: the aeries have a mastery of our kids' voices. They use their cries to bait us into traps." Thomas' changed expression showed he hadn't understood the enchantment until just now.

"You're brave," Adelaide continued, her rickety voice slowly finding stability. "On the rare occasion we come across others, they're terrified. But I don't want you to worry, dear; we owe you thanks, not harm. Rest assured, Thomas here won't lay a finger on you. If he does,"—she looked up—"I'll bite that finger off." Thomas smirked, deepening large wrinkles across his head that reminded Sera of Opa. "Anyway, you lost? Those boys a threat to you?"

Boys? Sera turned back to find Enry teasing a copy of himself, stumbling about with his arms outstretched like an undead faun while his body double did the same. With the blazing bonfire behind the two, the collective scene looked apocalyptic. "Oh! Not at all," Sera laughed. "One's actually a dead-ringer. No, I'm right where I want to be. I'm here to speak with you."

"A deadringer!" Adelaide remarked in awe. "Well, I don't know why you'd seek us out, but if you want the truth, we have no shortage. What do you say we retreat to the safety of the mine?"

The safety of the mine. Sera winced as she noted more evidence of Wilford's betrayal. "Okay, that sounds good."

…

After a brisk hike, the group reached their target; beyond the last of the trees, a near-blindingly bright, empty space awaited. *The clearing.* Sera suspected it had been felled for lumber back when the mine was being excavated—and aerie encampments we're being erected.

Outside an entrance to the mine, Sera, Enry, and a re-goggled Pterus took the chance to eat for the first time in a day. Afterward, Sera stepped away for a stroll with Thomas and Adelaide while Enry kept watch over Pterus.

Sera recounted for her new company the bizarre state of the world. From a broad strokes summary of modern life to a detailed retelling of the past week, she brought Thomas and "Addie" up to speed on the insanity that had forced her present hand. In the process, she realized a liberating silver lining in her new outlaw status: *I no longer have to cloak talk with other outlaws!*

At the end of her retelling, Thomas looked bothered. "We're not the monsters they've made us out to be. They held our kids as hostages while forcing us to hunt for the Yantra. We broke our bodies searching. It just wasn't here."

"And they endlessly torment us with those spirits." Addie inserted.

Sera nodded. "Yeah, the first time I encountered one, I had no idea what to make of its childlike cries. But today, I realized the cries are an enchantment. Pterus copies things as they *truly are*, not their enchanted form. When he copied that kindread spirit, he mimicked its squeals and hisses, but not its faun-like screams. I don't think he actually heard the voices we heard, because the cries weren't real—at least they weren't really present. If I had to

guess, I'd say those sounds are the summoned echoes of children long ago taken. I imagine your kids were taken to the same place my older brother and so many others get imprisoned. We're told they ascend to the Grand Sorcerer, but I doubt that. What I do know is that this deity's tied to tremendous forms of power, he's connected to the abduction of our kin, and the manipulative aeries are desperate to keep him safe. It's clear to me that the prophecy and the Yantra exist for one reason: to correct this otherworldly imbalance."

At Sera's pause, Thomas leaned in. "You're not like other kids, are you? Sera considered an answer. *I'm not, and I never have been. It's not like I haven't tried though. My whole life I've tried.*

Thankfully, Addie was quick to help: "No need to answer, dear. Maybe we can offer *you* some answers. We've spent a lot of time with the Queen's Corps, and we *did* steal their Horroscope." She flashed a devilish grin. "Just don't expect too much from it. Without the right date and time, without transport or an army, it isn't an asset."

Sera warmed at the refocusing. "What can you tell me about the prophecy?"

"Not a lot to share. While we were slavin' away in the mines all those years ago, the aerie supervisors would occasionally talk about it. They say the lore was born on Mons Olympus. In time, the prophecy gave way to an extensive search across both planets. As I understand it, there are a few other spots, just like this mineshaft, always around the equators of Earth and Mars."

"Why around the equators?"

"It's in the prophecy. Let's see, …

> "The shortest span from three to four, two points in space, in one much more. But when and which must be known to deny a sorcerer their throne."

Sera considered the riddle carefully before asking to hear it once more.

"So, I get that it's referencing the third and fourth planets from the sun," Sera admitted. "I also imagine that, depending on the point in time, their rotations line up differently, meaning different points on each planet will be closest to one another. What I can't tell is whether you're saying 'w–h–i–c–h' or 'w–i–t–c–h.'"

Addie look stunned as Thomas once again jumped in: "You know, you really are sharp, Sera."

"That's why the mine is precisely *here,*" Addie explained. "Some other perceptive folks picked up on that too. The Coven is led by the aeries' supreme ruler, the High Priestess (also known as the 'Queen Witch'). Like us, she's immortal. Unlike us, she's supposedly a medium to the Grand Sorcerer. So, folks started asking themselves, 'What key date can be associated with the Queen?' There were only two days that measured up: her birthday and her coronation."

"So, each of those two dates translates to a pair of sites on Earth and Mars?" Sera asked.

"Yes. Four sites in total, two of which are on Earth. At the time the aerie were giving up on this site, we'd heard they were similarly fruitless in their search of the other sites."

"Maybe it's 'w-h-i-c-h' then."

"Why don't you come with us to our lair, to the Crimson Core? Our collective wisdom may shine new light on the darkness you're facing."

Addie waited, noting Sera's hesitation. "You aren't sure you can trust us?"

"I mean, my intuition tells me I can trust you. But I trusted Wilford, and

that nearly got Enry and me killed."

"What did your intuition tell you about Wilford?"

"I had a feeling I couldn't trust him. But my 'logical' half won out. He was saying all the right things—even while my intuition remained unsettled."

"Sera, your intuition is grounded in logic—it's just reviewing the world at a level of detail your conscious mind can't. But when your conscious mind is calling all the shots, it's easy to reach a point where you're blind to danger."

"Like allowing an alien race to physically tamper with our minds."

"Indeed."

"My intuition is telling me, in no uncertain terms, that we need to join you in your lair."

Addie smiled. "There's hope for you yet. Now, before we get going, you and your boys are going to need some light. Bring a lantern, a torch, whatever you have, but try to make it fast. We have less than an hour before the sun sets."

"Okay, we'll work on it."

A few minutes later, Sera brought Enry up to speed on her exchange. "Addie says we'll need light to venture through the mineshaft. I think firefleas

will work, but we don't have much time. I'm going to see what I can catch." She lifted her lantern to show the container she'd be using to hold the bugs. "Want to collect some too?"

"Sure!" The idea of venturing into the mineshaft by the light of an insect was clearly thrilling to Enry. "I'll be right behind you. Going to see if I can find a container of my own."

"Okay, I'll be just inside the thicket."

...

A while later, Sera returned with a brilliant lantern full of firefleas she'd gathered by her lonesome after failing to locate Enry in the thicket. She found Addie and Thomas with Pterus, just within the mine. A dozen paces onward, she finally found Enry as well; Head-to-hoof aglow in the juices of firefleas, his smile was the only part of his body not illuminated as he too discovered a friend in the darkness.

12

THE SACRED GESTURE

The mineshaft's main lateral tunnel delivered an otherworldly experience. By the green glow of her new fireflea lantern—and her equally energetic, luminescent friend—Sera observed all manner of strange details: long-rotten crates bearing alien markings, metal tracks running along the ceiling, and, at one point, a group of ultra-realistic aerie statues that seemed to be fused to the mine's rock wall. Disturbingly, there were holes bored into—or out of—the rock, in some cases boring right through the stone aerie figures.

Sera pulled Pterus' tight leash even tighter. She had already re-goggled him so that the entourage could focus on the trek at hand, but now that he'd been rendered blind by the darkness, it was crucial that she act as his eyes.

After ten minutes trekking inward, the tunnel they had been following opened into a large chamber. Faintly visible on the other side of the cavernous space was a peculiar rock wall. As the light-bearing group neared, Sera realized what she was looking at: a carved stone monument of an aerie staring forward. Though it only started mid-torso, featuring its arms laid flat on the ground, the scale was quite unlike anything Sera had seen before. As tall as five or more fauns, the craft required to carve such a huge stone figure, particularly the curling horns atop its head, was hard to fathom.

"Many years ago," Thomas explained, "when we first started mining, the plan was to dig at these precise coordinates until either one of two things happened: we unearthed the Yantra or we reached a ridiculous, full-league's depth. Every tenth of a league we excavated—every two furlongs or so—was marked by a monument to one of the Royal Coven's witches and warlocks. This here is Winnie Bellows. As far as wicked witches goes, she's probably the *least* bad.

"Now, watch this." Thomas carefully handed Addie to Enry. Then he positioned his arms as though they were lying flat—just like the aerie monument and incanted a spell new to Sera:

"Eviscera!"

Next, he rotated his arms about his elbows to form an implied triangle as his fingertips touched his chin. Sera felt the ground beneath her hooves

rumble while Pterus squealed in alarm. The huge stone arms of Miss Winnie Bellows were rotating just as Thomas' had. As they swung upward, they revealed a pitch-black void in the space below. The arms stopped only once they had formed the same triangle Thomas was maintaining. That's when Sera realized Miss Bellows was no longer staring coolly ahead. Now her head was craning down with her eyes fixed directly on the crew. Sera felt extremely uneasy, as though the eyes were looking at her in particular.

Thomas ushered the crew forward. As he entered the newly-exposed archway, he was careful to maintain the odd triangular gesture with his arms. "These partitions were constructed to ensure a collapsing segment of the shaft never destroys those segments that've been excavated beneath it."

Once everyone had made it over the threshold, he reversed the motion with his forearms, and the triangular portal behind them reverted back to a stone wall. On the inside, an identical monument was present. It too was once again stationary, staring forward composedly.

The landing before them turned out to be the top of a staircase—one that spiraled into the depths of the earth. With Enry leading the downward procession as a headlight of sorts, each traveler stayed glued to the outside edge of the staircase. The going was dreadfully slow and repetitive, but the stakes left little room to feel bored.

The all-stone staircase had been carved from the earth with astounding precision. Sera imagined an alien machine chewing its way down, the steps serving as mere remnants of its bite. Interestingly, every 10-20 steps, holes had been bored into the surrounding rock. As Thomas explained, the holes were "feelers," drilled to check for any change in rock consistency that might reveal underground pockets, resins, or other treasures.

"I understand the Sorcerer's Yantra was never found," Sera commented. "Did you find anything else?"

"While under the Queen's Corps' rule, we unearthed a few rare resins used to make helixirs—which is how we came about our immortality. And in the centuries since they departed, we've continued searchin', hoping we might actually find a way to undo it. We once uncovered a small pocket of muddle resin. About a century ago, we found a sliver of reality resin too. The helixir it yields will let you rewrite your reality—or even strip away others' alterations. Never used either of 'em though; we can't agree who should benefit from these single-serve potions."

Sera continued to prod for answers while they descended. Eventually, they reached the bottom of Miss Bellows' segment. A second gargantuan stone figure was waiting. This one was gaunter, with sunken eyes and scary, misshapen horns. "Persnissa Pale," Addie noted. "Not as nice as Winnie Bellows."

Thomas frowned while incanting the "Eviscera" again. "Yes, she's a mean one." Once the group had resumed their descent, he explained: "She's more like the other members of the Coven. She believes we exist for her gain."

As the group continued downward, Sera's ears popped more than once. She was finding it harder to catch her breath—as though the great depth was winding her as much as exhaustion. Gate after gate, they met stone versions of the Coven's witches and warlocks:

Ambrose Morose, Bronwyn Were, Roald Ephrem. Somewhere between Rieger Mortis and Luci Defile, the group took an overdue break.

Now not moving in circles had become dizzying. Sera's legs felt like noodles. At once, she collapsed, claiming the step beneath her to lie on.

After a moment, a hand brushed her arm, stopping only once it had found her hand. Sera didn't have to sit up or turn to know the source; a greater glow of green light told her Enry was reaching out. In the calm, in the dim light, she gently squeezed his hand back.

Perhaps Opa's stoicism had shaped her, channeling a penchant for silent strength. Perhaps early intellect had driven a wedge between Sera and the raucous kids her age. Whatever the cause, she had come to prefer a measure of restraint in her company, prizing measured actions over mindless impulses. But now it was Enry's gentle impulse, a hand held, that threatened to destabilize Sera, coaxing her to the edge of a new form of dangerous cliff.

A moment later, Thomas rose to his hooves. "We should be gettin' a move on." Without another word, he scooped

Pterus under one arm and Addie the other. Sera reluctantly rose as well, forced a deep breath, and followed suit.

Down, down, down they descended. It didn't take long for the spinning to feel like status quo again, their brains reacclimated to the consistent motion. Eventually, they passed the enchantingly beautiful Sedicia Sodomier before reaching Raveneve Isle. "This one is our penultimate partition!" Addie announced. "After Raveneve here, the final gate will be marked by none other than High Priestess Maeve."

"So, there are ten members of the Royal Coven then?" Sera asked.

"That's right," Addie replied. "Unless the High Priestess finally had her baby."

"And I take it a witch or warlock joining the Coven is a rare event?"

"Most definitely." Thomas chimed in. "They're immortal, so there's simply no opportunity for a refreshed guard. That's part of the reason they're crazy —part of the reason our lot's crazy too. Our minds aren't made to last forever. We might be incapable of dying, but too much time ain't good for the mind. The older you get, the more desensitized you become. Eventually, little

delights you, scares you, or makes you laugh. You outlive your wit, your kin, love of life, even love of yourself."

"Good grief!" Addie exclaimed. "Will you give it a rest already? 'N we thought the mine was dark!"

"They ought to have realistic expectations before they meet our lot, Addie. Not everyone's as chipper as you." Addie didn't challenge Thomas' rebuttal which was enough for Sera to assume some truth to his counsel.

"Anyway, when you meet our lot," he continued, "just know they're good folk underneath their tough exteriors. They never interact with anyone else —and I mean ever. So, you know, most have long forgotten what it's like to be young, full of hope, ambition, or love." Thomas glanced at Sera and Enry but found the boy's attention lay elsewhere.

"Ah, good eye." Enry was studying a hole in the rock wall quite unlike the others they'd been passing. "That's no feeler. That's a Martian worm hole. Don't worry, we hadn't heard of 'em until we reached this depth either. You have to get beneath the upper Earth crust before you reach their domain."

"Shouldn't Martian worms be found on *Mars?*" Enry pressed.

"Oh, they are. But they're *also* here now. The aeries brought 'em. Kinda make our earthworms look like a joke, eh? They chew their way through stone, lookin' for nutrient-rich resins. Funny, I hadn't thought about it, but they're actually not all that different from us." Thomas paused to appreciate his comparison. "One difference, I suppose: they produce a sticky, black mucus that hardens anything it touches into stone. We think it's to reinforce the integrity of the earth as they bore through. You know, so the rock doesn't cave in on 'em in the future."

"So black ooze is bad?" Enry asked.

"Right. That means we need to be vigilant. At the height of that hole, the worm must've been coming rather than going. Check the steps ahead of you from here on out. If you step into fresh mucus, it'll quickly cement you to the ground in a bond of stone."

"Excellent, now things are getting interesting," Enry observed without a trace of sarcasm.

For Sera, this latest hazard underscored just how dangerous their path

had become. Not only did they have to navigate an oppressive darkness with alien monstrosities lurking, but a single misstep guaranteed either a perilous drop or petrification.

A few steps later, Enry leapt sideways to avoid one such string of slime. His out-of-rhythm jump would prove to be the first of many awkward maneuvers as the group ventured deeper and deeper, down to the final portal.

At the bottom, Sera was taken aback by the stone likeness of the Queen Witch. The High Priestess had an odd beauty to her, but more than that, her expression was unnervingly intense. Just looking at her inspired the urge to look away—an urge Sera resisted.

Thomas set Addie down before performing the Eviscera spell. Once again, alongside rumbling and animated stone limbs, the monument craned downward to focus on Sera. But unlike their prior encounters, this time the figure also spoke: "Young Sera, you are brave but foolish, well-intentioned but ill-informed. You seek to disrupt a system you do not understand, that you cannot understand. Because a system's beyond your faculties does not make it evil."

The stone head craned closer. "Consider your destructive intent carefully."

Sera's entire body went cold. Maeve's subversive words stood to catalyze a self-doubt that she'd been struggling to suppress. While she considered the counsel, Sera maintained her firm posture, staring brazenly back at the craning stone figure. *What if she's right? There surely IS much more to the aerie control than I understand. There may have been, at least at one time, good intent behind their actions. And what if the Grand Sorcerer has no role to play in their actions, well-meaning or not?* An incapacitating wave of worry flooded over Sera.

But she recognized the feeling. It was one she'd felt many times before;

She was exposed to real danger, forces she couldn't see and didn't understand. Her instincts told her that the danger was unnatural, that a veil of dishonesty was masking something that fundamentally held her interests apart from the High Priestess'.

Then Sera remembered Addie's sage advice—that she must always trust her instincts. She hadn't yet betrayed her confident façade, … and now she was determined not to.

After a deep breath, Sera responded with absolute calm: "You're right, I *will* consider my destructive intent carefully." Then, without waiting for Maeve to fire back, she stepped forward, leading the others through the final gate.

THE HIGH PRIESTESS

As Sera stepped over the threshold, the familiar stone portal rumbling returned—but it was happening too soon. She turned to Thomas and found he was still maintaining the triangular gesture. Suddenly, Maeve's stone arms began careening downward. "Get in!" she shouted.

Thomas abandoned his triangle and dove to pick up Addie. Enry scooped up Pterus while barreling under the falling stone limbs. Sera's companions were lucky to avoid getting squashed, but there would be no time for relief; as soon as she tumbled through the collapsing portal, she found the inside version of Maeve just as perturbed.

"SHE'S PULLING FREE FROM THE WALL!" Thomas roared while launching forward. Rounding the first complete coil of the staircase, Sera saw what she had feared: Maeve's gargantuan stone likeness was clawing down the shaft. A split second later, Thomas leapt out of rhythm as he narrowly avoided a pool of black mucus. *Skip three steps, dart to the side, skip two steps.*

Horn shards were raining down, making as much a racket wrecking the floor below as Maeve was making above. Then one of the horns crashed into the staircase ahead. On impact, it obliterated a huge stretch of stairs just before Enry. "Jump!" Sera screamed.

In the last second before they would have to leap, Thomas thrust Addie into Enry's hands—atop Pterus—and catapulted the bunch across the divide.

Still flying downward, Sera watched in horror as Thomas himself leapt only to reach the other side of the gap at chest level. The brute roared as he hit the stone and flailed to keep ahold.

A second later, Sera was forced to jump the same gap. Like Thomas, she failed to reach the other side. But as she plummeted, sure of her imminent death, the relic thrust forth an arm and grabbed her. A brilliant clatter below signaled Sera's lantern meeting its end. But Sera was safe. Single-handedly, the relic hoisted her onto the staircase he himself couldn't scale.

Once again on her hooves, Sera resumed her frantic downward flight. Suddenly, Thomas slammed into the steps before them, having fallen a full revolution of the staircase. Sera could tell at once he was badly injured.

Fortunately, she could also see the final floor below. *Skip two steps, dodge the goo, skip three steps.* It took all of her concentration to plot a path fast enough to keep pace with her hooves.

Soon thereafter, Sera and the others were down and racing for cover. But as they reached the far side of the chamber, a thunderous boom and walloping wake rocked the mineshaft.

Whether stone Maeve had lost her grip or intentionally let go, she'd managed to destroy the last revolution of the staircase on her way to the bottom. Amid a pile of arm and horn rubble, a hornless bust was cratered into the ground. All about, the firefleas Sera had collected were crackling about, free of their confines. Most remarkable, the stone figure's head and one of its arms were still animated.

In the dim light, it took Sera a moment to process what she was seeing; the stone abomination had seized a Martian worm from the chamber floor. To her dismay, it had begun swinging the worm like a weapon.

Then, seemingly out of nowhere, the worm smacked into Enry's torso. It hit him with such force that it sent the boy flying. Sera leapt to stay at his side. The two skidded to a stop just beyond Maeve's reach. Enry was still conscious but now immobile as Sera scanned for injuries only to find a tar-like mucus bubbling across his torso, very rapidly bonding him to the ground.

"We're going to have to break you loose!" Thomas boomed from a few paces away. Then the relic sprang into a limping run across the chamber. A few breaths later, he was gone from sight, lost to the shadows.

…

Echoing hoofsteps and an emerging roar of fearsome voices announced Thomas' return—along with the rest of his circle. "NO!" someone screamed. "WHAT'VE THEY DONE?!"…"MY GOD, WE'RE TRAPPED!"

The horde's cries continued escalating until the entire chamber had filled with their ravenous fury. And while Sera could barely see, what little she could discern was enough to send a bright chill down her spine. The relics were terrifying. Some were spider-like, served by unnaturally lanky limbs. Others cowered like undead ghouls. Every one looked murderously angry.

Then one voice bellowed above the rest. "THESE. FOOLS. WILL. PAY!" Sera gnashed her hooves firmly into the ground to quell a stirring tremor. Before her, the fiery crowd had begun to make way for something colossal. An enormous, cane-wielding relic was entering view.

"NEVER—not *ONCE* in centuries," the relic roared, "have the Crimson Core compelled the stone clergy to give chase! NEVER have we seen such devastation!" At the edge of the rocky ruins, the beast stopped to marvel at the possessed monument before him —and its captive worm.

"Careful, Oren," Thomas cautioned, "that's how she took 'im down." The gargantuan relic was now marching straight toward Sera, and before her, Enry. Sera was about to lose her nerve when Oren finally stopped and handed Thomas his cane. "*YOU* brought this trouble into our home! *YOU* get it out!"

Thomas accepted the cane without rebuttal. The object he'd received shimmered unexpectedly. *Metal.* Then he whisked a mallet from his belt and knelt before Enry. "You ready, bud?"

All of a sudden, a thunderous clap erupted a mere pace away. In the wake of the attack, a storm of rocky particles

showered down over Enry's rescuers. Stone Maeve had adjusted her grip of the worm, unlocking new reach. Sera dove for cover among the wreckage.

With rock dust raging in her lungs and sweat-infused mud dripping from her brow, Sera turned back for Oren. Sadly, the latest attack had brought a boulder down on him, pinning him into the surrounding ruins.

Meanwhile, the injured worm had begun doubling back, using its own body as a brace to reach its captor. By the time Sera had found a place to hide, the worm had found what it needed: the leverage to escape stone Maeve's murderous grip.

Once free, it deftly slid up its assailant's arm. Stone Maeve thrashed her head and flailed her working arm to stall the worm's attack as it concentrated on her face.

Soon, its horrific mission was complete; the worm had forced itself into her mouth. Seconds later, it re-emerged through the top of Maeve's barren stone head. Sera teetered on the edge of shock.

But Thomas' sonorous voice forced her attention back. "ENRY'S FREE!"

With the still-petrified boy under one arm, the relic launched into another limping run, this time to clear stone Maeve's dangerous reach. The rescue came not a moment too soon. As Thomas neared the others, Maeve's eyes ratcheted back behind her lids. A second later, a torrent of black, bubbling mucus blasted from her mouth.

Then a second worm burst from the top of Maeve's head. A moment later, a third. A fourth, fifth, sixth, seventh. So many worms were sprouting from the once-barren crown it appeared to be alive with serpentine locks. Sera's arrival had become a nightmare.

"Send 'em back!" a voice screeched.

"Now wait just a minute!" Thomas fired back. "Do you have any idea what they've been through to see you?"

"I DON'T CARE!" the shrill voice retorted. "Just LOOK at this mess!"

"I'm tellin' you, this girl has what it takes to shake things up!"

"She's clearly a much *bigger* threat to us than the aeries!"

"So get her on our side, Phaedra! She's here to help!" Thomas was practically glowing with white-hot anger. The wriggling veins in his temple and

those throbbing from his neck looked as though they were one shrill denial from springing their own attacks.

Thomas' opposition plowed forth. "You say she's here to help us, so let her prove it. Let her restore our access to the outside world. If she's successful, I, for one, will hear her out. If she's unsuccessful, then we'll know she was unworthy of our time." Gritty cheers of agreement erupted from the crowd.

Thomas scoured the twisted faces before him, searching for the slightest lack of resolve. Slowly, his shoulders slumped. He turned to Sera. "I told you, they mean well, but my god do they have a crusty exterior."

The consolation did little to satisfy Sera who marched forward to face their adversary. "Do you know *why* this staircase is in ruin? It's not because I've arrived or because a monster fell from above. It's because Maeve fears me. She sees me as a threat, … and she should. I aim to shine a light on the parasitic system that enslaves our kind.

"I understand your fear; they've trapped, maimed, and shamed you. I get your anger; they stole your kids and taunt you with their cries. Keep your anger, but shed your fear. If a faun of my status and stature can incite the High Priestess, together, we can send her running."

Several horned heads quietly nodded approval for Sera's rallying speech. "This is the worst entrance I could have made. This situation is appalling. I could really use some support as I try to remove this *thing* from your one and only path to the surface, but even if you choose to retreat, I'm going to confront the danger. That's why I'm here, why *we're* here." Sera motioned to Enry. "We refuse to hide anymore. But if you retreat, ask yourself: how will we ever be free of this tyranny when we lack the will to support one another?" A flurry of hushed utterances swirled through the mob.

"Then it's settled!" Phaedra fired back with a sneer. "The girl will SAVE THE WORLD, and we'll all feel the shame of having stood by! Have at it, *GIRL!*"

Phaedra turned and marched back toward the far tunnel. Not far behind, the raucous assembly followed suit, leaving only Thomas and Addie as ambassadors.

"I'm so sorry, kid," Thomas seethed.

"This is total hogwash."

"It's fine," Sera lied.

"Well, how about I work Enry here free of his confines?"

Enry was quick to answer for him-self: "Sounds like a plan, mate."

As Thomas carefully chipped away at Enry's stone wrap, Sera ventured as close as she could to Oren—who was still stranded. She was careful to side-step pools of ooze while staying beyond reach of the still-swinging stone arm.

"Who's there?" Oren demanded.

"My name's Sera. I'm one of your new visitors, escorted by Thomas and Addie. They're still here with us. The rest left."

"THE REST LEFT?!" Oren craned backward, attempting to see the girl addressing him.

"Don't worry, I'm going to get you free of this. I don't know how yet, but I'm working on it. I can tell you it's not as easy as marching over to you and removing those rocks."

"AND WHY NOT?" Oren exclaimed.

"Because even *if* I could somehow join you at your side, I would still be exposed, surely next to be attacked. Then, there'd be no one to save you."

Sera waited for a softening acceptance in the relic's contorted face. "But that's my pledge: I will do everything I can to slay that beast. Then I'll come for you, to set you free."

Sera returned to the edge of the chamber to crouch near Addie while devising a plan. After a moment's silence, she raised the relic's heavy head to meet her at eye level. "Does it seem strange to you that more worms just appeared alongside the first one?"

Addie furrowed her brow. "I don't know, Sera. Every bit of this is absurd. Should you set the deadringer loose?"

"He *is* a force to be reckoned with. And he would help us discern the en-chanted bits of this monstrosity." Sera paused. "But he'd only be copying the un-hexed version of Maeve. She would definitely have the upper hand."

Suddenly, a body knelt next to the two. It was Enry. "You're all right!" Sera exclaimed.

"Well, I bashed his shins in pretty good," Thomas joked as he too joined the group. "That was for outrunnin' me on the stairs." Then he turned to Sera, arm outstretched, to bestow a small, canvas bag. "Dinner is served."

SORCE

Thomas' pride spanned his face with a delightfully devilish, ear-to-ear grin. "When I left earlier, I also grabbed a few things from our lair."

Inside the bag, Sera found an assortment of roots, nuts, and some sort of Earth-native worm, presumably for Pterus. Underneath it all, she found a small, glass object. "What's this?"

"I broke a cardinal rule; I snagged our disenchantment helixir for you."

"You did what?!"

"Don't bother arguing. The way I see it, if you use it and you still die, they can't exactly punish you. On the other hand, if you use it to *successfully* slay the beast—and save Oren—then you had a good excuse for using it."

"What about *you?*" Sera retorted. "Whether or not *I* make it, you're sure to face some very angry company when they realize it's missing."

"Yeah...." Thomas shrugged. "But what are they gonna do, execute me?"

The implications were dizzying; *unhexed vision would help. Much of this mess is surely crafted. But this potion's not mine. If we're here for help, thieving from our hosts won't improve our odds of a warm reception.*

As Sera's mind raced ahead, her eyes suddenly went wide. "Does anyone in the Crimson Core own a hand mirror?"

Thomas hesitated. Then his sinister smile returned. "There is *one* among our circle. Can you guess whose it is?"

14

PHAEDRA'S MIRROR

The echoes of an ungainly trot announced Thomas' return from the relics' lair. Strangely, he didn't slow his limping run until he was fully upon Sera. In one hand, he clenched the hilt of a weapon. Given his large stature, the blade looked like a knife, but Sera knew better: *A sword when wielded by a faun of my frame.* In his other, he held an ornate mirror.

"You're gonna need to make it fast," he barked as he thrust both into Sera's arms. "They don't know exactly what's up, but I certainly attracted attention."

"Thanks!" Sera sat Phaedra's mirror down and uncorked the disenchantment helixir. Then she very carefully poured the magickal fluid over the mirror's glassy surface.

The potion immediately pooled up, contained by the mirror's ornate wooden edge, but disappointingly, nothing more happened.

Now what? Sera's eyes panned from the mirror to the empty vial to Thomas and back to the vial. Her palms were sweating, her heart sinking to the floor. *I've just WASTED a potion the Crimson Core have saved for a century!* "Well?" Enry asked. "What are you waiting for?"

Oh, right! "Deguile!" At once, the pooled liquid simmered as though brought to a boil. Then a brilliant blue flash scintillated from its bubbling surface. The effect was truly magickal.

As a plume of smoke lazily cleared, Sera found the mirror once again dry. Without explaining herself, she grabbed the mirror and rose. Then, to the concern of her company, she marched toward the ever-irate, serpent-haired head of Maeve.

Sera stopped just short of the worms' reach. Then she turned to face her worried friends and raised the mirror to her face. With it now blocking view of her expression, Enry and Thomas waited anxiously for an update.

For a moment, Sera turned her head —and with it, the mirror—in various directions. She was careful to move in such perfect sync that the mirror may as well have been attached to her face. Then she lowered it to reveal an ecstatic expression of pride. "It works!" Despite the chaos still raging behind her, Sera had been restored, fueled by new optimism she might yet succeed.

Sadly, her deserved delight was cut short as Phaedra and the rest of the

relic circle rushed into the chamber. "MY MIRROR! THAT LITTLE *THIEF* PILFERED MY MIRROR!"

There would be no negotiating. Sera was out of time. "The sword!" she cried.

Enry was ready. At once, he darted to her, the fiery mob mere paces behind.

But they were too late. The moment Sera seized the weapon, she stepped backward toward the swinging arm and writhing mess of worms. All the while, she was relying on the mirror's reflection instead of direct eyesight.

Backward she ventured, bound for a danger no one else dared near. The absurdity of her actions had forced a lull upon the mob. But as Sera backed into a pool of goo, it gave way. Seconds later, so too did the nearest worm. As it whipped at Sera, its appearance distorted. Somehow, the worm appeared to get squeezed when at its closest. Enry would later describe the effect as akin to peering through thick glass.

With another stride, another worm struck out before similarly distorting. At the edge of the chamber, a mix of awe and horror blanketed the crowd. The girl hadn't yet used her sword, but she was holding the mirror as though her life depended on it.

As Sera neared stone Maeve's destroyed right arm, the monstrosity's left swung out, narrowly missing her. Unlike the worms, it hadn't bent to Sera's mirror-guided will. Slowly, she climbed the dead arm to reach Maeve's head.

Then, out of sync with her movements, Sera thrust her sword upward. She had seen something no onlooker could. Like Maeve's arm, one of the many frenzied worms had penetrated her invisible bubble of distorted space. But with Sera's ready defense, the worm struck her sword to gruesome effect. A burst of shrill hisses made clear Sera's small victory as it recoiled. Hastily, she advanced, scaling the stone head. Amid a tangle of worms, a sphere of impenetrability seemed to surround her.

Again and again, only a single worm was having any luck entering Sera's bubble. Through every step and swing, she stared myopically into her mirror, tracking the bug's reflection. Each time it attacked, she struck back.

After several close calls, Sera let slip a short, hoot-like scream, reflecting both fear and triumph as the worm brushed past her sword-wielding arm. From a distance, those watching could see her adversary's bubbling mucus cauterizing the sword to her forearm.

A moment later, Sera thrust herself into another full-force swing. This time, she connected directly with the worm's soft middle. Her devastating strike let loose its innards, and with them, an ensemble of cheers from those paying witness. Voices that had howled in anger now bellowed in celebration.

But gaining the upper hand brought Sera no joy. She pitied her mangled adversary—even as they sparred to the death. She understood the unfairness of its circumstance as much as her own, each crushed between colliding celestial bodies that cared not for softer constituents. With a conscience as heavy as her sword, Sera swung hard and halved the beast.

All about, strange phenomena coincided with the deadly blow. Instantly, the other serpent worms disappeared. The ooze too. As Sera scanned the scene, she found little remained: only an expressionless stone monster still swinging its sole arm erratically.

Sera had accomplished the impossible, but she wasn't done. Wearily, she slid down now-dull stone face and carefully stepped out onto its shoulder. After tucking the mirror into her belt, she raised the sword with both hands, and paused for a breath. *This I can enjoy.* Then, with all her might, she drove the sword down. As metal collided with fractured stone, the last-moving arm crashed to the ground.

Whether she liked it or not, Sera Skohlidon had become the quintessential hero. Enry and Thomas rejoiced as their friend slimbed down—and they weren't alone; even the once-bloodthirsty relic horde was now cheering. Still, Sera paid little notice. Her work wouldn't be done until her promise to Oren had been fulfilled.

Upon reaching the relic, she slid her sword under the biggest rock pinning him. Utterly depleted, she slumped her body over its hilt. The boulder lifted, and Oren scrambled free.

Braced by one another, the two staggered over the wreckage to rejoin the group. As they neared, Phaedra snatched the mirror from Sera. "YOU STUPID WRETCH, YOU STOLE MY MIRROR!"

"Hold on now," Oren rebuked, "that's no way to talk to the girl who saved me.

Besides, technically, *Thomas* took it.

This girl figured out what none of you had; that the monster blocking our path to the world above and keeping me captive was an enchanted illusion."

"It was enchanted," Sera clarified, "but for you it wasn't an illusion. As long as the enchantment was maintained, its effects *were* real."

Oren turned to Sera. "How did you manage to get Phaedra's mirror to show things in their un-hexed state?"

Thomas jumped in: "I gave her the disenchantment helixir too."

"YOU DID WHAT?!" Phaedra's rage was now boiling over.

"I believed in her when none of you did—and it was worth it! She saved Oren, and we're no longer trapped."

"AND SHE USED OUR HELIXIR!"

Sera stepped between Thomas and Phaedra. "Well, ma'am, you have something nearly as magickal. I applied the helixir to your mirror so that its effects wouldn't stay with me. I wanted to return the borrowed magick once I was done slaying that monster—or getting devoured by it." Sera looked up at the matriarch. Phaedra's unfazed expression was utterly unnerving.

"I'm sorry. This is no way to make a first impression. I came here because I was told you have experience with aeries, that you're wise, and that you haven't been corrupted by the Grand Sorcerer's supposed gifts."

"Dear, *you* don't need to apologize," Oren pressed. "We all know this mess was the Coven's making. You stepped into their disaster, faced an unwelcome reception from our lot, and still, you cleaned up the mess and saved me. You are a hero," he looked around for all to see, "and you deserve our PRAISE." Oren's words drew wild approval.

Phaedra spat and turned to leave, but none among her company made way. Oren then motioned an invitation for *Sera* to lead. This time, all made way.

With her arm fused to a sword, a decapitated serpentine beast behind her, a fluorescent friend by her side, and a fearsome horde leading her into total darkness, Sera realized she had never felt more at home. This was the strange reality she knew existed, long ago buried and forgotten beneath her world's bizarre surface. Here, in the depths of the earth, she could find answers. Here, she could discover herself.

15

THE CRIMSON CORE

As Sera entered the tunnel, Oren re-hooked his elbow around hers. Enry's fireflea body paint had mostly dimmed and she no longer had a lantern, so the extra support was most welcome. "So how do you do it," she asked, "function in total darkness?"

"In the decade after the Queen's Corps left, we trained ourselves to navigate with less and less light. We used their remaining fuel supply to ease ourselves off of our light dependence. In time, we learned every inch of the mine, this tunnel, and our lair. And since then, day after day, year after year, we've continued to use the same pathways. In time, we learned to depend on other, heightened senses to see. There's no chance I could trip in here. For us, these spaces are so rich in known contour and detail that our perception is nearly like seeing."

"I'm so impressed!" *Seeing without sight, like a bat.* She was reminded of Enry's recent success seeing more with hyperspectral imagery than was readily apparent through visible light.

In the same vein, I wonder what I can do to improve my current predicament. Quietly, she accessed OmniSync, ask-ing the network to replay her prior exchange.

In an instant, she was treated to the sounds of echoing steps, distant voices, and an up-close exchange with Oren as he once again explained growing accustomed to the darkness.

Is the audio from logs preserved in 3D form? she asked OmniSync.

"Logs do not compromise the fidelity of the original experience," the network confirmed.

Okay. Without OmniSync, if I were to focus on a single sound, I think I could roughly estimate its direction and distance. Let's see if OmniSync can do the same but for ALL surrounding sounds at once. Sera gave the order: *Continue playing this log but replace the dark visuals with a spatial recon-struction using the estimated depth of all audio sources.*

At once, Sera's pitch-black experi-ence took on rich detail. She could see the top half of Oren as he spoke, Phaedra's legs as she angrily clopped along the tunnel ahead, and Enry and Thomas as they threw covert karate chops in Phaedra's direction. The sen-sation was magickal.

Sera logged out to refocus on her present walk with Oren. A return to total darkness brought a tinge of disappointment, but she didn't dwell. "When we reach your lair, Oren, do you think your friends could do me a favor, please? If we could get them to distribute themselves about the space and clap for a few seconds, that'd give me a way to effectively *see* the space."

"Looking for more applause?" Oren teased. Sera felt like sinking into the floor as she stuttered and fumbled to return a coherent explanation. But a reassuring pat on her elbow-hooked arm told her there was no need to fret. "Sera, I'm just kidding! Of course, that won't be a problem."

…

Once they'd reached the relics' lair, Sera and Enry were led down a disorienting series of staircases to a lower level. An echoing of hoofsteps suggested the space was monumental. Oren then organized Sera's peculiar clapping activity just as she had requested.

After a few seconds of clamor, Sera explained herself and thanked the participants for their support. Then she and Enry accessed the event through OmniSync, using her "echolocation" technique. Finally, she set the sequence to loop endlessly. As long as she stayed in one place—while in OmniSync— she could see a 3D-view of her otherwise imperceptible environment. Dual presence was as tricky as always, but given the alternative—seeing nothing at all—she was happy to embrace the challenge.

The relic's lair was astounding, not at all the sad, cave-like domain she'd imagined. With multiple levels united by a variety of different staircases, the central hall was chapel-like, except that little of the space was symmetrical. From each level, a myriad of different archways led to countless chambers beyond.

At the two lowest levels, where the group had stopped, the theater found a circular shape. Its floors were covered in straw, offering a welcome respite from all the endless stone. Strangely, in the middle of the straw on the bottom level, a large moat separated a central stone podium from the rest of the floor.

"Welcome, friends, to the Crimson Core!" Oren bellowed.

Enry marveled at the space before them. "This place is incredible!"

"It really is!" Sera giddily agreed. Below, a circular podium at the center of the room was surrounded by a ring of water. "What's the moat for?"

"It keeps us safe from our fire," Oren answered. "Tellin' stories around a bonfire is about all we have going for ourselves these days. In fact, with your brave show today, I imagine it won't be long before we're retelling your story."

"It's gonna put our old stories to shame!" Thomas' unannounced presence startled Sera because her auto-looping log hadn't shown him coming. "We sometimes weave refraction into our own stories," he explained, "but to see it again in real life—"

"Thomas is referring to the bubble that *we* saw surrounding you," Oren clarified. "The un-hexed reality you were seein' through the mirror—where just *one* worm had sprouted from Maeve's stone head—had to be reconciled with the enchanted reality *with many worms* the rest of us were seeing. Whenever realities collide, all manner of spooky phenomena are possible. Tonight, we witnessed refraction."

"I think I've seen it before," Sera remarked. "At a—a Soliday festival—" *Oh no! Soliday's in two—*

Inexplicably, the world had started tilting. Sera innately knew the space above her was "up," but gravity begged to differ. Suddenly, her knees buckled. As vertigo nudged her off her center, Sera fell from her senses and collapsed to the floor.

…

"Hey dear, it's okay. Take it easy." An unfamiliar voice was doing its best to comfort Sera as she wriggled.

"I'm sorry, Mother," Sera mumbled.

"She's burning up," the voice cried. "Bring water."

Soon, Sera felt big, rough hands lift her head. Then water spilled onto her lips. She welcomed the water in, and passed out.

…

"Oh joy, you're awake!" As Sera came to, she found her body drenched in cold sweat. "Hon, you want another blanket?"

"No, thanks." In time, Sera accepted the disorienting darkness and sat up. Right away, she noticed her arm had been cleared of its bonded weaponry. "How long was I out?"

"Nearly a day, I'd say. Hard to know for sure with no daylight to judge by."

Another day! My poor family must be worried sick. An image of Bram popped into Sera's mind. She imagined him waiting for her, wondering where she was, whether she was okay. What she would have given at that moment to hug him, to reassure him.

Then the same big hand reached out and touched Sera's. "We didn't get to meet, hon. My name's Goldie."

"Nice to meet you," *though I wish I could see you.* "I'm Sera."

"Of course you are, darling. You're all anyone can talk about. Folks have slowed their clocks to take you in."

"Good or bad talk?"

"All glowing praise, dear. Well, from everyone 'cept Phaedra, but don't pay her any mind."

"So, what happened to me?"

"Accordin' to that handsome boy, you hadn't slept in nearly two days 'n you'd eaten next to nothing. On top of an exhausting trek and a staircase sprint, you had that battle with a— well, a monster. It's no wonder you passed out, dear; your body needed the rest. You *still* need to take it easy."

"Mm," Sera croaked. "You mentioned others slowing their clocks. What does that mean?"

"Oh, it's a form of legacy magick," Goldie explained. "It predates Omni-Sync. With it, we get to perceive time at faster or slower speeds. Given that we're immortal, most of us have opted to speed up time—it makes our endless routine down here more bearable. But you've given us reason to break from our typical drifting."

"Dazzling," Sera gushed. "I've never heard of such a thing. And, come to think of it, I didn't know there even *was* magick that predates OmniSync."

"There's quite a bit, in fact. The form we're discussing is part of a class of 'mindful magick' that can be used to affect how you perceive time, the world, our even yourself."

Mulling over a new form of magick was proving a welcome distraction from Sera's queasy disorientation. "Do you need helixirs for mindful magick?"

"No, you don't." Goldie paused. "That might be why mindful magick was outlawed once upon a time: the clergy can't easily track it through OmniSync or regulate it like most helixirs."

"Would you be willing to teach me mindful magick?"

"Did you … catch the part about it being forbidden, sweetie?"

"I did."

"Just checking." Goldie laughed bashfully. "Then yes, I'd be delighted!" She then proceeded to indulge the request.

As Goldie soon explained, mindful magick spells work in various ways to expose "the truth of the present." They are part of a magickal class called "Bone" that serve forms of enlightenment. Goldie went on to outline the few forms of mindful magick their circle knew of:

Mindful Magick

Uncommon Sense, Chronillogical Perception, & Extraspection.

"Uncommon Sense enhances your senses. It's real easy. You touch part of your body—like, say, your nose—and then you say 'Sensorius.' While all your other senses fade away, whichever one you were touching becomes super sensitive. So, for example, you can smell flowers from a league away or hear hushed voices in a far-off room.

"With Chronillogical Perception, you can speed up your sense of time, makin' years feel like months or even weeks. You can also slow time, but that gets really … weird." Goldie giggled. "Anyway, you set the speed by first saying 'Tempus' and then following with either 'Citius' to speed things up or 'Tardius' to slow things down.

"Finally, there's Extraspection. To be able to see yourself as others do, to better understand yourself as just one character in a larger story." Goldie paused, searching for the right words to describe an out-of-body experience. "You'll just need to try it. You trigger Extraspection by saying 'Forasui.' And then, when you're ready to go back to seein' things normally, you just incant 'Intersui.'

"But take it easy with those spells, okay?" Goldie laughed nervously. "I feel like I may've just walked a babe up to a cliff or something."

Sera was about to reassure her host when echoing voices pulled her attention away. *Not just fauns,* she noted. *Something lighter and faster.* Sera studied the approaching sounds. *Pitter-patter-pitter.*

Suddenly, a wet snout nuzzled itself into her face. *Pterus!* Sera snuggled her companion back as the voices came into focus. *Enry … and Thomas.*

"Sera? You in here?" Enry certainly wasn't convinced they were yet in the right place.

Thomas, however, was surer: "How are you feelin', kiddo?"

"Much better, thanks."

"So, guess what?" Enry pressed. But before Sera could respond, the boy spoiled his own quiz. "They're going to let us see the Horroscope!"

Sera laughed. "Great. I was hoping we'd get to see it!"

"She needs rest," Goldie cautioned.

"Thanks Goldie, but don't worry, I'll take it easy. I just don't know whether I'm more excited to see this ancient device,"—Sera rose to her hooves— "or to simply see anything at all."

The group of five left Sera's resting chamber with Goldie and Thomas leading the way. Halfway down their first staircase, Sera noticed a faint light below. By the time they'd reached the vaulted room beyond, that light had grown to an impressive brilliance.

All about the central hall, lanterns had been raised, some on posts, others hanging from chains. Just as Sera had done with hers, each had been filled with firefleas.

But what most caught Sera's eye was the moat-enclosed podium at the center of the room. It was ablaze with flickering firefleas. Like a large, green fire, a thousand frenzied insects

danced atop the podium. Sera stood in awe. *It's beautiful.*

"She lives!" Oren called from below.

"I do!" Sera outshined the bonfire as the two met on one of the hall's many seating tiers. "A day in the dark will work wonders on the fatigued."

"You make it sound as though we were bein' cordial. But now that we've bought your good graces, you have no choice but to listen to us old timers tell stories all night."

Irving—who'd already been poking fun at Oren before they'd noticed Sera—could no longer help himself: "Boy oh boy, what I'd give to undo this immortality when you get going on them stories: 'Ooh, refraction…. Oh, what's this, Poseidon's trident? Pew pew pew. Just picture it. Amazing, huh? I said it's AMAZING, huh? Yep, … it's amazing. Okay, the end.'"

Irving tried to hold a deadpan expression, scrunching his face until it had shriveled and twisted like a raisen. "Pew pew pew," he repeated. His ridiculous retake proved enough as both he and Oren burst out laughing.

Thomas shook his head as though the impersonation was one he'd heard before. "I got a feelin' these two are up for it. But before our dinner, I was hopin' to show 'em the Horroscope." Thomas turned to face Goldie. "Would you please watch this pig thing while we go below?"

"Happy to watch the 'pig thing,' hon." Goldie rolled her eyes and smirked before crouching to lure Pterus over.

"Thanks a bunch. Now come on, you two! You're about to be the first outsiders to witness Crimson Core's sacristy, our room of sacred, magickal treasures."

16

HORROSCOPE

As they descended a final flight of spiraling steps, the room that entered view surpassed Sera's grandest imaginings. All about, glass and metal objects sparkled as Thomas extended his lantern forward. Across shelves and shelves of artifacts, dozens of strange, alchemical instruments, oddly shaped crates, and bottles of every size begged to have their stories told.

At the far end of the room, Thomas retrieved a hefty crate and brought it to a central table. Dust exploded outward as he set it down. From within, he carefully removed an ornate, pie-sized apparatus with a metallic sheen. Gingerly, he laid the device on the table.

The Horroscope hosted a complex system of concentric rings, some extending beyond its main body. In its middle were a number of pronounced, orbital gears, among which, three had been given specially distinction: a big one in the center had been etched to look like the Sun, and two medium-sized gears in the outer rings represented Earth and Mars. Finally, spanning the entire outside edge were clusters of bulbs whose filaments all faintly looked like eights.

While Thomas twisted a fin on the Sun gear, the orbital gears surrounding it, including Earth and Mars, also turned. At the same time, some of the peripheral bulbs illuminated, revealing numbers that continuously changed in response to the twisting. When he stopped, the filaments in these bulbs rested on "3106-05-59." Then he pulled the Sun gear upward, and additional bulbs lit up to the right of the shown numbers. As he turned the Sun gear in this raised state, the newly illuminated filaments cycled through their own whirlwind of numbers. Thomas slowed his twisting before stopping as the bulbs flickered to "21:36." Last, he pushed the Sun gear down once again, causing all remaining bulbs to light up. The balance of the device's outer edge now showed: "+00.124322 -57.647138 « E" and "M » -00.161894 +19.504923."

"This is a 'Horroscope.' Right now, it's set to the date and time the Queen Witch was born. The Earth coordinates represent this very location. The Martian counter-coordinates indicate the closest spot on our sister planet at the same time."

"I've never seen *anything* like it!" Sera exclaimed. "May I give it a try?"

"Absolutely. Just be careful."

Sera nodded. But just as she'd begun to twist the Horroscope's Sun dial, Goldie's voice rang out from the stairwell. "Maybe you all could bring it 'n try later? Everyone's ready."

Thomas turned to Sera. "Okay, you hang onto it tonight."

Up a level, the central hall had taken on a new light. Across the bottom two floors, the relics were now gathered in even distribution. Each looked totally relaxed, as though they had just happened to be seated as such. But something about the arrangement gave the room a sense of occult significance. Spots for Goldie, Thomas, Enry, and Sera stood out. Goldie invited Sera and Enry to sit next to the blaze.

At the base of the great "bonfire," an etched—and painted—emblem caught Sera's eye. Its form looked a bit like the Coven's, but its inner details were different, marked atop by an explosive black force that seemed to burrow into the earth. At the lowest point of the void it carved, a red diamond held some great significance—though Sera had no idea what that was. Just then, Thomas leaned in. "Ah yes, its resemblance to the Coven's crest is by design," he explained. "'The Crimson Core' is a reference to the undying wrath the Queen and her Sorcerer unearthed in the depths of their malfeasance."

Before Sera could press for a better explanation, Oren's voice interrupted the exchange: "To our guests!" As he saluted Sera and Enry, he raised his mug to a chorus of cheers.

The acoustics in the great hall were phenomenal, as though it had been designed with crisp sound amplification in mind. At her side, Sera found a platter of plums, walnuts, and greens.

As bellies filled, so too did the hall swell with chatter and laughter. Sera realized this was a moment she'd love to be a spectator to the full experience, unconstrained by her own perspective. *Why not?* Excitedly, she incanted the spell she had been so eager to try:

"Forasui."

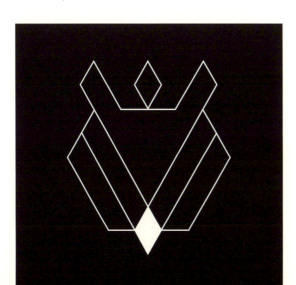

In an instant, her experience of the dinner was altered. It wasn't that her vision actually changed—rather, she found herself freed from her body and its limited perspective.

As though metaphorically floating above the fire, Sera took in all parties equally—including the girl known as "Sera." She noted Irving and Phaedra locked in a fierce debate while Addie and Goldie were quite the opposite, exuding sweet love for one another.

But as she observed the circle, Sera naturally gravitated to Enry. Despite the ordeal they'd endured to see her safely reach the relics' lair, he still looked effortlessly put-together. His carefree demeanor, in contrast to his sharp, perfect features, was hard to deny; he was dashing. Enry leaned to the girl at his side and smiled softly. "Try your birthday on that thing."

Sera watched her character roll her eyes. Still, she seemed to entertain the prompt, briefly going still. Sera suspected her character was checking for her birth time. Then the girl refocused on the device in her lap. Just as she had begun twisting its dial, a shrill call rang across the chamber: "HA-YOH!"

All conversation stopped. A surreal silence blanketed the room. Then a response boomed from the other side of the circle, this time a much deeper "OY-YAH!" One could hear a pin drop.

Next, quite unexpectedly, nearly all of the hooves in the space clopped on the ground, twice in unison. This was followed by a deep, drum-like resonance as the same relics slapped their chests in perfect time. All about, the once-jovial exchanges had taken an elegant swan dive into reverence.

There was rhythmic beauty to the orchestrated exchange, but it seemed neither Sera nor Enry were sure what to expect next. Enry looked enthralled by the unannounced shift, while Sera seemed unsettled, her focus on the Horroscope momentarily sidelined.

What followed was entrancing: a harmonic stream of voices calling out from various sides of the circle. Like a single voice bouncing about the hall, the speech shifted from high-pitched to low and back to high as a story was told, piecemeal, by all gathered relics. Between lines, calls of "HA-YOH" and "OY-YAH," along with clops and chest thumps, served as rhythmic interludes.

Centuries ago, life above was sweet 'n slow,
No secrets on the surface, no demons down below.

But our neighbors came to preach, to caution and beseech,
That deep within our core, lurked an evil out of reach.

An end to our maker, endowed upon the taker,
Unless we worked together to preempt such a caper.

By trial and error, paid in blood of the bearer,
We sought sin within, but our deeds were the terror.

No mantras, no yantras, no tantras, no tombs,
What we lacked in artifacts, our land witnessed in wounds.

Work started as a partnership to avert disaster,
Turned into dictatorship with servant serving master.

"Until you're successful, we're keeping your kin,
Work harder, blast faster, dig deeper within."

Our lives etched in stone, our offspring alone,
Our oppressors, frustrated, made plans to go home.

HORROSCOPE

"Return us our kin," we begged and we pleaded,
But our cries went unmet, unheard or unheeded.

Then we found a resin—a prize promptly seized,
Reduced and transformed—our captors were pleased.

"We've searched as you said, carved our land to bits,
The least you can do is return to us our kids."

"If you'd wanted the Yantra as badly as your kin,
We wouldn't today be in the position that we're in.

"But we'll throw you a bone, heck, a whole body's worth!"
Then down flew a faun who fractured the Earth.

With no time to waste, in desperation and haste,
We stormed the killa's keep, to afford our faun a taste:

Immortality brew, drawn from the resin,
Is what it would take to keep our own in the present.

Twix us and the bottle, stood a captor enraged,
With blood on his hands, failure fueling his brain.

SORCE

We struggled, tackled, pinned the ram in a pile,
But he dropped the prized potion, shattered the vial.

Life slipping away on this floor and below,
We dropped to the ground to lap up and stow.

Then down we flew—though not as fast as the ram—
Down to the bottom to finish our plan.

Lips wet with life, we kissed the limp lass,
We coddled, we swaddled, we wept as she passed.

A rumbling like thunder announced the away,
As *all* of our children departed that day.

Deep in our world, our pain and regret,
We discovered the yantra they'd set out to get.

We are the weapon, we are the scorn,
We'll end our oppressors by wit and by horn.

This marks the moment our neighbors will mourn,
This marks the spot rebellion is born.

As the impassioned poetry came to an end, Sera watched her own character slowly stand. She was obviously moved, but more than that, she was stunned. The girl, "Sera," turned to face Thomas. Without due care, she handed him the device in her arms. For a second, he simply studied it. Then, as if her disbelief were contagious, he haphazardly reassigned the priceless device to Enry. His expression showed he too was struggling to process something. "*This* is when you were born?"

Slowly, the girl nodded. "Mhmm, and that's *this* site?" she countered.

"It is," Thomas confirmed.

"What are the odds my birth time would match *this* site?" she prodded.

"Impossibly small."

Sera, while still out-of-body, imagined what this girl must be feeling as she processed the crushing burden just dropped on her. There was undeniable prophetic significance behind the fact that her birth time, as entered into the Horroscope, pinpointed their present location—the exact Earthly counter-coordinates also implicated by the High Priestess' birth time.

While word gradually spread and the room filled with animated colloquy, Sera, still extraspective, remained fully focused on the girl. It wasn't that she'd sought herself out. Sera was simply, impartially most drawn to this against-all-odds girl, inspired to help her face forces and worlds beyond her station —because the girl must. She had been thrust into a terrifying confrontation, and her response had been directness, to stare bravely into the darkness and denounce its vile offenses. For this girl to fulfill her destiny, she would need the unwavering commitment of many. The first would be Sera herself.

"Intersui."

17

THE RELEVANCE OF SCALE

Sera's revelation had spawned a lively discussion. After a few hours, it was settled: She was "destined to bring about the liberation of all fauns." Sera couldn't deny *some* significance to the discovery, but she was more careful than the rest in assigning meaning.

After what resembled a night's rest, the relics and their guests gradually trickled from various dark corners to reconvene in the central hall. Enry was seated at one of the chamber's upper balconies, idly engaging Pterus in a bit of play. As Sera neared, she realized the play was merely a distraction; the boy was troubled. "What's wrong?"

Enry glanced up, discovering Sera's eyes on him, and sighed. "Sometimes it's really hard just being friends. You're just so—I mean, who wouldn't want to be with a girl like you? You're fiercely intelligent, you're enchantingly beautiful, you have a heart of solid gold and the will of ten titans. You have it all."

Enry looked away. "I try to keep these thoughts to myself. I really do. It's just too hard keeping this bottled up."

Sera reached out, gently guiding him to face her. As their eyes met, some unknown force within her stirred. A feral beast rousing. Its strength scared Sera for she innately knew it bent not to her will, its compulsions driven by some deeper truth, a baser instinct.

"Mornin' you two!" Thomas rumbled from a few paces away. "Hope I'm not interruptin' anything. Wanted to see how our plan is comin' together."

Sera exhaled shakily. "It's coming. Enry and I were—" Sera began braiding hay into a crown loop to calm her trembling hands. "Well, I've been pondering what it would take to force the aeries to play nicely. It's not like we can appeal to them on some basis of decency. The only thing I can see working is intimidation. We need to organize. We need our kind to see the truth so clearly it can't be dismissed. If they witness their own children being abducted—if they understand that their kids *aren't* being divinely chosen to ascend—I think they will finally come around. Get our kin to acknowledge the ugly, parasitic truth of the matter, and you have a real force to be reckoned with."

Sera shifted her gaze up to Thomas. "Soliday's tomorrow. We know sacrificial offerings typically coincide with the event, with induction campaigns. If I can attend the ceremony, I think I can reveal what's really happening—maybe even broadcast it. I just need to figure out how to cloak myself from spying eyes now that I'm an outlaw. The problem is, I know so little about how they're accessing my logs."

Thomas' head rocked back as his his mind chased some fleeting idea. "Sera, may I see the port behind your ear?"

While perplexed, Sera obliged. The girl lifted her hair and turned so that her OmniSync port faced him—and the dwindling bonfire. Out of the corner of her eye, she caught Thomas nodding to himself. "What do the aeries tell you about them ports?" he asked.

"They're supposedly a rite of passage, a magickal endowment which unlocks a connection between us and the Grand Sorcerer's immense power."

"And do you question this?"

Sera felt chagrined. "Probably not as much as I should have."

"I'm no warlock, but I suspect aerie design behind this 'magickal endowment.' I doubt the Grand Sorcerer himself manifested OmniSync just so some dastardly aeries could track fauns.

But before we go any further, I want you to jump into your cloaked state, okay? This next bit's gonna help you."

"Sure." *As above, so below.* Sera pulled up a serene experience. "Okay, I'm in."

"So, how might you retain Omni-Sync's benefits *without* being tracked as a now infamous outlaw?" Thomas asked. "You'd need someone else's port."

"Enry's the only other one here with a port, but swapping between the two of us isn't going to be of much use; He lives in the same guild, and by now they must have figured out we're friends." Sera continued playing out the bad idea. "Worse still, I'd likely just be drawing attention to him." She turned to Enry. "Drawing attention to *you.*"

"Mostly correct. Except he's not the only one here with a port. Contrary to what you've been told, OmniSync's been around for centuries. Even the aerie excavation crew had ports. That's how they stayed connected with their higher-ups on Mars. So, let's say we had an aerie you could swap with…"

"The fallen ram!" Sera interrupted. "Your chant last night mentioned an aerie throwing one of your kids down the main shaft. You all had to confront

him to get to the immortality helixir that you hoped would save her. If I heard the story correctly, after the ram smashed the helixir vial, you all said something about him plummeting to the bottom of the shaft too."

"Very good. Unlike the others who fled that day, that particular aerie—the dead one—stayed behind. There's not much left of him 'cept a crate of bones. But his skull still has a port embedded —one we've crafted a key to access. Once unlocked, we're able to remove the port's central cylinder. That tiny contraption is definitely the heart of your induction."

Sera was giddy with excitement. "Well then, what're we waiting for?"

"Attagirl! I'll go get his remains. With a bit o' luck, it'll work for you. But you should stay cloaked until the very moment I unplug you," Thomas advised.

A minute later, she and Enry caught Thomas huffing into earshot. "Without all their trimmings," he bemoaned, "these guys still weigh a ton!"

Then, Sera heard—and felt—a dull thud as something landed in the hay. She abandoned her braided loop to find a ribbed, curling horn before her.

"Meet 'Molwart.' He always was a nasty one. Today, Molwart starts makin' amends. Now, hold on tight to his horns."

Sera obliged. Soon, she felt great tension as Thomas twisted the cylinder —and to a large extent, the skull with it. Then, in an instant, the tension was gone. A tinny scraping sound followed as Thomas removed the OmniSync cylinder from Molwart's housing ring.

"Now, Enry," he announced, "we're going to need your help as we do the same to Sera here."

Enry's hand slid over Sera's clenched fist. "You okay with this?"

"With you looking out for me, yes."

A breath later, Sera felt metal-on-metal contact as the relics' handcrafted key found its place, then immense pressure as Thomas twisted the key and Enry held her horns firm. Abruptly, the pressure stopped—as did Sera's leisurely stroll along a distant, moonlit beach. The girl's vision harshly transitioned to her real surroundings while a tinny scraping sound confirmed her own cylinder's removal. Then Sera felt another cylinder take its place, pressure pushing inward, then twisting to the right. Enry held her horns firmly as Thomas twisted it into place. A sub-tle *Pop* could be heard and felt as the cylinder locked into position.

"Alright, you bastard, time to rise!"

A surprised laugh nearly escaped Sera's pursed lips as she unpacked Thomas' harshness. *Oh right, a ruse, a show for spying eyes. This is the rude awakening Molwart would face.* "How long 'ave I been out?" she croaked in her grittiest voice.

"A long time, you scabrous mutt. We forced you into hibernation so we wouldn't have to deal with you." Thom-as poked Sera aggressively. "Consider yourself lucky we're wakin' you. You are gonna lead an expedition up top for us."

Now I'm a grimy, centuries-old aerie soldier in a faun's body! Sera wanted so badly to smile without betraying the act. Without hesitating, she logged into OmniSync.

At once, she was surprised by how very different the experience was. The old visuals she'd grown so accustomed to were gone, replaced with a set most alien. *Show me a calming experience.*

What OmniSync returned was not at all like the sort of serene experiences Sera had grown accustomed to. Rather, she was treated to a view of a smokey, indoor lounge. The ugly sounds of a raucous crowd demanded attention from beyond a drawn curtain. "I'm in."

"I should have warned you," Thomas confessed, "from here on out, you're 'Molwart.' Let's make sure you reach the guild without being recognized. To that end, I'm gonna go bring the others up to speed. And I have an idea how to make you more Molwart-like."

Thomas groaned as he rose to his hooves. "Enry, mind takin' that skull to the sacristy, please?"

"Aye," Enry agreed. Then he soften-ed his voice: "See you in a bit."

Sera took a deep breath. By the time she'd exhaled her anxiousness, she and Pterus were alone. Free from Omni-Sync, she gazed out at the dulling "fire." Sera recalled its effect the night prior as it shimmered across Enry's sculpt-ed face. But now it was meager. She wondered whether the captive firefleas had the sense to know it was daytime up above, whether they were deliber-ately dulling. *Or is the answer more macabre?* she pondered. *Maybe their light just fades as they die…. What if*

they're ALL dying? At the relics' scale, the fates of a thousand firefleas are basically inconsequential—and yet I can't really fault our company for such decimation. Without common perspective, real empathy is surely impossible.

Soon, Sera's unsated mind moved onto the broader relevance of scale: *What if, to the Grand Sorcerer, fauns are just a fascinating blaze of firefleas? Could he even truly care about the well-being of a single faun any more than I'm capable of empathizing with a fireflea?*

Sera decided to get more acquainted with the very old, very alien form of OmniSync. But just as she'd jumped in, she heard voices approaching. *Thomas and Goldie.* Not sure whether they'd be addressing "Sera" or "Molwart," she accessed a serene experience.

"Listen up," Thomas boomed, "here's what's happenin': you're gonna eat this root or it's back to naptime for you."

"Thomas, I'm cloaked!" Sera volunteered. "You can speak normally."

"I am."

"Darlin', that's not funny," Goldie rebuked. But Thomas was already chuckling at his own crass joke. "Love, don't pay him any mind. We brought you something: 'hoarseradish'—a nasty root we sometimes eat. It's good for you. More importantly, it alters your voice." She handed Sera a fist-sized bulb. "We didn't always sound like this."

Sera took a big bite as though eating an apple. The root was extremely bitter and crunchy. She was about to go for another mouthful when a hand hurriedly pushed the bulb away. "Oh no, dear!" Goldie was notably alarmed. At the same time, it sounded like Thomas was now laughing even more heartily.

"What? What did I DO?" To Sera's great distress, her voice had just taken a sharp turn. By the time her question landed, her voice was already much deeper, grittier, and far louder.

"It's just that you only need a nibble."

"OH NO!" Sera groaned. Her voice was now so different she sounded like a monster—even by relics' standards. Absentmindedly, she reacted to her own appalling voice with another "OH NO!"

The effect was too much to bear. At once, Goldie lost her usual composure to a fit of cackles. Thomas fared even worse, shedding tears as he howled and wheezed uncontrollably. "That's going to work … just fine."

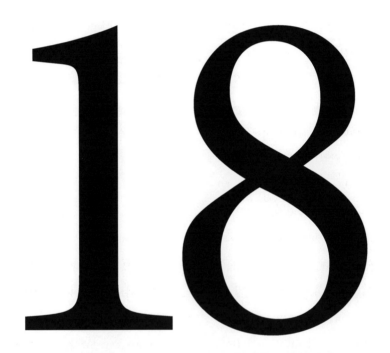

18

THE ONE WHO WHIPS THE WINDS

Sera avoided interaction as the relic horde filed in and preparations were made for a return to the surface. Unconcerned with her staunch refusal of gifts, the relics ultimately insisted Sera take their sole remaining potion: a fuddle helixir. Concocted from muddle resin, the magickal fluid was a staple among the clergy. Fuddle helixirs were used to turn inoculated parties temporarily more complacent, more accepting of the clergy's smoke and mirrors.

Within an hour, plans were settled; two groups would escort Sera, Pterus, and Enry back to Haveroh. Splitting in two would ensure Sera's extradition —where she'd carry on her Molwart charades to venture unseen—wouldn't be complicated by Enry's presence.

Soon, the two groups were ready. Sera would return with Thomas and Oren while Enry and Pterus would be accompanied by Irving and Phaedra.

With dimming lanterns in hand, the two groups ventured through the dark caves to the bottom of the mineshaft, and then up, up, up.

At the first gate they encountered —formerly guarded on both sides by Maeve's stone likenesses—they found no such gate guardian on the inside. Most surreal, the stone wall looked as though it had been stretched when the now-legendary stone abomination had pulled free to give chase.

The balance of the spiraling trek brought little of note—but that didn't mean the climb was easy; by the time Sera staggered out, into the sun's dying light, her legs were on fire. A dozen trembling steps further, she tumbled into the sun-singed grass.

Sadly, Sera's swoon delivered no respite from the inertia. In fact, her woozy head had begun to spin faster.

'Round and 'round she hurtled. After a few disorienting seconds, she realized she'd been plucked from the clearing by a mysterious vortex. Below, a stormy cyclone hungrily sucked up other souls from the land. All about, their agonizing cries whipped past Sera with horrid speed. But above the calamity, a worse destiny awaited: the mouth of Maeve bore down, inhaling shame-stricken prisoners with carnal delight. As Sera approached the same fate, a deafening howl of winds eclipsed all sensation.

This is it.

Sera was shaken into consciousness. For a few seconds, she struggled to find her bearings. For one thing, the deafening roar was still present. For another, the world truly was shaking. Sera realized she was being handled —very roughly—as Thomas sprinted toward the tree line. And then there was sky: whereas it should have further darkened since she'd last seen it, the heavens were a fiery shade of orange.

"THE QUEEN'S CORPS ARE HERE!" Thomas roared.

Still in a daze, Sera's gaze landed on the immense, metal spaceship bearing down on them. It was rotating such that its nose would soon face the great void from whence it came, and its thundering rockets would soon greet the ground. As the ship's explosive flames inched closer, she understood the primitive urge to flee; the ship was about to eclipse the sky itself. Its flames were incinerating most of the clearing.

Then its rockets went dark. In that moment, before the ship reconciled its great weight with its celestial target, there was peace. Thomas deposited Sera within the tree line just as the ship too touched down.

The landing may have constituted masterful aeronautical handling, but a shockwave of displaced energy offered rebuttal. Sera and company were all knocked off their hooves.

After a few seconds, a discordant mix of mechanical noises began clicking and buzzing behind the ship's vast, metallic hide. Then a ring of exterior lights fired on. A breath later, a fine seam appeared on the ship's hull. As a forming lip pivoted outward, an arch-shaped gap formed. Then the separated metal surface touched the ground. Sera realized it had become a ramp.

Suddenly, a metal wagon raced out into the clearing. It was unlike any Sera had seen before. Its wheels weren't wooden or rickety, its coach had a perfect glass wall at the front, and it moved faster than any of the simple, magick-imbued ones that occasioned Haveroh. Once the wagon skidded to a stop in the clearing, Sera noticed a high-pitched hum emanating from it. "We'd best get a move on," Oren announced.

As her group turned to leave, Sera caught the briefest, distant glimpse of Enry and his crew a furlong away. It seemed they too had made it to safety.

...

Counter-intuitively, the Grimwoods turned out to be easier to navigate at night than day. With so many pockets of firefleas about, one could see a great distance in all directions. Sera and her crew retraced her earlier path from the clearing to the brook, racing as fast as their bodies would allow. But they were careful to circumnavigate the pyramid-shaped encampment in the middle. With the Queen's Corps arriving, aeries would soon be moving into the woods. And the Child Processing Center, with its proximity, was sure to hold gravity.

After several hours' journey along the brook, a caterwaul of hums whirred past one side of the stream. Several wagons were zipping through the woods en route to guilds such as Sera's. Meanwhile, dimming pockets of firefleas offered similar warning: the group would have to pick up their pace if they intended to deliver Sera to Haveroh before Soliday festivities started.

Shortly after sunrise, they reached the edge of the thicket. As they neared, Sera discovered the field beyond was far from clear. Judging from the many, once again old-looking wagons parked—and the many aerie soldiers congregating in its center—the clearing seemed to have been designated an official staging ground for the big day.

Sera pulled up a serene experience to shroud her imminent reunion with Enry's group. The brief moment of calm would serve as a welcome chance for Sera to catch her breath. *My heart's REALLY racing,* she observed.

She recalled a study block when she'd learned the three reasons a heart beats fast: exercise, anxiety, and desire. An all-night run had checked one box, but she suspected anxiety was playing as much a role as exercise. *Two reasons.*

The blinding world ahead, in fact, the day ahead, would be marked by fiery confrontations, exposed truths, and if all went according to plan, an Earth-shattering reckoning of perspectives.

A moment later, Sera recognized Enry's voice: "Oh no! It's your grandpa. They're leading him to one of the wagons and it's, um, distorting!"

"Seems we're no longer able to see the real form of the wagon," Oren observed. Sera's company watched as the back of the wagon stretched, revealing a rear door. Then one of the soldiers opened the door and shoved the old faun inside.

"Can we STORM THE WAGON?" Sera blurted.

"Not a chance. Not while the clearing's full of soldiers. We're gonna need you to go play your part, Sera. You have a crucial role to play today—and it's not here. Leave this 'Opa' fellow to us."

Sera bowed her head. She couldn't see the company before her, but she faced them all the same. Then an unannounced party hugged her. For a moment, they said nothing. Without sight, Sera focused on the feel of their frame, the warmth of their breath. As she realized who it must be—a faun so comfortable with her that they were willing to invade her space when she couldn't see them back—Sera found Enry's stolen intimacy both calming and exciting. "Be careful out there," he whispered. "I'll be waiting." Then he placed Pterus' lead in her hand. At the touch, she nearly grabbed his hand and pulled him back to her side. She was finally ready to accept the truth of her feelings—that a *mutual* attraction existed. Despite his immaturity. In fact, because of his easygoing whimsy, Enry was exactly the sort of company she preferred. A familiar image settled in her mind: it was Enry, aglow from the flickering fire, as he turned to take in Sera, to stare at her fully through resolved, immodest eyes. *Three reasons,* she admitted with a flutter.

With a deep breath, she turned away from her friends and exited OmniSync. While staying within the thicket, Sera carefully circumnavigated the clearing.

She wasn't the same faun who had entered the Grimwoods days earlier. In the depths of the Earth, she'd shed a calloused hide of self-doubt to find her vibrant inner self. With every breath, Sera exhaled captive fears. With every step, she was discovering new strength.

As she strode from the thicket, a furlong from the aeries' staging area,
Sera adapted the relics' impassioned liturgy to make it her own:

"Through smoke 'n thunder, you pillage, plunder.

You suck up souls you do not own.

But I will not pray. I am not prey.

I am the truth, and I will be known.

You'll fear this fury you have born,

This seed that you have sown.

For I'm the one who whips the winds,

Your reckoning
cyclone."

19

THE FACE OF DANGER

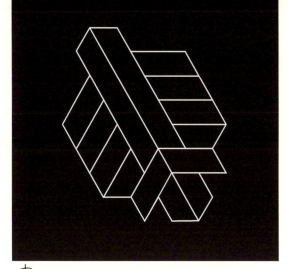

Crucial work awaited Sera, but before any of it, she'd settled on seeing her family. Rounding the last corner on her way home, her heart dropped; a wagon bearing the Queen's Corps emblem was parked in front of her house. The rarely seen symbol carried such powerful associations that the mere sight of it was known to make stoic fauns flighty, dry palms clammy, and confident voices tremble. Sera veered into nearby foliage for cover.

After ten minutes, two robed aeries emerged, hunched over so that their spiraling horns could clear the front doorway. To her relief, they weren't escorting anyone out. Once the alien visitors had departed, gone from sight, Sera and Pterus ventured in. Dust from the road swirled like embers as warm light invaded her home.

Mother and Father were in the kitchen. At the sight of Sera, Mother's knees buckled and body crumpled.

Sera and Father dashed to Clementine's side. A second later, Bram raced into view. Already, he was drowning in tears. Sera outstretched her arms to make room, but as the boy threw himself into her embrace, he pushed Sera and Father off their huddled bases. At once, the entire Skohlidon family tumbled to the floor. Sera held tight long after their bodies had settled. This was the reunion she'd needed.

In time, Mother's voice croaked from the pile. "We were so worried."

"I'M SORRY."

At hearing Sera's hideously gritty response, Mother's eyes widened, but her daughter just grinned and shook her head dismissively. "It's temporary. I ate HOARSERADISH."

Sera proceeded to share her adventure with her parents, carrying them through tale of Wilford and his devious plans, the relics, her battle with a stone incarnation of the Royal Coven, and the stunning, Horroscope-enabled discovery that her own birthday held prophetic significance. She also used the opportunity to come clean regarding Pterus' true nature. While he was still wearing goggles, his exposed ribs

SORCE

and wings left no room for continued deception; This was no injured pig.

Afterward, Sera studied her parents' faces. She could see each struggling to process what they'd learned. *There's no hex here, no magick holding you back. You must choose: comfortable denial or uncomfortable acceptance.*

Sera still wasn't sure which half was winning in Father's mind when he began recapping the Queen's Corps' visit to their home. As she learned, the aeries had appealed to her parents on the basis of "concern" for her. They'd explained how she'd fallen in with dark-magick-wielding beings, that she was in great danger, and that as soon as she returned, they had to report her to the nearest authorities. Father looked torn as he relayed this to Sera.

The aeries had promised that Sera was not to be harmed, that they merely intended to question and caution her. But a particular part of their message had really troubled Father: they had also cautioned that failure to report her return could put the entire family at risk. As they'd put it: "The Grand Sorcerer himself is known to intervene in times like these. Let us address this excusable misstep before it escalates to a level that garners *his* interest. Particularly around Soliday, his eminence is known to play a more *active* role in our plane."

"He looked at Bram. The aerie officer looked right at him when he said that." Bram's jaw dropped as Father carried on with the retelling: "We're compelled to bring your brother out to the guild square this afternoon for Soliday inductions. I'm just concerned," Father confessed. "We may be tangled into something truly dangerous."

"The danger's always been there, Father. We have to remain strong. Real strength is finding the resolve to carry forward in the face of danger." Sera studied her father as he mulled over his regurgitated counsel.

After an uncomfortable silence with little expression to judge by, Sera sprang the question she'd been dying to ask: "Why was Opa taken?"

Mother's eyes filled with tears as she shook her head. "'Coercion,'" she squeaked through feeble air quotes.

"There's only one side guilty of coercion here." Sera waited for looks of acknowledgement. "As you say, Father,

we're tangled into something truly dangerous. If I blindly comply, I'm sure to be arrested, just like Opa, but I don't want to endanger you." She paused. "Do as the aeries have advised: report my return, attend the ceremony as expected. I'll emerge from this all right." Slowly, Father nodded. There may have been more he wanted to say, but nothing more was offered.

...

Before heading out, Sera grabbed some fabric to re-wrap Pterus' midsection. She also stopped at her room for a ceremonial garb. A remnant from her younger years, the robe she had grabbed didn't fit well, but it did conceal. What's more, it made her look a lot younger. *Better than nothing.*

Then Sera gave Bram a hearty hug and bid him farewell. She promised she'd see him again later that morning, that she'd be present, "front row," to watch the induction ceremony.

Back on the road, she and Pterus headed for the guild square. Sera was careful to keep her head low in the old robe. With flags lining Haveroh's main streets, fauns filing out of their homes, and a band trumpeting in the

distance, it seemed the celebrations were already kicking off. The closer she got to the square, the more fauns she encountered—and the more aerie invaders she had to carefully avoid.

The square was framed with various kiosks and tents. Amid a suspended web of colorful streamers and cobblestones littered with confetti, overly animated vendors were peddling sun-themed wares, fortune-telling services, fake wands, and confections.

To one side, a gigantic, stone stage had appeared. It looked as though the land around the stage had been carved from naturally rocky terrain. *If they're going to nab a child, I need to be ready to broadcast it. I need to anticipate how and where they might take the child.*

After a few minutes, she'd convinced herself that the inductions would be performed on the grand stage itself. While timing her movement carefully to avoid attention, Sera ascended stone steps at the back of the stage. Given the relative sparsity of fauns thus far gathered, she hoped to steal a minute to examine the stage without attracting attention.

As Sera soon observed, there was

nothing noteworthy about the structure. Whatever magick the aeries had used to erect it, she found no detail to suggest ulterior, kidnap-conducive underpinnings. *Maybe there won't be any sacrificial offerings this year. Even if there are, who's to say they'd happen during induction? As accepting as Haveroh is, abducting kids in broad daylight would certainly be pushing it.*

Sera was about to slip off the stage to investigate how aeries might *move* an abducted child when she realized a mindful magick spell might be useful. Quickly, she touched her eyelids and incanted:

"Sensorius."

At once, the sounds of the festivities faded away, as did the smells, even the feeling of the stage under her hooves. Sera peered about the bustling square like an eagle in the sky. She could see so much, as though focusing on all details at once. In the distance, she spotted a squadron of aerie soldiers approaching the square. *Time to pick up the pace.*

Sera soon abandoned exceptional sight, touching her ears as she recited the spell again. This time, all went dark as she traded sight for hearing. She could hear a mother reprimanding a child, Pterus' snotty breathing, even individual flags rustling in the wind.

This is amazing, but I don't have time. One more, and it's time to move on. Let's see: smell, taste, or touch? Heightened smell with Pterus next to me? I'll pass. Let's go with … touch. Sera put her hands together and recited the spell again. Still in the dark, but now without the ability to hear, she immediately regretted the choice. But as she stepped forward, ready to return to Common Sense, she felt something: a hollowness beneath her. *How is that possible?*

She walked a couple of paces to be sure. A cavity within the stage was giving unexpected resonance to her steps. Then she walked to the edge of the stage. There was no such resonance.

Sera returned to Common Sense. With her sight restored, she knelt down to inspect the stage's stone surface. Pterus puffed air at the ground as well. *Nothing.* There was no seam in the stone to suggest a trap door. She hopped down from the stage, grabbed Pterus, and carefully examined the stage's perimeter. *Still nothing.*

Just as she'd finished studying the stage, Sera picked up on a faint, high-pitched hum. She scanned about for a wagon. One was pulling up nearby.

Casually, she backed into the crowd, pretending to admire wooden trinkets at a vendor's table while a few soldiers passed. *There it is: means of transport. To most, that wagon looks like nothing —certainly not something that would conceal an abducted child. But we know better, don't we, Pterus?*

The wagon had stopped with its rear side between two buildings—notably away from the festivities. The way it was parked would make it difficult to follow its occupants' actions, but Sera soon watched two aeries emerge from the narrow nook with a wooden crate. Despite their hulking physiques, the two were struggling to carry the over-sized item to the stage. In time, they managed to get it up the rear steps and situated at back of the stage.

The ceremony would start soon. Risking recognition, Sera craned her head to review the crowd. There were now a number of families present,

most with at least one young child in their company.

Sera's craning ended as she spotted Enry's parents: Commissioner Fenora and her husband Naden. They were on the far side of the square, standing watch over their two youngest, Fay and Gordy. To Sera's relief, Enry's parents seemed at ease. *I wonder, do you still think your eldest is off camping?*

While watching Fenora and Naden, Sera spotted her own family farther down the street. Unlike Enry's folks, hers looked pale and skittish. They moved nervously with heads low, as though each step through this mine-field would be their last.

Sera pitied them. Jack and Clementine were so mangled by fear that they had lost the will to stand tall, to crane their heads with due skepticism and confront the vile charades before them.

But as Sera tracked her parents' death march, she also sympathized with their plight. They'd seen more than Enry's parents. They understood more. And that knowledge had cost them every-thing.

20

SOLIDAY

In time, the band's grand trumpeting reached its crescendo. Those present turned their attention to the stage as one of the town's elders stepped out.

"Friends, thank you for joining us in this splendid celebration of Soliday, the Grand Sorcerer, and the many blessed gifts he bestows. This year, we're going to be inducting your sweet kids here on the stage! What's more, the Coven's Herald is here to mark the occasion!"

Cheers erupted from the thickening crowd as parents shared their wild approval. Sera's stomach turned as she marveled at their stupid denial: *you're cheering for a system that STEALS your children!*

On-stage, the elder continued, highlighting important news and outlining the afternoon's schedule. From Sera's position at the front of the stage, she'd lost sight of her parents.

"Compassus Māter,"

a wayfinding spell, brought a humming to her ears that resonated loudly as she turned in the wrong direction and dulled to an inaudible level once she'd spun to her mother's heading.

Sera studied the crowd before her until she eventually spotted them. They were escorting Bram to queue in behind an already-long assembly of other children. The line was a mess of kids—most of whom were too small to have any sense of a proper formation—bobbing out of queue. Fortunately, Bram was wearing a bright red jacket, so he was easy to spot. After a second, Gordy plowed through the line to stand next to him.

One by one, the kids were invited up the steps at the rear of the stage. With the inductions imminent, Sera switched to super-sight to watch with eagle-eyed focus. At the processing station, each child was subjected to the jarring procedure, handed a sweet bribe and an entrancing device, and asked to take a seat on the stage.

Eventually, Bram was ushered up. Sera held her breath watching the robed facilitators, how the OmniSync port was implanted, and studying the toy Bram was handed. Nothing about his treatment was exceptional.

Soon, the last of the kids had been inducted. Sera assessed the little ones seated around the upright crate in the center of the stage. Squeals of delight filled the air as the kids got acquainted with a virtual fairy that danced about their devices. Sera eased a bit noting Gordy's spot next to Bram. *Strength in numbers.*

The two robed aeries were making their way around and over the seated kids to reach the upright crate. Delicately, they pried it open and pulled an aerie-sized mannequin out. Proud parents beyond the stage broke into another enthusiastic uproar while the seated kids remained focused on their devices. True to the sacrosanct order of inductions, one of the aeries then anointed her hands with a helixir and performed the "Animoto" spell on the mannequin. Behind her, the other carefully worked their mannequin's crate back to the edge of the stage.

At first, there was no indication the spell had worked. Only the surrounding crowd had changed as parents in attendance went completely silent. Anxiously, they studied the mannequin for signs of transformation. More than a few craned their heads for a better view.

Even with the help of Uncommon Sense super-sight, it was hard for Sera

to pinpoint when the transformation occurred. What started as a subtle, windblown rustling of the figure's feathers seemed to become, gradually, more. The feathers began shifting in ripples as if muscles under the surface were moving. In time, these tectonic movements appeared more deliberate. Then the towering figure stretched her wings and opened her eyes. The Herald was alive.

It took a few seconds for the kids to notice, but one by one, their attention shifted from the virtual Herald to her true form. Now the newly inducted —like their parents—were entranced. Sera studied the crowd. Dumbstruck and slack-jawed, those in attendance were giving every indication they had been hypnotized, rendered blind by an all-encompassing sense of euphoria. *THIS is how the clergy do it, how they reset parents to accept what follows.* Sera shook her head in disbelief. *They have just muddled most of my guild without the constraints of helixirs.*

Sera's extra-capable vision *shouldn't* have helped. With all she could appreciate at once, it should have been easy to slip into the same mesmerized state.

It seemed something about Uncommon Sense, an exclusion of all senses but sight, had made her immune to the Herald's crowd commandeering. *The clergy must be seizing control through one of the other senses.*

Sera studied the spectacle before her, serving witness as the only faun with eyes un-hexed. At nearly twice Sera's height, with ruminant legs and wings like a swan, the angelic Herald had begun to prance and pirouette about the children, praising them for reaching such a milestone. Imbued with the same elegance, the kids were rising to join the Herald's waltz.

Then, just as the Herald twirled past Bram, Sera witnessed a strange twiddling of the fairy's fingers. It would've been all too easy to miss the subtle gesture, but foresight and super-sight had endowed Sera with the extra focus to see this out-of-rhythm movement.

The gesture had been intentional, and in that light, most alarming. *This is it, my sole chance to broadcast an abduction. The world NEEDS to see what's happening.* Sera hesitated for a second, torn between broadcasting the abduction and rescuing Bram. *But I am NOT leaving Bram wriggling on the hook.* So she plowed to the front of the crowd, dropped Pterus' leash, and waited. When Bram next neared the stage's edge, she leapt up and seized him. Her sharp movement left no time for the aeries to notice, let alone intervene. A second later, she and Bram had disappeared back into crowd.

Crouched among the onlookers, Sera hurriedly examined her brother to be sure he was all right. In doing so, she realized her senses were still strictly limited to sight; she wouldn't be able to hear the aerie facilitators if they were calling her out. Quickly, she touched her eyelids for a return to Common Sense. Unfortunately, just as she incanted "Sensorius," a body behind her jostled forward. Sera's hand was flung downward, brushing her nose at a most inopportune time. Instantly, the world went dark as her vision was replaced by an exceptional sense of smell.

Pungent odors abounded. Faun sweat, swine sweat, sweet perfumes, and buttery foods filled the air. But something else was overpowering the aromas: *Something pheromonal. What-*

ever it is, it's extremely close. Sera leaned forward until her nose was on the odoriferous object. Then she reached out to grab it, but without sight or tactile sensation, she still no idea what it was.

Sera incanted a return to Common Sense. As she regained her senses, she realized what she'd grabbed: the strong pheromonal scent was coming from the back of Bram's jacket. *What would cause this?* she questioned.

Then a chill shot down Sera's spine. *The Herald just charmed the exact same spot! She's tagged Bram for ascension!* At that moment, Sera knew for sure: her family was under attack. At once, she commanded OmniSync to broadcast her current experience:

"Impertius!"

"Broadcast privileges are restricted. See your superior officer for exceptional privilege." *Argh! Of course, Molwart's restricted from broadcasting an ascension. What was I thinking?* While frantically considering next steps, Sera simultaneously stripped the tagged jacket from her bewildered brother and threw it back to the stage. Then she recited the compass spell again to

be guided to her parents. With Bram under one arm and Pterus under the other, Sera plowed through the mindless mass of onlookers, chasing a heading of minimal hum.

Only once she'd reached the rear of the assembly did she spot her parents. As she approached them, an uproar of applause signaled the ceremony's end. Father's sleepy expression roused a bit as he spotted Sera and Bram. "Oh, he's here.… I was confused," he confessed. "I thought that boy was Bram." Father pointed weakly to the stage.

Sera turned back to see Gordy at the stage's edge, holding the magickally-tagged jacket as he whirled circles of his own in search of Bram. Sera dove back into the thinning crowd.

By the time she'd reached the front of the stage, only sparse pockets of fauns remained. There, she frantically spun about, scanning for anything red. *Shoot! Shoot, shoot!*

Sera sprinted to the back of the stage. There, she found Enry's parents and sister standing idly, as though waiting for Gordy to miraculously appear. But there were no children left. The stage was deserted save for the aerie clergy repacking their cases.

Sera approached Gordy's mother. "WAS HE WEARING BRAM'S COAT?"

Expectedly, Fenora was taken aback by Sera's voice. There was no time to explain; she turned to Gordy's father next, but Naden too was dumbstruck. Only Gordy's sister, Fay, accepted Sera's pleas—and their thunderous delivery. "Mhmm," she affirmed with eyes aimed at the ground.

"THEN THEY'VE TAKEN HIM! THE AERIES TOOK GORDY! THEY WILL SAY HE ASCENDED, THAT THIS IS A VOLUNTARY SACRIFICIAL OFFERING—BUT IT'S NOT! HE'S NOT GONE, NOT YET!" Sera frantically scanned their faces for any sign of skepticism. There was none. "FOLLOW ME," she commanded.

Gordy's family stuck with Sera as she found a hiding spot twenty paces out: a produce wagon on the side of the road. Not only did it offer cover, but its position between the stage's rear and the aeries' own wagon was ideal.

After a few minutes, she and her company watched the robed aeries run their crate down the stage's rear steps. But then, a surreal twist: the rear wall birthed a doorway. Sera and the others witnessed the two aeries step into the exposed cavity, still carrying the crate. Once through, the opening receded behind them.

"BROADCAST THIS!" Sera ordered. Out of the corner of her eye, she noticed both parents fumbling through OmniSync, attempting to live-share.

"It won't let me," Fenora lamented. A second later, Naden reported the same.

"WHAT DO YOU MEAN?"

"It say broadcast privileges are suspended." Sera's urgency seemed to be rousing the Vintallos from their stupor.

All of a sudden, the stone at the rear of the stage distorted again. The clergy were emerging. A moment later, the two resumed their march to the wagon. "HE'S IN THE CRATE!" Sera cried.

For Gordy's father, the moment was too much. Without warning, he burst from their hiding spot and charged the two aeries, screaming maniacally.

Unfortunately, in his blind fury, Naden had lost reasonable judgment. The aeries saw him coming from too great a distance, affording ample time for them to rest their crate and ready themselves. While Gordy's father raced forward, the lead ram hunkered and charged to meet him. On contact, Naden was thrown back violently.

As he crashed down, the sound of bones yielding to cobbles made Sera's stomach lurch. Fenora rushed to her husband, only shifting her attention as the aeries marched past. "You WILL *NOT* get away with this! Your actions will be known by every faun in the guild. My son will be returned, and YOU will face judgment!"

"Judge away," the lead ram shot back as he continued his steady advance.

From their vantage point, Sera and Fay could see the back of the aerie wagon grow as the clergy approached. Then they opened its rear door and slid the crate in.

"I KNOW WHERE THEY'LL GO!" Sera put her hands on Fay's cheeks and stared into the girl's terror-stricken eyes. "I'M GOING TO GET GORDY BACK." Then she kissed Fay's forehead, grabbed Pterus, and began an all-out sprint back to the clearing.

21

O'KILLA

This is pure failure. Horrible, stupid, utterly avoidable failure. Deep down, I KNEW Gordy and Bram were in peril, and YET I allowed them to get up on that stage. My greedy quest for proof outweighed basic concern for others. I'm so sorry, Gordy. I'm so, so sorry.

As she neared the soldiers' staging area in the Grimwoods' outer clearing, Sera took a tangent into its adjacent tree line to reach her friends unseen. Light under the canopy was again scarce, but the veil of darkness offered a renewed sense of security. After a minute marching inward, Sera came upon two, hog-tied and unconscious rams.

"She's back!" Enry called out. With the all-clear, Sera's gang emerged from concealed spots in the thicket. For a second, she panicked; she hadn't yet cloaked herself. But then Sera realized the game had changed; Enry's parents had just squarely taken sides in the eyes of the clergy. They, like Sera, were now the enemy.

Oren stepped forward, visibly frustrated. "We cleared the damned guards around that wagon, but we can't get the confounded mirror to work—and

we need it to. We have to see the wagon with un-hexed eyes just to access the blasted door."

"Listen, we have no time for—Wait, …YOU BROUGHT THE MIRROR?"

"I wasn't gonna let it leave my sight," Phaedra rebuffed.

"Well, you've got to hold the mirror right up to your eyes. You should only be seeing the wagon as a reflection. Only *then* does the reflected world become your reality." Sera reached out her hand. "Let me do it, … please."

Phaedra reluctantly handed Sera the mirror. *That's progress.* In return, Sera handed her Pterus' leash. Then she darted into the clearing, bound for the wagon that had swallowed her grandfather.

As Sera approached the wagon, she raised Phaedra's mirror very close to her face. But to the onlookers' surprise, she didn't stop at the back of the wagon. Instead, at one of its forward doors, she used the mirror to reveal a hidden handle. Sera pulled up on the lever, and the door swung open.

Within the front cab, she was astounded by the differences observed as she lowered and raised the mirror.

Without the mirror, the cabin was a simple, rustic space, trimmed with splintered wood and rusty parts. It was covered in a layer of dirt and marked by a pungent mix of mildew and sweat.

With the mirror, the cabin was an otherworldly space, trimmed in glass, shiny metals and rubbery materials. It was cleaner than its rustic form, and it didn't stink. In this state, a prominent button sat between the front seats. Sera pushed it.

"Where shall I take you?" a familiar voice asked. It sounded like the voice of OmniSync.

Woohoo! Sera rejoiced. "Take me just within the tree line."

The wagon responded immediately, generating a high-pitched purr as it moved forward. Once it had rolled about ten paces into the thicket, the vehicle eased to a stop. Satisfied, Sera jumped out to a barrage of enthusiastic hoots and hollers.

Without paying her audience any attention, she turned to the rear of the wagon. Once again, she raised the mirror. To her onlookers, the back of the vehicle abruptly grew to twice its height as realities collided. "Refraction is blowing my mind," Enry muttered.

Sera revealed and pulled another handle. As the wagon's rear door swung open, she found Opa huddled in the back of its containment area. His face immediately lit up.

"OPA!"

The old buck pulled back. "Sera?"

"Yes, it's me. I ate hoarseradish. I've picked up some new skills in the past few days." Sera swung both doors open so her friends could peek in. "And I made some new friends."

A look of deep pride spread across Opa's face. "You're incorrigible."

"And *you* are welcome. Sadly, I'm also in a huge rush. Enry's brother's been abducted." Sera turned to Enry. "It's my fault. I should never have let him and Bram take the stage. I was so blinded by the need for proof…. But now Gordy's been nabbed, and still, we have no proof…. I went out there and accomplished nothing! I feel absolutely terrible."

Enry stood motionless, expressionless as the profundity of Sera's words settled over him. Slowly, he shook his head. "Don't—don't blame yourself.

Let's just get him back. Do you think they've taken him to the Child Processing Center?"

Sera nodded solemnly. "Yes, I do."

"Well okay, what are we waiting for?" Enry jumped into the containment area with Opa. "You okay joinin' us, Mister uh—Mister 'Opa?'"

"I am, lad." Then Opa turned to Sera. "I was wrong when I said there wasn't a resistance. I'm right in the thick of it—and there's no place I'd rather be."

Sera shot Opa an approving nod as Oren and Irving climbed in behind Enry. The wagon's prisoner storage area was now full. Carefully, Sera backed out, still looking through her mirror to maintain its tall, rear opening. As soon as she was out, Thomas squeezed in, leaving Phaedra, Pterus, and Sera remaining. With a mighty, backward shove, Sera forced the rear door shut. "Looks like you're riding up front," she commented while opening one of the vehicle's front doors for Phaedra.

Once she, Phaedra, and Pterus were seated, Sera used the mirror to expose the wagon's big, red control button.

"Where shall I take you?"

"The Child Processing Center," Sera commanded, and the vehicle promptly took off. Sera then exhaled and handed the mirror to Phaedra. "Thanks."

"So, what's the plan, girl? Do you really expect us to bring the battle to them?"

"Where, to Mars?" No sooner had the question spilled forth than Sera realized her confusion. "Oh, you mean to the Child Processing Center!" Sera laughed at her own telling mix-up. "No. I know you all are very strong, but I don't think we can out-muscle the aerie fleet. We're going to have to out-wit them. At least we've got some decent ingredients for concocting a ruse: Molwart's identity, a deadringer, an aerie wagon. Each suggests I'm an aerie. Plus, I have your fuddle helixir. Should be able to organize a pretty convincing illusion."

"Well, if you intend to play Molwart," Phaedra replied, "you'll need to *know* his identity."

"Good point." Sera promptly immersed herself in OmniSync. *Show me my records,* she commanded. The network obliged:

Molwart O'killa
Staff Sergeant
in service of Her Majesty's Royal
Queen's Corps
Earth Fleet 6, Born 4-10-3389

Then something landed in her lap. "WHAT'S THIS?"

"Another ingredient. I want you to make a 'killa' cake."

Sera slipped out of Omni-consciousness to see the unannounced object. *The mirror.*

She turned to face Phaedra. With so much going on, Sera hadn't noticed the big changes happening right next to her, in the Crimson Core's matriarch herself; Phaedra had softened. Gone was her persistent, scornful expression, her vitriol and selfishness. There could be no greater proof than the present gesture. Sera offered a heartfelt "Thank you."

But the moment was not meant to last. Their wagon's hum seemed to be growing louder. Another wagon was quickly approaching. *Gah! I'm just getting started, and already I've been found out.*

But as a bout of panic took hold of Sera, the other wagon pulled away. Those within apparently hadn't noticed her.

"I think we're getting close," Phaedra announced.

Sera pulled Pterus over and removed the wrap from his torso. A moment later, their wagon slowed as it neared the Child Processing Center's security checkpoint. Sera turned to Phaedra. "I'll meet you all at the mineshaft's entrance."

"You don't want help?"

"I've got a crazy plan, and I think I'll get further if I minimize the attention I draw."

"But, girl, you're Sera Skohlidon, the long-prophesied deicide. You'll be recognized at once. You can't just roll up, demand they give you the kid, and march out."

"TRY ME. MY NAME'S MOLWART O'KILLA, AND I WON'T ACCEPT INSUBORDINATION!" Sera flashed a demented smile, grabbed Pterus'

lead, and opened the door. Before shutting it, she leaned forward with the mirror to reveal the wagon's control button yet again. She pushed the button.

"Where shall I take you?"

"TAKE THESE *PASSENGERS* TO THE EXCAVATION SITE. UNLOCK ALL DOORS WHEN YOU ARRIVE."

CRAFT

Don't slow. Keep your chin high. Grimace and sneer. Sera's nerves were frying as she approached the Child Processing Center's security checkpoint. A few strides farther, she found herself arm's length from an inattentive guard. At sight of Sera, the boy jerked backward and raised his rifle. "Freeze! This is a restricted zone!"

Then a second soldier, farther back, noticed. "It's the wanted eerie witch!"

"Eerie?" I think I like that. Sera continued her advance. She even fired her own audacious demand back at the soldiers. "WHOA THERE, BOYS. YOU HAD BEST STAND DOWN!"

The first guard, not a day over sixteen, continued to yield. "I said hold it! Don't move!" His voice cracked as he tried to sound as tough as Sera.

"HEAR ME, PRIVATE, if you lack the sense to question this obvious hex, at least summon the *WILL* to FOLLOW PROTOCOL."

"I am! You're the wanted witch." With every word leaving his mouth, the boy sounded less sure. "You need to—to hold still so—so that I can—"

"You're going to do your job, SON. That eerie witch cursed me with this blasted appearance. But her offense needn't force your folly. Do as you're expected: CHECK MY RECORDS!"

"Yes—yes, ma'am."

"WHAT'D YOU SAY?" Sera barked.

"Well, I mean I don't know who—"

"STAFF SERGEANT MOLWART O'KILLA. Check the system. Check my location. You'll realize you are WAY out of line, Private."

"Oh—oh—"

"O'KILLA. What's your name, boy?"

"Mangus, sir."

"Listen DINGUS, I've had enough incompetent, sniveling—"

"It's 'Mangus,' sir."

"Okay, MANGO, here's what you—"

The second guard was now nearing as the first frantically verified Sera's "Molwart" claim. At the last second, Mangus put his hand up. "It's okay, Ledbetter, what we're seeing here is a cursed illusion. This is Staff Sergeant Molwart Oh—"

"O'KILLA," Sera finished for him.

"Are you sure?" The boy, Ledbetter, pointed his rifle straight at their visitor while Sera took another defiant step forward. "I'll shoot you if I have to!" he shouted. "We need credentials!"

Sera sneered at the guard while her sweaty hands fumbled to uncork the fuddle helixir. Then, with her heart in her throat, she whipped the contents at the boys. As they stared back in disbelief, she finished her unholy anointment with the helixir's incantation:

"Befuddle!"

At once, the stunned faces before her went limp. The boys' rifle-wielding arms drooped, and their rigid bodies slouched. Sera barreled on. "PRIVATE LEDBETTER, have you ever seen an eerie with a deadringer?"

No response.

"Ever heard an eerie sound like me?"

Still no response.

"Ever seen an eerie pull up in one of *our* vehicles?"

Nothing.

"You know, for all your bravado, you seem to have no substance."

Ledbetter mumbled something too quiet for those paying witness to hear.

"What was that, SON?"

The boy slurped a string of drool into his mouth. "I said 'I'm sorry, sir!'"

"That's better, soldier. Now listen, the witch may still be here. We suspect she's taken the form of a child; some boy going by the name of 'Gordon Vintallo.' If she has, there's no telling what trouble she's got planned. She may even be aiming to free your prisoners." Ledbetter was quickly growing pale. "So let's go see if it's indeed her."

"Yes, sir," the boy agreed.

The exchange's newfound momentum seemed to rouse Private Mangus too. "I'm really sorry, Sergeant. We'll keep this from happening again."

"I SHOULD HOPE SO," Sera and her military escorts strode up to the building's entrance. Fortunately, Sera knew the space. With a confidence born from her prior stay, she stepped into the facility's cavernous main hall and resolutely marched up its steps to its second floor.

There, she found the barracks—the same ones she and Enry had explored days earlier—each now had a labeled clipboard hanging from its door. *This place is FULL of abducted kids!* Sera checked every clipboard until she had found her target: "GORDON VINTALLO," she announced.

As if on command, the door donning Gordy's clipboard opened. To

Sera's dismay, a physician was inside. Gordy, on the other hand, was not.

"Guards!" the physician howled.

"Oh criminy! Why'd you have to call for backup?" Mangus turned to Sera. "I'm sorry sir, I'll take care of it." A second later, a rumble of hoofsteps signaled two more inbound soldiers. Before Mangus could slow them, he, Ledbetter, Sera, and Pterus had all been shoved to the floor, barely a half-pace from the physician. In the commotion, Sera's mirror was knocked free of the belt loop that had held it.

"It's the Skull-whatever witch they've been reporting on! Arrest her!" the portly physician shouted.

"I CERTAINLY AM NOT! HELP ME UP AT ONCE, AND STOP THIS COMEDY OF ERRORS!"

Ledbetter was the first to rise, quickly extending a hand to Sera. Mangus retrieved Sera's mirror and handed it to her. The others weren't sure how to proceed. "I'm sorry," Ledbetter offered. His apology was echoed by Mangus.

As the two soldiers attempted to explain Staff Sergeant Molwart to the incredulous physician and officers, the physician waved her hands at them,

as if to shoo them into silence. She addressed Sera directly: "If you're actually who you claim to be, you should be able to see this room's true form."

"I DON'T THINK *YOU* COULD SEE THE TRUTH IF IT JUMPED OUT 'N BIT YA," Sera snapped. "But yes, *I* can. What do you want me to say, that there's a stretcher in here?"

"And what?"

"That ridiculous doll." While the soldiers behind Sera nodded as if vindicated, the physician plucked the mirror from Sera. "You see this? I bet it's enchanted! Why would a high-ranking officer carry a mirror like this? This is something a *witch* would carry."

Sera snatched the mirror back and offered it to the officers behind her. "Does that look enchanted to you?"

The closest officer accepted the odd mirror and very carefully examined it. To him, the room reflected everything as he saw it. "Nope," he admitted.

"Of course it doesn't, you bloody fool, you can already see this room in normal form!"

"Good grief," Ledbetter gasped, "now the mistress is accusin' *you* of witch-craft, sir!"

"What, no! It's her, you damn fools!"

"That's enough," the officer with the mirror announced. Then, directing his attention to his partner, he issued an order: "Please see Mistress Pogwollow outside. She clearly needs fresh air."

Sera turned to face the senior officer and review his uniform's name tape. "Thanks, 'Corporal Dade.' So, where can I find this 'Vintallo' boy?"

"New arrivals are bein' processed. By now, they're likely queued upstairs. I'm going to escort you."

"Okay, then let's get on with it."

The Corporal made way for Sera and handed her back the mirror. Sera almost let slip a sinister smile as she headed back to the stairs, now escorted by a full entourage of aerie soldiers.

But as she climbed the stairs, an emerging sound of sobs made her heart sink. At the top, lined up from one side of the building to the other, stood two dozen kids. Sera scanned the line and quickly spotted Gordy. Just as the boy was about to run to her, Sera opened her eyes wide and shook her head. A bead of sweat dripped from her brow as she fought every instinct to look around, to assess whether the

small exchange had drawn notice.

"Is there a 'Gordon Vintallo' here?"

Gordy wasn't sure how to respond, so he did nothing.

"GORDON VINTALLO, YOU ARE COMPELLED TO STEP FORWARD!"

Gordy did as commanded.

"I need to determine whether or not this is the witch. Let's get him downstairs."

As the group escorted Gordy to his cell, Sera once again carried Pterus in her arms. Casually, she shifted his goggles up from the back of his head to the point that they were bound to fall off. She also unhooked his lead and simply tucked it under his collar.

Back in the processing cell, she put Pterus down and handed his leash to Private Ledbetter. "Keep an eye on 'im, will you?" The soldier was happy to prove helpful. But as he accepted the leash, he discovered that it wasn't properly connected to the animal he was supposed to watch. Quickly, he knelt to reattach it. Just as Sera had intended, the slightest touch knocked Pterus' goggles off.

Pop. Hreee. Snap. Snap. Now there were two Ledbetters.

"Good grief, son. I just asked you to hold him for ONE SECOND!"

"I know sir, it's just that—"

"It's just that y'all are gonna make this very difficult. I'm gonna need you boys to step out."

Ledbetter nodded and retreated to the door, followed in tow by the other soldiers. Once the door was closed, Sera approached Gordy with a proud smile. Then she turned Pterus around so that he was facing the boy.

Crack. Snap. Squee! Pterus had just taken the form of Gordy. Were it not for his maintained spot in the room, Sera could have easily mistaken him for the real boy.

"Thank you, buddy," she whispered. It took tremendous determination for Sera to avoid tearing up as she then confronted the darkest part of her otherwise solid plan: to get Gordy out, she was going to have to leave Pterus as a decoy in the custody of the aeries.

Sera kissed the top of his head and pointed him at the corner. "I'll see you soon, friend." Then she turned to the real Gordy and addressed him with great intensity: "Don't say a word, Gordy. Not one word. No matter what

someone says, I want you to stare blankly and follow this lead, okay?" Gordy looked as though he might cry. "I'm sorry. Stay strong. You're almost free," Sera reassured. Then she put Pterus' lead around the boy's neck and opened the door.

"FALSE ALARM! You all are lucky you aren't harboring that witch. I think I scared the wit out of that boy, but he ain't no witch."

The corporal seemed appeased.

Just keep it up, Sera coached herself. *We're almost free.* Channeling all the strength she had, Sera stayed in character as she and her full entourage returned to the first floor.

Unfortunately, Mistress Pogwollow spotted the group on their way out. "WITCH!" she shouted. "That's no officer! That's the EERIE WITCH!"

Corporal Dade whipped back to face the physician. "Are you daft? Enough of this nonsense!" Then he turned to Sera as the heckling continued. "Do you need a ride?"

"I have mine waiting. Thank you."

Sera stepped past the checkpoint before gradually picked up her pace. "Don't run," she muttered to Gordy in

the quietest voice she could manage.

That's when she heard what she'd feared: a brilliantly high-pitched trill echoed from the encampment. Then a siren wailed. "STOP HER!" someone shouted.

More whistles and yelling. Sera knew she was beyond the point of bluffs. *Now IS the time to run!* She grabbed Gordy by the waist—as she might do with Bram—and sprinted toward the nearby central clearing.

Sprinting with a child under her arm was physically harder than anything she had ever done before. Harder even than a league's climb up a mineshaft. Legs pumping, heart racing, and lungs burning, Sera pushed herself to the point of nausea as the high-pitched hum of aerie wagons reared up on her. Still, onward she raced, weaving among the dense trees to slow her pursuers.

As Sera neared the clearing, she howled for help: "GET HIM! GET GORDY!" Within seconds, the relics erupted from the mine's entrance. At the same time, several wagons were closing in, positioning themselves between Sera and her rescue party. Soldiers had begun springing from the vehicles to physically give chase.

But Sera was out of energy. She had nothing left. As she gasped for air, mucus flowing from her eyes, nose, and mouth, she charged a few final strides and collapsed into the grass. Gordy tumbled as she hit the ground. "GET UP!" she demanded. "RUN TO THEM!" The boy was seconds from being nabbed, and yet he stood frozen.

It's not over until I say it's over! With strength she again didn't recognize, Sera forced herself back to her hooves. "YOU WANT THE EERIE WITCH? THEN COME AND GET HER!"

With each passing second, the closing soldiers tightened their perimeter. Like hands squeezing her neck, Sera could feel the grip of the aerie army preparing to choke her out. And so, out of options, she charged forward, away from Gordy and his only escape path.

This time the young boy found the necessary strength to act. He darted toward a gap behind Sera as his older brother and the relics charged to meet him. Bolting ahead, Sera did her best to draw the soldiers away. Those closest to her hesitated, unsure of who to pursue.

They chose the witch.

Once one had committed, the rest aligned, descending on her like a pack of jackals. While bodies piled on to suppress her, she detached from her egocentric view with a bit of help from Extraspection.

Sera may have been caught, but that didn't mean her aerie adversaries were in control. She had successfully whisked Gordy to safety—and managed to do so without compromising her other, more covert and ambitious objective: securing a Mars-bound ride on the Queen's Corps' departing ship.

As soldiers dragged her depleted body through the Grimwoods' central clearing, Sera turned her focus to the sky, to the heavens and beyond. She wanted Earth's alien oppressors, those wielding deceptive magick from afar, to know they were no longer veiled, that they were being addressed: "It's 'w-i-t-c-h!'"

23

HARVEST

Wails of the abducted forever rang in Sera's ears. As days bled into weeks, every prisoner aboard the Bostromo spiraled into despondency. Sera ached for the children, each someone's brother or sister, a son or daughter, now grieving miserably without hope of rescue. Within her first day aboard the aerie ship, Sera had understood the implications; The captive kids were inventory to the aeries with little pretense to suggest otherwise.

And so, to stem a growing void in each child, Sera had assumed a maternal mantle. Her newfound purpose while aboard the ship was to show all 216 of her "eerie" cellmates the genuine concern and care they so desperately needed. With the transition, her gritty voice had gradually given way to a softer presence. Sera had become an unofficial ambassador to the young—and in this role, part of her volunteer duty was to meet with the children's alien captors. Most notable among them, Mistress Pogwollow, who was responsible for overseeing the young prisoners aboard the ship.

"Mistress, you and your orderlies check on us every day, but all you do is weigh and measure these kids. Yes, Constantine here is losing weight," Sera pulled the girl at her knees close, "but what she needs most is *reassurance,* not reassessment."

"About that, Miss Skohlidon, we're kicking off secondary inductions today. So rejoice, we're moving past 'assessment.' Henceforth, we'll be excusing two fauns a day for the procedure."

Sera felt a knot in her stomach as Constantine trembled with newfound anxiety. Sera cupped her hands over the girl's ears. "What are secondary inductions?"

"Divine endowments, prepping those of your plane to assimilate with ours."

"I don't understand. Aren't 'eeries' and aeries *both* children of this plane? I thought it was strictly the Sorcerer who ordains from a higher plane."

"Uh, that's right. But enough pesky prying, girl." The mistress looked past Sera to the cowering kids beyond as her expression morphed to delight. "Children, I've just been conferring with your guardian angel here. She and I are pleased to inform you that the Grand Sorcerer's given his blessing to proceed with secondary induc—"

"What?! I had NO part in this!"

"One moment, children." Mistress Pogwollow craned back to Sera, dropping to a hushed tone as she cupped Constantine's ears. "Your call, missy. Either we give 'em the unbridled truth 'n see how they respond, or we offer 'em the more of the fairytale they're already used to. Which would you prefer?"

Sera was dumbstruck. *It's always been easier with morality on my side. But the mistress has a point; these kids lack means to resist. What help am I if we merely highlight new, inescapable terrors?* Sera hung her head in silent acceptance. Realizing her protector had somehow been outdone by their mistress, Constantine tightened her death grip around Sera's leg.

"I thought so." Mistress Pogwollow turned back to the cowering kids. "As I was saying, *WE* are pleased to let you know the Grand Sorcerer's sanctioned your secondary inductions. This is an honor to be celebrated, not a thing to fear. Now, Petunia Tin and Dora Dae, come join us."

Among the vast sea of little, horned heads present, none of the kids identified themselves, but a unison of quick glances from those surrounding Petunia and Dora made it impossible for the two to go unnoticed. As the room watched in horror, the first-selected children were cornered, pinned, and dragged from sight.

…

The first few days of this new routine were emotionally overwhelming. But in time, secondarily inducted kids started trickling back. Beneath a thick wrap of head bandages, they bore extra horns. And these out-of-place appendages—as well as the children's original horns—had been reshaped, curled to point inward. "Why do they do it?" Constantine had once asked. Despite the mistress' assertion that secondary inductions were the work of the Grand Sorcerer, the precocious child had not been swayed from the truth, that the Queen's Corp were responsible for the deeds at hand.

Sera studied Constantine's wise eyes. This withering, sepia-skinned girl of exceptional intellect would not be fooled. Since their first day aboard the ship, she'd singled Sera out as an ally of similar mind. "I'm still trying to figure that out," Sera confessed.

Sera struggled to keep her chin high as secondary inductions raged on. But a month into the procedures, her anxiety was coming to a head. Several of the "excused" had failed to return when they should have. With each passing day, her hope and morale dwindled.

The only motivation carrying her through this tough period was to focus on those still present. Sera spent her days tending to the kids, attempting to lift their spirits. Constantine needed her help the most. Steadily, the girl's state was worsening. Sera had recently noticed a thin streak running vertically through her horns—a telltale sign of malnourishment.

On the inevitable day Constantine's name was called, Sera's sobs briefly echoed the child's own. Of course, she fought for composure, to suppress her emotions, but the damage was done. "It's okay, sweetie. You'll be fine," Sera cooed. "We'll see you in a few days. Stay strong." She stayed by her terror-stricken protégé until the orderlies had dragged her little friend from the cell.

…

Not long after, the front door to their holding cell reopened. Given the odd time of the visit, Sera knew the matter would be one of grave consequence.

It was Private Ledbetter. "Miss Skohl-idon, your presence is required. His holiness, Roald Ephrem, would like to speak with you."

"One of the Royal Coven's warlocks?"

"That's right."

As Ledbetter guided Sera through the ship's labyrinthian maze of corridors, Sera got a chance to take in some of the finer details she'd missed on her fiery entrance. For one thing, the public spaces were unlike anything she'd seen before. In stark contrast to the holding cell, they were not simple. Every wall had a different texture, each corridor marked by architectural nuance.

The cast of characters she and Ledbetter passed were equally intricate. There were large, lumbering aeries who studied Sera with unnerving intensity. There were adolescent eeries of roughly Sera's age who altogether avoided eye contact. Like secondarily induced fauns, their heads bore many horns, but more strangely, these horns were shrouded in a web of moss-like material. There were also flickering aeries who seemed to defy the laws of

nature. They reminded Sera of the way the Coven's crest appeared during supper summoning—as though they were both present and yet not really.

"Some form of magick?" Sera asked. They had just passed an alcove occupied by both physical and flickering aeries engaged in a conversation.

"Sort of. They're 'holographic.' They *are* real. They're just not really *here*."

For a moment, Sera walked in silence, attempting to process the new magick she'd witnessed and how it was seemingly commonplace in aerie culture.

"So, about your crazy stunt at the Child Processing Center—the CPC—" Leadbetter resumed, "I just wanted to say that your whole 'O'killa' act was pretty bold. It caused a helluva lot of trouble, but to show such commitment to such a crazy plan—well, that's how legends are born. Your acts weren't that far removed from the sort of heroism we idolize—except you were supporting the wrong side.

"Anyway," the young soldier turned to Sera, sincerity shimmering through his emerald eyes, "you may have made a fool of me, but I'm not above appreciating the skill that must've required.

Through-n-through, Skohl 'n Bones, you are crafty to your core."

Despite her purported bravery, Sera felt the odd urge to look away from the handsome soldier complimenting her. "So, I caused some trouble?"

"That's an understatement. Corporal Dade was beside himself. Mangus too. He seems to think this'll affect his ability to move up or some nonsense."

"Yet you're not worried about such 'nonsense'?"

"Nah. It takes a pretty narrow mind to think you're defined by how others view you. There's a whole universe of different perspectives out here. Why should I worry about the perspectives of a few minds on this ship?"

"Because distorted minds on this ship are imprisoning more open ones."

"Maybe." Ledbetter looked pensive. "At least you have a chance to speak with a controlling mind. Most folks never get the chance.

"Well, we're here. Talk to him. See if you can sort it out. Then let me know if your perspective changes. I'm bettin' things aren't as simple as you think." Ledbetter knocked on the huge door markeing the end of their corridor.

After a lengthy wait, it opened. As it did, the ram who peered down on them took Sera's breath away. He was enormous, with a head as big as Sera's entire body. Like the relics she'd come to know, he was obviously ancient, as evidenced by sagging skin that had withered and drooped well beyond normal.

"Your holiness." Ledbetter bowed.

"Thank you, Private," the old beast rumbled. "You're dismissed." Ledbetter glanced at Sera as he turned away.

"Hello, young lady. Do come in."

"Is that an order or an invitation?"

"It's whatever you'd like it to be." The ram, who Sera surmised to be Roald, opened the door and shuffled inward. The dimly lit room, which had walls lined in velvety fabric, was punctuated by the two biggest chairs Sera had ever laid eyes on. Between them sat a marble block. As she approached, Sera realized the cube was an altar.

Roald reached one of the chairs and motioned an invitation for Sera to sit in the other.

"Why am I here?"

Roald glanced up, confused, as he eased into his chair. "How could you *not* be here? Wasn't this your goal—to confront the Coven? You strike me as a faun who will stop at nothing to see her goals realized."

"I aim to see eeries treated justly or left alone entirely. We're not crops to be harvested."

"'Harvested.' Roald chuckled. That's a peculiar choice of words. Say more."

Sera furrowed her brow. "I'm not going to tell you anything you don't already know—"

"Mm." The warlock leaned forward. "This isn't a matter of establishing what *I* don't already know; I'd like to determine what *you* don't yet know."

"Your use of fauns is … parasitic. Your vile actions serve only yourself."

"Is OmniSync not reciprocity?"

"OmniSync's a gift from the Grand Sorcerer."

"Is it?"

Wow, I'll need to unpack that later.

Sera attempted to seize back control. "Do you only speak in questions?"

"No, Sera. My intent is not to riddle you. It's to surmise *your* understanding without first tainting it. Answers are coming, but first, please, tell me more about this 'parasitic' behavior."

"The Queen's Corps visit every four years to collect eerie kids. You're careful to spread out harvesting so that you don't incite an uprising. You veil your actions under the guise of inductions—'primary inductions,' I suppose. You want something these kids' bodies have to offer, something aeries can't easily collect on your own."

"Not bad." Roald leaned forward more, his hulking horns now blocking out light from above most ominously. "What we seek is marrow." Wearily, the lumbering beast slapped one of his forearms. "It's the spongy substance in your bones. Marrow holds the rare ability to produce stem cells, a special type of cell that can adapt to meet a host body's needs in a variety of different ways."

Sera's face had lost all color. "Our kids really are a *crop* to you."

"Effectively, yes. As bodies mature, these cells become less adaptable. So, to 'harvest' stem cells, we must focus extraction on young beings—yours or ours—taxing as that may be. It's true, we lost many lives as we initially pioneered marrow mining, but over the years, we've improved our approach.

Our yield is quite high these days as we've found stronger bodies prone to repeat success the second, third, eighth time around. We've also perfected the practice of surgically appending horns —the bone of choice. Plus, we've unlocked the secrets of fungal therapy, where mycelium fuses with the host body to block immune defenses while accelerating cell growth. In short, we extract more marrow from fewer kids."

Sera felt her body grow rigid as she forced continued eye contact. "Your directness makes me uncomfortable."

"As has your directness caused me discomfort, yet here we are, Sera. I'd have been fine learning some sprightly kid from who-knows-where was poking around with questions, pressing cave dwellers for inconsequential answers. But you weren't content with answers. You sought a ride aboard this vessel, to pillage my armory. You had to have confrontation and resolution—"

"Your armory?"

"You're here for directness, Sera, so let's not play games."

What the heck are you talking about? Sera grimaced as she studied Roald's face. Whatever he was referencing, he

believed he was speaking the truth— but he was also unwilling to discuss the matter any further. "Well, in the spirit of directness, what do stem cells offer you?"

"Progress. Your kind has benefited immensely from our inventive magick. But it comes at great cost. Ironically, the most significant cost of progress is time itself. Everyone starts with some, yet no one can buy more. Consider the plight of the royal clergy—mortal leaders who elevated the quality of ruminant life across several planets— as they neared the end of their own lifelines. Sure, we'd have gladly settle for immortality resin, but there's just so little of it in existence, and unlike the amount you need to see results, we require great quantities of its distilled form—"

"You make me sick." Sera's arms had started trembling. "I don't need any more directness; I've heard enough to understand who I'm dealing with."

Sera began to rise, but Roald motioned to stay put. "Please, don't go down that path. We both know where it will lead you. On any other vessel, you'd already be dead. Lucky for you,

you're on *my* ship, in the company of a warlock who truly prizes exceptional intellect. As soon as you were boarded, I knew your perspective would be a treat. I may not agree with your coming observations, you certainly won't enjoy your enlightenment, but to lay my cards out before you, explaining and demonstrating how we play the game, to then discuss with a bright mind how the experience has changed you—that's an opportunity no purveyor of progress should deny.

"You're a bit old, but you too will join our harvest. The experience shall fulfill your quest for answers. You shall *know*—" Roald motioned with his hand again, "what role your kids play in the greater good, in buying *me* time."

Sera was still questioning his repeated hand gesture when an unseen entity jerked her head backward. She screamed as multiple sets of robed arms restrained her, pinning her head and shoulders into the seat of the chair.

As she thrashed about, biting and scratching every restrictive limb within reach, one set of hands managed to force a wet cloth over Sera's face. A second later, Sera's world went dark.

ROOM ELEVEN

I need you to wake up. PLEASE."

Sera squinted. The world before her was too light, her eyes too crusty and clouded. At least her inner ears told her she was lying down, facing upward. Gradually, a dark blob overhead was coming into focus.… "Enry!"

"Shhh—shhh." Enry gently cupped his hand over Sera's mouth. "We should be safe as long as we stay quiet." Then he returned attention to her restraints.

Sera crackled with energy. "How?—How are you here?"

"When will you learn you can't shake me? You tried to ditch me before the Grimwoods, then you tried to lose me in the clearing to board this ship—"

Suddenly, a squeal and a grunt from below announced another party. "Hang on, he's just—he's pulling on his lead." The boy leaned down, momentarily out of view, before resurfacing with a goggled Pterus in his arms.

Sera teared up. It was too much. The last time she'd been conscious, she was nearing an alien world, very far from home and loved ones with no hope of reunion. Yet miraculously, she now had both Enry and Pterus back, the latter wiggling and whining ecstatically.

"Shhhhh. Come on, boy. Take it easy." Enry attempted to calm the beast. "I'm going to set you down. Give me a sec so you can have your reunion." He subdued Pterus and shifted his attention back to Sera's bindings. Soon, he had her free of the straps that had bound her to the hospital bed.

With his help, Sera shakily slid down to the floor to sit next to Pterus. The beast nuzzled into her with intensity. Then she turned back to Enry as he too settled claimed a spot on the floor. "Tell me everything."

"Well, while you were getting yourself captured—which, yes, I assumed was by design—the relics and I got Gordy to safety. I asked Thomas to see Gordy back to my folks. Once the sun had set, I snuck back to one of the aeries' wagons parked in the clearing. I rested under it until I heard voices approaching. As they loaded into the wagon, I hooked myself to its underbelly and joined the ride up the ramp.

"Over a few hours, the ship's loading bay filled with wagons. Eventually, it emptied of soldiers, and I was left alone to explore the bay. That's when I found this little guy tethered to a staircase!

"He and I made the bay our home for the past month. Of course, it isn't meant to serve as quarters; it has a latrine, but no provisions. Pretty soon, Pterus and I were facing starvation. But then, on what should've been our last day, I woke up to a note. I still have it." Enry fished through his pockets, retrieved a stack of papers, and started shuffling through them. He handed one to Sera.

Check 37 again.
It's no longer locked.

"Someone had stocked a locker with water bottles and military food packets. Pterus and I did much better from then on. We still had to be careful since soldiers would occasionally barge into the bay, but we had the place to ourselves at night—or whatever you call the time when folks sleep in space.

"One day, our secret supporter gave me and my 'rescue Sera' scheming a boost. They left us this one. Let's see...."

"You know what we found? A wealth of stuff!" Enry fished within his jacket and pulled out the disenchanting hand mirror. "I bet you thought you'd never see that again."

"Amazing. You're amazing, Enry."

The boy laughed. "Well, like I said, we have help, it seems. Anyway, that's not all we found. The aeries had all sorts of contraband in that armory. For example, I found this kit." Again, he went searching through his jacket.

"How many pockets do you have?!"

"Yeah, I can't leave stuff in the bay, so I'm kind of a mess, but I always have what I need on me. Anyway, here it is." Enry pulled a wooden box, about half the size of a cigar box from his jacket's front pocket. "Best I can tell, it's some sort of permanent cloaking kit. It was in a locker full of stuff the military must have confiscated from some of the less loyal guilds. See?"

Enry opened the box. Inside, Sera noticed a key that looked similar to the hand-crafted one Enry and Thomas had used on her. "This thing came with instructions. Basically, you remove

65-68 are locked but worth it.
Lay low after opening them. You'll attract attention.

your cylinder. Then you use this pin to connect two of the little metal nubs in it. Once done, you put the cylinder back, and you're no longer traceable. So, you know, I did that right away."

Sera shook her head in disapproval. "How do you know it actually worked?"

"I don't know for sure, but it made a little spark and left a smokey smell in the air. After that, my life meter showed I'm basically facing imminent death."

Sera laughed. "Welcome to the club."

"But I figure the aeries wouldn't have bothered to confiscate it if it wasn't a real tool. So yeah, I was still working on a plan—a *bad* plan—when we got a final note from our supporter." Enry handed it to Sera.

> **Miss Skohl 'n Bones will soon be in the hospital wing's recovery**
> # room 11.
> **You must go tonight.**

Sera sat studying the parchments, momentarily speechless, as Enry studied her. "You know, you've got to stop passing out on me. Looks like you must have really hurt your head this time."

"My horns!" Sera reached up and felt a huge wad of bandages wrapped about the top of her head. Panicked, she seized the mirror. As she'd feared, her crown was heavily bandaged. "Hold this! I need to get these bandages off!"

"Are you sure that's a good idea? … You know what, just let me do it. You can keep a hold of the mirror." As Enry proceeded to unravel the wad atop her head, his shocked utterances conveyed as much confirmation as a mirror's reflection. "I don't … understand what I'm looking at. What did they do to you?!" He gently brushed his fingers along Sera's temple. "Seriously, what is this?! Oh my god!" Enry pulled back to look Sera in the eyes, his face pale. "You've got—" he paused to count, "you have at least six horns now."

Sera gave a nod, acknowledging that the horror was one she'd anticipated. Then she slumped against the bed. "I need to fill you in on my half of this adventure. I'm apparently part of the aerie crop now. It's the same reason the aeries steal our kids. They're using us to harvest bone marrow.… The Coven have figured out how to use the cells in our marrow to achieve immortality."

Enry's eyebrows furrowed and his face reddened. As he knelt before Sera, she raised the mirror to examine her mutilated crown. Indeed, her original horns had somehow been altered to curl inward, stripping Sera of her most basic self-defense: the power to impale. Worse still, her two original horns were not alone: two additional sets now extended from her crown. Among the six horns, a scaffolding of crude braces held the transplanted additions in place as anchored by Sera's existing horns.

It took a minute for Sera to process the horrors reflecting back at her. The first thing she noticed was that her hair had been twisted into a bun atop her head, leaving notches of shaved-bare skin around its perimeter. This was where the surgery had been performed —as evidenced by a grotesque collection of stitches and staples.

Sera studied the horns at the front of her crown. *They're so small, and that striping— the horns of a malnourished—* Her mirror crashed to the floor as she made a devastating connection.

These are … Constantine's … horns. Bile burst from Sera's mouth.

For a few minutes, she remained slumped, soaked in tears and phlegm. When she finally looked up, her sad gaze found Enry. "The weak ones— It's where they get the horns," she croaked, every word a battle. "These are the remains of a sweet, very bright little girl."

Enry stared into Sera's miserable eyes as his own welled. He clenched his jaw and a tear spilled free. Then he leaned in and wrapped his arms around her.

In time, Sera caught her breath. Her cries faded to weak sobs. She found her heartbeat slowing to match Enry's.

"You're here for a reason," he cooed. "These kids need your help." Then he pulled back to face Sera again, to fully connect with the girl trapped behind her harrowed eyes. "Let's give them the help they need. Let these be the last horns ever taken."

Sera was at her weakest, her lowest low. It took all that she had to peer back. Through bloodshot eyes and swollen lids, she found Enry waiting.

You have always come for me. You chased me across the solar system. But your journey's more than a torrid hunt. I see now that you cherish me. You are the one with the heart and will to move mountains. You move them for me.

25

ROALD'S GAME

"Around this next corner, the hall-way straightens, so we'll be stuck in the open if we're spotted," Enry explained.

Before heading out, he had used the cloaking kit on Sera. True to his claim, the application was marked by a spark and a small plume of smoke.

The boy had also removed Pterus' goggles and shown him a pair of shiny surgical pliers. To Sera's amazement, her deadringer hadn't transformed at the sight of Enry—like her, the boy had managed to get Pterus accustomed to his appearance—but Pterus *had* transformed at the sight of the pliers. Sadly, this meant they were even more press ed to get to the loading bay; The pliers were in one of Enry's front pockets.

About halfway down the corridor, his pocket started swelling. "We have to move faster," he complained. "I can't let Pterus out." As Enry spoke, he shifted from shuffling to speed walking.

Soon thereafter, a group of heavily-horned fauns entered the opposite end of the corridor. *At this pace, Pterus is going to give us away,* Sera anguished. *But if we move any faster, we're going to draw too much attention!*

Then, just as they were about to pass the group of fellow fauns, Pterus let out a wild squeal. He was simply too restricted. Enry's leg appeared to have formed an immense growth—an immense, *squealing* growth.

Hreeeee! Reeeeee!

Sera glanced sideways only to find all three of the passing fauns staring back, mortified. "It's okay, George," she improvised. "We'll just let *ROALD* know the experimental therapy isn't working." In an instant, each of the craning heads became *un*stuck as the nosy passersby realized the spectacle was beyond their privilege.

"I have no idea what that's supposed to mean … or why your impulse for a pseudonym is 'George,'" Enry whispered, "but thanks."

Seconds later, a loud rip announced Pterus' return to their company. As he rolled out, onto the sterile floor, Enry grinned with embarrassment. He had been left with shredded rags where pants had once covered his legs. Sera snickered as she shifted her attention from Pterus to Enry. "You alright?"

"Well, I'm a lot better now. I never knew what childbirth is like."

Sera couldn't contain a good laugh.

"I'm pretty sure that's *not* what child-birth is like." Then she scooped Pterus under one arm and darted ahead.

To their great relief, Sera and Enry managed to reach the loading bay without further incident.

Enry opened a locker and retrieved a jumpsuit. "You really seem to know your way around here," Sera observed.

"Well, as I said, I had help."

"About that, could I see those parchments again, please?"

"Um, sure."

Sera sat at the base of a metal staircase studying the stack while Enry changed behind her. Then she nodded and turned back. "I know who your mystery supporter is. He's a member of the aerie military. He seems to be quite open-minded." Enry's face dulled.

"Anyway, he's the one who escorted me to meet the head warlock aboard this ship, Roald Ephrem. On the way there, he called me 'Bones.'"

"And *why* would you trust him?"

"He helped you get me out, right? ... And got you the cloaking kit?" Sera caught Enry shaking his head as he re-stowed the parchments. "But I am bothered by something," she admitted.

"When I met with Roald, he accused me of raiding his armory. I realize now that meant his *lockers,* that the raid was actually your doing, but Roald claimed I had done it. So, either he really thinks I raided these lockers and I had his missing contraband like that cloaking kit—which I'd clearly use—or else he already knew I had an ally aboard this ship—an ally who raided his armory. Either way, he knew more than he let on. He was playing me."

Sera stared into space for a minute. "Hey, let's leave a note for Ledbetter. There were a couple hundred kids in the holding cell with me. As soon as we land, we need to free them—and there's no way we can do it alone."

Enry sighed and sat on a metal step next to Sera. "Listen, I'm glad you're letting me in on your planning now. Thank you. And I don't mean to be super pessimistic or anything, but—well, I have questions. For instance, we're bound for a planet *full* of aeries; how do you intend to rescue the kids when there's nowhere to take them?"

"I'm not sure yet. Still forming a plan, but I'll tell you one thing: We lack the resources to save those kids ourselves."

After a few minutes, the two had their note for Ledbetter, stowed in the same place Enry typically found his. They used cryptic language in case it happened to fall into the wrong hands.

If you're here alone, request a Bone. You'll find you're in good company.

With their plan underway, the two retreated to a crawlspace Enry had long since discovered beneath the loading bay. The space was very broad but also far too short to stand within. In one corner, he'd fashioned a makeshift bed out of a pile of towels and jumpsuits. The arrangement wasn't much, but his nest was still incredibly inviting, offering measures of safety and comfort.

Soon Sera's lowered guard brought an acceptance of her exhaustion. With Pterus on one side and Enry on the other, she drifted to sleep.

…

"Sera? … Sera?" A hushed voice was calling out from above.

At first, Sera mistook the voice for Enry's, but as she found her bearings, she realized Enry too was just stirring. *Someone else…. Ledbetter.* She looked to Enry, and he nodded back as though he suspected the same.

Cautiously, the two crawled out from the space under the loading bay and crept along one of the aisles formed by rows of parked wagons. "Ledbetter?"

"Hey, Bones."

At the front of the bay, their aerie supporter stood waiting. He was out of uniform, which made him harder to recognize, but there was no mistaking his emerald eyes. As he stared fixedly at Sera, her pulse found a new tempo.

"So, you're our mysterious ally?" Enry stepped into Ledbetter's line of sight, forcing the ram to redirect his gaze.

"You could say that." The boy nodded. "Nice work freeing Miss Skohlidon."

Sera stepped back into Ledbetter's view. "I recall you saying things weren't as simple as I thought … yet, you've taken sides."

"I have," he shrugged. "What can I do for you?"

"We need to keep the eerie kids from becoming Roald's next harvest. How long until we arrive?"

"Isn't it obvious? The ship's already slowing. We'll be entering our Martian atmosphere within the next hour."

"Then we have no time. I need you to orchestrate a diversion, please. Anything that'll pull attention from the detaining cell long enough for Enry and me to get the kids out of there."

"And where will you take them?"

Sera hesitated before confessing her half-baked plan: "Here. We'll load 'em in these wagons. Eighteen-to-a-wagon, twelve wagons."

"Seriously?" Enry exclaimed. "When did you have time to count wagons?"

Sera rolled her eyes. "You have no idea how busy my mind stays."

"How do you expect to escape with two hundred-some kids?" Ledbetter asked, clearly concerned.

"We'll use the cloaking kit to render the kids untraceable," Sera explained. "As soon as the ship touches down, we'll open the loading bay and hightail it. We have to. We have no choice. If we flee before anyone knows what's happened, we'll at least stand a chance.

We just need to get far enough away to ditch the wagons and lay low."

"I don't know…" Enry's said gravely.

Ledbetter looked more pensive as he considered their options in silence. "That could work. You'd need to get fifty leagues west of our landing site, out to Old Town, and immediately disband. Not easy, but yeah, that's likely your best chance at freeing the kids."

"So, you'll help us?" Sera asked.

"I will." Ledbetter paused. "We really are short on time, but I think I've got a good diversion to offer. On our initial voyage to Earth, one of the rookies tripped a fuse by overloading the lower levels' power supply. See, these levels house a lot more than just your holding cell. They're also home to many of the soldiers' barracks. So as long as—"

"Wait, what's a fuse?" Sera asked.

"Let's just say it's part of the magick that keeps lights shining, doors locked, and cameras running.

"Anyway, I can help ensure we 'accidentally' trip a fuse, giving you two a veil of darkness to quickly round up the children and get 'em back here. You'll only have about ten minutes to get through the corridors though.

Any longer and the folks higher up will start to get suspicious."

"Nice thinking," Sera praised.

"Thanks. Okay, give me a few minutes to make the tripped fuse look like an accident. These lights are going to go out too since we're also on one of the lower levels—the lowest level, in fact. Do you two know how to get to the holding cell?"

"I do," Enry offered dryly.

"Alright. Just know those corridors won't be much fun when they're pitch black. Not that corralling that many kids would be easy in the light. Okay," Ledbetter turned to Sera, "I had better get moving. Good luck."

…

A short time later, as promised, the lights went out. Sera and Enry were ready. With flashlights nabbed from the armory, the two ventured into the corridors beyond. This time, they left Pterus behind to forgo the added complexity—but doing so also meant they were traveling without his support.

The corridors were completely dark. Thankfully, they were also empty. It seemed no one else was eager to venture through the ship's dark hallways.

Within minutes, Sera and Enry had reached the holding cell. From outside its door, they could hear the howling of dozens, possibly hundreds of kids. The children were terrified, surely triggered by the sudden darkness.

But as Sera entered, their woeful sobs quickly transformed. "She's back! … Mama Sera!" Soon, she was completely surrounded. The children were still sobbing, but now, theirs were cries of happiness. Sera teared up too, feeling the warmth of their love for her, their dependence upon her.

"Listen, my friends, we have little time." She wiped her eyes. "I need you all to hold hands to form one super-long chain of bodies. We're going to lead each other out of here to safety. When we leave, you're going to have to be brave. You'll have to be very, very quiet. You won't be able to see since the hallways are dark, just like this room. But I'll be at the front of our line with this flashlight … like the front of a train." Sera pointed her light at Enry. "And my friend here will be at the back of the line, like the caboose of the train. So, you'll all be safe between us."

Sera looked around. Most of the kids were still whimpering, too young or upset to understand what she had just asked of them. But enough of the older kids were paying attention that she was hopeful they could lead by example. "Okay, everyone, grab the hand of someone else whose hand is free." Sera turned to Enry and nodded.

It was nerve-racking having to lead so many cumbersome kids through the winding hallways—and slow going. After five dreadful minutes, Sera and the front of her procession reached the bay. She led the kids down its stairs and had them wait in front of the wagons.

A minute later, Enry arrived with the tail end of their caravan. "Enry, I have a huge favor to ask: I know we're running out of time, but can you check the recovery rooms? I don't think I'd ever be able to forgive myself if we were to leave a child there, destined for a life of servitude."

"No worries." Enry looked frazzled, but he didn't hesitate. At once, he grabbed the cloaking kit from one of his many pockets, tossed it to Sera, and darted back through the door.

As soon as Enry departed, Sera realized she'd traded one dread for another. *What if he doesn't return? Our ten minutes are nearly up! What if I've sentenced him to join the harvest instead?* But the urgency of the moment forced her to set aside her fears. Sera turned back to the kids, determined to forge ahead with the next phase of her plan.

"Great job, you all! I'm super proud of you. Now comes the cool part: I've got a special kit here that's going to make it hard for the bad guys to find you. I want you to keep holding hands, just as we just did. As you stay lined up like train cars, I'm going to work my way down the train, helping each of you. Don't worry, I promise it won't hurt."

Sera had never used the cylinder removal key, yet she now faced the neigh-impossible task of using it hundreds of times in rapid succession.

After performing the procedure on a dozen children, the lights came back on. Sera was at once both relieved to be able to see clearly again and fraught with renewed anxiety. *Where's Enry?! Where is he? Please let him be okay!*

Still, she carried on, deftly advancing down the line. With each child, her skill improved until she'd reached a point where she was clearing one child every ten seconds. The hurried routine seemed to go on forever, but eventually she came to the last child, the only one with an un-held hand. Sera shook her head as she tried to ignore a stifling guilt. *Not now,* she rebuked, *I have to stow the kids.*

26

PRECIOUS CARGO

Clunk. Sera shut the door on the last of the wagons. Though she couldn't see the outside world—there weren't any windows on the lowest level of the ship's loading bay—the thunderous rumbling of descent rockets and an immobilizing vertigo left little doubt that their landing was underway.

A metallic squeal announced some unseen party's arrival as the loading bay's primary door, located on its second floor, creaked open. From Sera's position on the lower level, there was no way to tell who had just entered. But the girl was too anxious to hide, … so she didn't.

After an insufferable pause, a little body stepped into view at the top of the staircase. Scared and winded, the child scanned her surroundings before a look of great relief washed over her and she rushed down, open-armed to "Mama Sera." Then another child reached the landing. Again, a moment of ovewhelming relief. And another. Finally, a full-sized faun strode into view.… *Enry!*

The boy held a grin from ear to ear as he helped the last of his escortees down the steps.

"I was so worried!" Sera exclaimed.

"So was I. The lights came on while I was still making my way to the hospital wing. I was totally exposed.

"By the time I reached the recovery rooms, other aeries and 'eeries' had already started returning to the corridors. I had to bide my time as I ducked from one recovery room to the next, but I checked each and every one. It was very good thinking on your part. These three absolutely owe you their lives, Sera."

Enry looked up to signal his awareness of the landing. The sides of the ship were rattling violently. "But we're not out of this yet. Where are all the other children?"

"I have them stowed," Sera answered. "I've ordered each wagon to head to Old Town as soon as we land. You can leave these little ones to me, but I could actually use your help on one more thing, please: We need to figure out how to get the loading bay open as soon as we touch down. Got any idea how it's controlled?"

"I might." Enry glanced toward one end of the bay's mezzanine. "See that door at far end? I suspect it leads to the bay control room."

"Well, I sure hope you're right. Mind investigating?"

"On it."

…

As a newfound cloakmaster of sorts, a mere three additional procedures should have been a breeze for Sera. But the near-deafening roar of winds outside was impossible to ignore. It dominated Sera's senses as she futilely tried to calm each child.

No sooner had she stowed them than her stomach lurched. Additional descent rockets had fired up. In that instant, Sera crumpled to the floor. There was no point trying to rise.

Slowly, she wriggled back to Pterus —who was tied up next to the lockers— and held tight. Behind her, the kids' cries were so loud they sounded as though they, too, were huddled next to Sera and Pterus.

A dance of extreme G-force maneuvering continued for several minutes as more rockets could be heard and felt firing on. Then, like the landing Sera had witnessed on Earth, all of its rockets switched off in unison. The sudden silence was, itself, violent.

The ship's steel shell was still banging, bemoaning the extreme pressure and temperature changes, as Sera pulled herself up and ascended the staircase. From the landing, she turned and raced for what she believed to be the control room.

At its door, she stretched up to peer through a barred window. *Yes!* Sera could just barely see within, but indeed, she had found the right room; Enry was seated, his back to the door, shaking anxiously. *I know, I know. We have to go!*

Frantically, she wrestled with the door's unfamiliar latch to gain entry. It wasn't until she had succeeded that her misread became clear; the boy was bound to a chair. Regrettably, Sera's first impulse was to rush to her friend. A second later, the door behind her slammed shut. On the other side of the now-locked door, Ledbetter sneered vengefully at his prisoners.

Sera turned to Enry. "Just go along with it," she whispered. "Act terrified."

"I *AM* terrified! He's just opened the bloody loading bay door! But why?!"

Enry had apparently been too loud. "I'm glad you're both here," Ledbetter

announced. "You've earned front-row seats for quite the spectacle. You think those kids' lives matter, but they don't; in the big picture, they're irrelevant.

"Roald called on *me*. He's asked *me* to break you—to show you what happens when you tamper with his goods, be those the treasures in his armory," Ledbetter seized the cloaking kit from Sera, "or those in his holding cell. In a minute, the wrath of the Royal Coven is gonna rain down on those vehicles.

"You actually think you're 'crafty to your core,'" Ledbetter laughed, "that you can *outwit* the Coven. Well, 'Miss Marrow,' those kids' deaths are on your hands now! Sure, the lost harvest will sting for Roald, but it's going to cost YOU your sanity! THERE WILL BE NO COMING BACK FROM THIS!"

As Ledbetter continued his tirade, Sera had reason to break eye contact; Corporal Dade was approaching.

After a few more venomous words from the junior officer, the corporal let himself be known. Dade cleared his throat, stepped next to Ledbetter, and commended him on a job well done. Ledbetter proudly saluted his superior.

Then the corporal asked his junior to hand him something. At first, Sera couldn't tell what it was, but as Ledbetter handed over the device, she recognized it to be the cloaking kit.

What happened next perplexed Sera and Enry alike. As Ledbetter turned back to face his captives and finish his rant, Corporal Dade opened the kit, pulled out the cylinder key, and proceeded to use it on himself. After a few seconds, he had successfully removed his cylinder and put it in his pocket. *Why? Why do so?* Then the corporal grabbed Ledbetter about the torso and lifted him high. The boy struggled to resist. He was utterly enraged.... Then concerned.... Then truly terrified.

As Corporal Dade carried Ledbetter over to and down the staircase, Sera lost sight, but the junior's howls left little doubt his resistance was in vain.

"NO, NO, NO!" Enry, still tied to a chair, craned to face the nearest window. The wagons were now zipping away from the landing pad.

By the time Sera had reached the window, the procession of vehicles had grown. *Six, seven, eight, ten, twelve.* "They're all there," Sera confirmed.

"YES, THEY ARE ALL THERE! THEY'RE ALL BLOODY *THERE!* WHAT ARE WE GOING TO DO?!"

"There's nothing we can do."

"WHY THE HELL ARE YOU SO CALM?" Enry demanded. Before Sera could respond, a high-pitched whistle drew both kids' attention back to the alien world beyond. A cluster of black spots was racing down from the sky, bound for Sera's convoy.

Then, just above the ground, the spots fanned out before smashing into the vehicles with remarkable precision. As each was struck, it exploded into a fierce ball of fire and debris. Even at the great distance the electric wagons had reached, the shockwave from the blasts rattled the ship. Enry's face contorted to an expression of horror—a look he maintained as Corporal Dade entered the room.

"I am very sorry, Miss Skohlidon." The officer shook his head in dismay. "I didn't realize the kids were inside those wagons."

"It's okay, Corporal, they weren't."

"THEY WHAT?" Enry was beside himself. "WHAT DO YOU MEAN?! YOU MOST DEFINITELY LOADED THEM INTO THOSE WAGONS!"

"About that …" Sera turned to Enry. "I *did* stow the kids. I just didn't stow them *in the wagons.*" She turned back to Corporal Dade. "Thanks for taking care of Ledbetter."

"That boy ain't comin' back." The corporal offered a rare smile. "Anyway, I'm here to help, Miss Skohlidon. I've been impressed by your capacity for disruption. You've managed to fool nearly everyone aboard this ship."

"Even you?"

"Not me. I saw through your craft the moment you entered the CPC. But I went along with it. At this point, I believe you're the real deal; you have what it takes. So, I'm here to help."

"Thank you."

"His Holiness, Roald Ephrem believes I'm here to apprehend you. But as I just witnessed, the perpetually pesky Sera Skohlidon 'n her stowaway friend were blown to bits. Sadly, they kidnapped Private Ledbetter right before doing so." The corporal shook his head, feigned defeat. "There's nothing left…. Nothing left of you, your friend here, or the 200 kids you were rescuing. You are all gone…. Which means I might actually be of service to you. So now, what do you need?"

"Well, Corporal, I do have a couple hundred kids presently hiding in the lower crawlspace, so—"

"STOP DOING THAT!" Enry shook his bound body in furious frustration. "YOU HAVE GOT TO LET ME IN ON THIS STUFF!"

"I'm really sorry, Enry. The way I handled this was unfair. You've been an amazing partner with me, and I left you in the dark. It's just that we had no time.

"As we were making our way back here with the kids, it occurred to me that Ledbetter had to be in cahoots with Roald. It was the only way of explaining the bits still bothering me: why he would offer you help, how he knew which room I'd be recovering in, why he didn't just rescue me himself, and why Roald pretended he didn't know you were on the ship. Those details would have deprived Roald of a good show.

"But just as I witnessed when he took me through his sinister marrow-mining operation, Roald revels in drama, any chance to rip a mind apart and

then study it. So, I had to act fast. I left most of the plan intact; I just didn't actually load the children *into* the wagons."

Sera turned back to Corporal Dade as Enry's face faded from purple to red. "The kids have no trackers now. I didn't short them with the cloaking kit; I just used the key, like you did, to remove their cylinders before throwing eighteen cylinders into the back of each wagon. So, the children may be presumed dead, but they still have nowhere to escape to, not until this ship is ready to depart again. What would it take to get the Bostromo back into space?"

"You'd have to align with the next departure. That's the only way. But we run a tight schedule with these trips. Now that we've landed, they're going to promptly prepare the next flight."

Sera nodded. "Then it's best if the kids stay here, aboard the ship, until our business on this planet is over. You asked how you can help; can you keep a couple hundred children in the crawlspace, under the radar, until Enry and I return?"

"Yes, Miss Skohlidon, I can. I'll also

secure the necessary orders so that I'm expected to join the outbound crew."

"Thank you, Corporal. One more thing: do you happen to have a spare transport we can borrow for a day?"

Corporal Dade laughed. "I do indeed have something you can use for a 'sol.' So, what do you aim to do?"

"What I came here to do: find the Sorcerer's Yantra and end his reign."

OLD

With one arm gripping Pterus and the other wrapped around Enry's waist, Sera craned her neck to study their "one-wheeler." The strange vehicle was zipping them across the Martian countryside on a single, enormous wheel.

Her attention was split between the monolithic ship dwindling behind them and a cluster of glimmering spikes very gradually entering view on the horizon ahead.

The surrounding plain was alive with a red grass that rippled endlessly as a tailwind chased them. *Gorgeous,* she thought. *Like coasting over a fiery sea.*

They were bound for the Martian counter-coordinates that matched her birth date and time. As it turned out, this them back on a path to Old Town. Before leaving, Enry had used Omni-Sync to pinpoint their destination. Every use of the network made Sera nervous, as though it was only a matter of time before a frenzied battalion came into focus on the rear horizon. But as the triangles on the forward horizon took shape, Sera was relieved to find no new specks behind them.

The world ahead was not what Sera had imagined. On Earth, towns were small carve-outs that bent to the will of the terrain. By contrast, Old Town was an apparent metropolis that dominated the countryside, evidently born from many centuries of growth.

While hardly-durable encampments marked by tents, shabby shacks, and lean-tos were among the first notable dwellings they passed, the closer they got to the built-up town, the more the aeries' strange construction patterns found a sense of order and density.

Soon, there were no temporary dwellings to be found. The structures they passed reminded Sera of the Child Processing Center. Unlike the CPC though, none of Old Town's buildings were made of wood. Sparkly metal and glass surfaces abounded, giving the city a jewel-like sense of majesty.

The sun was setting, yet their surroundings remained well-lit. A plethora of different lights and signs had started to glow, projecting spectacular colors across the shiny, intricate world whirring by. It soon dawned on Sera: Old Town wasn't just a city that had evolved over centuries of growth, but also decay.

Throughout this perfectly imperfect

backdrop, a kaleidoscopic cast of residents bustled about. Enry marveled at their surroundings: "Any culture that can build such a place can't be *entirely* bad. The creativity, the ingenuity and coordination—our brethren have some undeniable strengths."

Sera considered his words. *He's right, actually. A good reminder not to vilify everyone here. There's plenty we could learn from aerie culture—as long as we're selective.*

Ahead, she spotted the first trees she'd seen on Mars. On Earth, it would have been impossible for any sort of grove to garner a second glance, but here, in the heart of aerie civilization, the trees they were quickly approaching seemed entirely out of place. Sera pointed to them. "I think we're going to somehow enter that thicket."

Just before the foliage, the kids' one-wheeler stopped sharply. "This is the closest-permissible drop-off for those lacking exceptional privilege," the voice of OmniSync announced. "Your destination is straight ahead."

Enry hastily dismounted. As soon as he had, the boy rejoiced with glee: "I still can't get over gravity here!"

With each leap, he lingered above the ground a full second longer than he would have on Earth.

As he then turned his joy to Pterus, throwing the deadringer into the air, Sera turned her attention to the wall of trees. "*It's there to keep you safe.*" She was reminded of her earlier counsel to Enry. These days, she knew better: *Thickets aren't there to protect; they exist to veil.*

After zig-zagging through the trees, Sera spotted an opening. She motioned to hang back. "Whatever this place's purpose is, its intentionally discrete."

From the shadows, the two studied a stone building ahead of them. Atop a gargantuan staircase at its entrance, two oversized rams stood guard. To one side, an intricately patterned cobblestone road guided a steady stream of vehicles to the building. As the occupants of each vehicle disembarked, she saw that they split into two groups: those aeries who approached through the front of the building and those eeries who approached through some yet-unseen rear access.

"I say we go for it," she announced. "When the next wagon pulls up, let's

just make our way across the road and head up the steps with those entering through the front."

"Are you serious? And just what do we say when they detain us?"

In sync with the next approaching vehicle, Sera stepped onto the road. She didn't turn back as she replied: "I don't know yet. We'll figure it out."

Enry rushed to stay in lockstep with Sera, flashing her a nervous smile as he caught up. Their timing was perfect. Just as a host of aeries exited the latest vehicle, Sera and Enry emerged from behind it. At such close proximity, Sera noticed something peculiar about the fauns bound for the rear of the building: they were much older than those aboard the ship.

Without breaking stride, Sera briskly marched up the steps behind a robed aerie who'd just left the same vehicle. At the top of the staircase, the guest was greeted and ushered inward. But as Sera nodded to the guards and attempted to follow suit, one of the hulking rams thrust an arm out to block her. "You tryna be cheeky? Yer about to meet the rude end of my baton if you don' cut the crap. Back a

the buildin' with ya." Then he turned his attention to Enry. "You too, lest you want a good whoopin' first."

Sera didn't utter a word as there was no point; whether or not the guard had any wit to begin with, the staunchness of his refusal suggested any effort to *out*wit him would be futile.

"Told ya," Enry muttered. Once they were around the corner, he knelt down next to Pterus. "May I see the mirror?"

"You mean, can *Pterus* see it?" Sera smiled, withdrew the shiny object, and placed it in Enry's open palm.

Unfortunately, as soon as he accepted the mirror, an aerie stepped into sight from the back of the building. "Where the HELL is your escort?"

Enry acted quickly, throwing his back to the approaching aerie to block his actions from view. Then he waved the shiny mirror before Pterus. *Crack. Hreee. Pop. Pop.*

Just as the ewe reached Sera and Enry, Pterus completed his transformation. Two mirrors lay on the ground —both of which Enry snatched up and threw into his back pocket. "It doesn't matter," the aerie seethed. "Just get back there NOW!" Both kids did as ordered.

At the back of the building, they filed in behind a queue of harvest fauns—all of whom were about Sera and Enry's age. Like the ones seen aboard the Bostromo, these too had a mesh of moss-like material over their horns.

As she took stock of the others in their midst, Sera was struck by two realizations: one, that she and Enry had the undivided attention of every faun in their company, and two, that each and every one looked defeated and depleted, as though the life that had led them to this point had been a very hard one. Then it dawned on her: *These fauns are slaves. Why truck in loads of worn out eeries? Why are their "masters" sticking around? Why such a formal facility?* Sera's brow nearly leapt from her face as the answer dawned on her. *This place is for slave trading. They're here to be traded!*

"Next group!" a voice rang out from a door at the front of the queue. While fauns filed inside, the aerie orderlies in their midst paid extra notice to Sera and Enry, but no one pressed for an explanation as to why they looked less haggard, why they were bandaged, or why their attire was so different.

Inside, Sera had the peculiar sense she'd visited this fortress before. Smokey swirls pirouetted beneath the dim lights. The walls and floors were soft. In the distance, she could hear glasses clinking and the murmur of many chattering voices. By ones and twos, the queued fauns were gradually led down a hallway before them.

In time, Sera found herself at the front of the queue. When called upon, she asserted that she and Enry were to be presented as a pair.

"Same master?" the orderly pressed.

Sera nodded. Then, without another word said, the two were guided down the foreboding hallway. After a stretch of silence, Enry leaned in to whisper: "I'm sure you have a plan, but I get the feeling *they* do too—and I'm sure it doesn't involve giving us the Yantra."

"If we're going to unearth this facility's darkest, innermost secret," Sera replied under her breath, "we'll first need to understand our environment. Let's play this out, Mister Fearless."

Beyond, the hallway was giving way to an abyss. The space was large, but with blinding lights pointed inward, Sera could only see a few paces ahead.

SORCE

A stage. Enry joined Sera at her side.

"Come forward," an unseen aerie demanded from the darkness, "into the light." Sera offered the slightest smile. Then, as she stepped forward, she started clapping. A clap later, Enry followed suit. After a few seconds of dissonant, echoing applause from the two, Sera stopped. Enry did as well. Finally, Sera silently asked OmniSync to reconstruct the last three seconds' sounds using her echolocation trick.

As a voice from the abyss chastised the kids for their "show of disrespect," Sera studied the once-black room in a now-visible, dimensional form. The space was full of tables and patrons. But instead of sitting in circles around each table, guests were facing forward, toward the stage.

Sera spotted the individual she surmised to be playing host. The ewe was standing tall, near to the stage. "It's okay, ma'am, you can take a seat," Sera teased. "We're done."

The room hushed. After a few tense seconds of silence, the same voice hissed at a level only meant for them. "Dearie, we are just getting started. You wouldn't be joking if you had any

sense, if you knew what awaits you after the bidding. But you don't have a clue. You think you can march out here and make a mockery of this institution. Well, I'm gonna start the bidding extra low for you!…And don't pretend you can see me. It's impossible to see from there!"

Sera pointed her head at the ewe. "For you, perhaps. I can see just fine." Then she raised her gaze and voice to address the rest of her audience: "Take this lot," Sera turned to face a group of very ornately dressed aeries on her left, "they definitely look like they know how to have a good time."

After a wave of gasps, Sera turned to the other side of the room. "Or this lanky bunch. Why are all your horns missing?" More stunned utterances.

"That's quite enough!" the familiar voice interrupted. Before Sera could get another word in, the ewe pressed on: "Bidding will begin at eight hundred ghora!"

"Eight hundred!" a deep voice rang out in response.

"One thousand!" another countered.

"Two thousand!" a third yelled.

"Three!" an earlier voice called out.

"I have three thousand. Do we have four?" the coordinator prompted.

Squeee! Enry's pocket cried out.

"Six thousand!"

"My, my!" the ewe exclaimed. "Seems these spritely kids are going to fetch a pretty price. Six thousand ghora, going once. Going twice—"

"Twenty thousand for the pair!" a gritty voice barked.

Squeee!

"Good sir, that's a remarkable bid. Okay, we're now bidding on the pair, my friends. Twenty thousand ghora! Going once.... Going twice.... SOLD! The disrespectful kids may now leave," the coordinator announced. "NEXT!"

Sera abandoned her reconstruction of the room. As she returned her focus to the blinding spotlights beyond, she found Enry leaning in. "Okay, so now we're *bought-n-paid-for* prisoners. I do hope this is the path to the Yantra. But whatever we're going to do, I first have to set Pterus free. He's ready to

burst out again—just like last time."

A second later, stepping backstage, Sera and Enry were met by a lanky ram with a sparsity of teeth and an abundance of thick, unkempt hair. His pale, gaunt face seemed reminiscent of a skull, except that it was framed in dark fur that glistened in the light, suggesting he was drenched in oil or sweat—or both.

As he leaned in to get a better look at his new prizes, Sera caught a whiff of his appropriately rancid breath. "Yer mine now," he asserted with grit and gravel that seemed to rumble from his bones.

Without turning to the lowly orderlies in his midst, he shifted his tone to address them. "This one 'ere 'as a fire in 'er belly. But ken she endure a baptism o' flames?"

The gangly figure then stood tall and turned to his orderlies. "Leave me an exam room so that I ken review my pricey prodigies."

COORDINATE

Squeee! Pterus erupted from the back of Enry's jumpsuit. The boy had just dashed to a corner of their exam room in a futile bid for privacy. But there would be no saved face; as their "master" locked the door behind them, the old tup laughed unexpectedly. Enry paid little mind as he frantically assessed the bottom half of his jumpsuit.

"Fantastic!" the ram exclaimed. In stark contrast to his previous rigidity, the aerie was now standing tall—and approaching with fluid ease.

"So, you're looking for the Sorcerer's Yantra?" the aerie pressed giddily.

"OH, *COME ON!*" Enry exclaimed. "It's really *THAT* easy?"

"Nothing here is easy, boy. But certainly, your quest would've been nigh impossible had we not crossed paths."

As the old ram spoke, something at Enry's ankles pulled his attention away. "Oh, my, the deadringer!" At once, he threw himself to his knees and leaned forward to coax the beast to him. Enry jumped as though he was under attack.

"I NEVER thought I'd see one—not before the Underworld. Pspsp, here, boy. It's okay, Nixie won't hurt you."

Sera wrinkled her nose at the zany personality contradictions they were witnessing. Then she too knelt forward, positioning herself beside their supposed new master. "'Nixie,' you say?"

"Oh!" The aerie flashed a sickly smile that, despite its authenticity, made Sera shudder. "I look ghastly, don't I? Just a second." With that, the ram raised his arms to his chest and stacked them atop one another. Then he rotated both about his elbows until his fingertips touched—forming the all-too familiar sacred gesture. "Deguile!"

In a flash of blue smoke, his form was replaced by a far smaller and younger aerie. At Sera's height and build with darker features and curling horns, the ewe standing before them took Sera's breath away. Like the Queen Witch, her exceptional beauty was punctuated by piercing, hawk-like eyes.

"Yes, my name's Nixie. I'm the High Priestess' daughter."

"What? ... Why? ... How?" Enry staggered back and slid down one of the room's blank walls as he grappled with the turn of events.

Nixie extended a hand to help Sera up. "It's time to start asking yourselves the obvious questions."

"Okay…" Enry replied incredulously, "are we really supposed to believe we just *happened* to cross paths with you?"

"Of course not, puppy dog, but that's not what matters right now. No, consider a more important question: If this place hides the Yantra, who do you expect would *own* this building?"

Nixie didn't wait for a response. "The Coven, of course. But are they really treating this place like a fortress, like it holds the one thing they most fear could fall into the wrong hands? Certainly not. The real question is 'why?' Why would they be satisfied with such a limited security detail?"

Sera paused to consider the prompt. "I suppose that's because they're sure the Yantra isn't at risk of being found. It's either no longer here, or they know for a fact that it never was here.… Have they found it and removed it?"

"It was never here, and yes, they found it somewhere else."

"That's … surprising." Sera shook her head. "I mean, it makes sense. It's just that the High Priestess' birth time coordinates—One of them matched one of my own. There was something prophetic about it, about the Yantra

hiding within a location we had in common. But I guess that wasn't actually the case."

Sera's unbreakable confidence was beginning to crumble. "So, where did they find it? Was it at some other site of significance to the Queen Witch? Maybe at the site that matches the date and time *you* were born?"

"That would've been nice," Nixie offered a glum, wilting smile as her shoulders slumped, "but no, it was discovered at the location matching the High Priestess' birth time."

"But you just said it's not here!"

"That's right, Enry, it's not," Nixie confirmed without an explanation.

Sera's mind raced to reconcile what seemed to be another contradiction. Then the answer dawned on her: "This site somehow isn't actually the one it's purported to be. The Coven's cheated. OmniSync tells us this site matches the coordinates we requested, but that's not true, is it?"

Nixie's exuberant smile and brow bounced back. "Shortly after they discovered the Yantra—at the actual site you're seeking—the Coven took some measures to thwart future seekers.

"First off, they propped up a bunch of scientists to report that our Martian coordinate system was flawed. Something about the true center of gravity, a need to accurately reflect our planetary rotation. Those 'scientists' put forth a global recommendation to re-register Mars' coordinate system. Then the Royal Coven ratified it. In the end, little changed except for a westward offset of twenty leagues. Of course, if you look that up on OmniSync, you won't find any record of the change.

"Once the dust settled from those shenanigans, low-and-behold the site of the Yantra—the *real* one hidden by a change in planetary coordinates—was obliterated by a nuclear disaster. Half of Old Town was wiped out, leaving little more than a crater. The thing is, those puppet scientists were the only ones able to detect radioactive fallout to back up the story.

"After that, life carried on for everyone else around the crater. Eventually the poor—typically those pushed to the edges of town—took up places inside the crater. That area turned into slums that, in time, became pockets of organized unlawfulness. Eventual-

ly, the whole area was built up again. Proper buildings covered the once-decimated land. And near the middle of it all, a magnificent academic institution was even constructed—by my father, no less. It taught fields of science and magick that bordered on the sort strictly outlawed by the Coven.

"At this point, the Coven had a *real* problem on their hands. They had a site of great sensitivity—the Yantra's real location—surrounded by a community proving unwieldy, anchored by a demigod wholly unconcerned with their propaganda and restrictions. It was only a matter of time before the Yantra would be uncovered. So, they flooded the crater. They claimed my father was responsible, but honestly, why would anyone trust them?

"Regardless, it's all submerged now. So many died. For years afterward, bodies floated up from below." Sera's skin puckered goosebumps at the image. "In time, the lake—which remains today—got a nickname: 'Corpsea.'"

Suddenly, Nixie shook her head in frustration. "For pity's sake, Mother, I can't even hear myself speak!

Mutus Māter."

While Nixie struggled to regain her composure, Sera considered the girl's words. She also considered her spell —one that was new to Sera—and what could have provoked her to use it.

"It seems this history lesson has upset my mother," Nixie continued. "She'll be sending her military legion for you now. And you know that table of robed guests you were mocking? One of them was a member of the Coven: Raveneve Isle. I imagine she may've figured out who you are too. If she has, the only reason Raveneve hasn't barged in here yet is that she believes me to be a well-respected member of the criminal underground. She can't see beyond my enchantment any better than you could." Nixie let slip the slightest smile. "There are some privileges that come with being born the High Priestess' daughter."

Sera smiled back. "So why help us?"

"Because I *think* I understand what's driving you: I believe you want your kind, your kin, left alone. But the Coven won't give you that, will they? They won't stop. I've seen it all before. They're going to press on, consuming and consuming until there's nothing

left of you, your family, or your home —just like there's nothing left of the cratered and flooded town beneath Corpsea. So, you've managed to get yourself here, to an alien planet, to the shadow of Mons Olympus, in search of a remedy. If I'm right about all that, I have tremendous respect for you, but I'm also scared for you. Lest you're extremely careful, you'll never escape this shadow. I want to help you finish what you've started. Then I want to help you get the heck out of here."

Sera bubbled with newfound optimism she might yet succeed. "You're right. You're very perceptive—"

Nixie threw her finger up in a gesture of caution. "I'm glad I've got it right, but PLEASE don't share any more than you absolutely must. Everything we're saying here is being heard and watched. If not from behind your eyes, then certainly through mine. I'm going to do the talking. Sorry, but it's for your own good." Sera nodded in silence as Nixie plowed forward: "So, here's what's going to happen; I'm going to leave *a thing* in this room as Sera and I leave." Nixie turned to Enry. "That thing will be for you, Enry.

SORCE

When you see it, I want you to think carefully about what it stands to help you accomplish and why I'd leave it for you. I want you to be careful as you use it, and when you're ready, I want you to take my personal transport out back wherever you desire."

"Okay," Enry replied. "Just to be clear, I don't have a flippin' clue what that *thing* will be, but sure." Then he turned to Sera. "And you're okay with this?"

"I am. Thanks, Enry. Are you okay with this leap of faith?"

"It's a bit late to be afraid of leaps."

"Okay, it's settled," Nixie announced. "Sera, you're headed with me. Enry, we'll hopefully see you soon. Now, let that deadringer get a look at you."

"He doesn't mimic me."

"Well, I suggest you find a way. Treat this as though your life depends on it."

Enry nodded, grabbed Pterus, and moved to the corner. There, he positioned Pterus so that the swine could only see Enry himself. Then he took Pterus' goggles off. Unsurprisingly, there was no shapeshifting response. Pterus waddled forward and nuzzled Enry with his snout. Enry laughed, gave Pterus a pat, and stood up.

Then he started clapping.... Nothing. He began jumping.... Still nothing. At last, Enry burst into an obnoxious mix of hooting, jumping, and clapping—a sight to behold. Sera felt embarrassed for Enry, a first.

Pop. It may've been ridiculous, but his performance worked. In an instant, there were two such fools, hooting and hollering obnoxiously. "Now, throw the goggles back on him," Nixie commanded. "He should come with Sera and me." Enry obliged. Then, as before, Nixie raised her arms to form the sacred gesture. Again, she used a spell altogether new to Sera:

"Beguile."

With a flare of fluorescent blue, her petite frame returned to its previous, twisted form. Sera admired how Nixie was able to carry herself so differently, standing as though every bone in her body hurt. From one of her pockets, Nixie retrieved an item she promptly tossed to the back of the room. As it hit the floor, it clattered brightly.

"Sera, get the clone. From here out, my name is 'Golamon,' and I am yer master."

29

A CRASH COURSE IN MAGICK

"Step aside," Golamon demanded.

A group of orderlies were standing in the hallway with one blocking the path forward. "Leaving already?"

"Gotta get 'em to my transport."

"Why's he got goggles on?"

"I don't know. But what my fauns choose to wear is none o' yer business." Golamon pushed ahead while keeping a fierce hold on his captives' wrists.

A minute later, they were exiting the front of the building. Sera sneered at the guard that'd given her a hard time.

"Look at this brat," he observed. "She has no idea what's comin'. I wouldn't be lookin' so smug if I was you."

The admonishment was too much for Golamon. In one impulsive swoop, he whipped back and clobbered the guard. "Mind yer station, you fool, 'r we'll find you a new one!"

The guard snapped to attention, his face flushed with embarrassment. A stream of effusive apologies chased Sera and Golamon as they then made their way down the grand stairs.

"For the first time in my life, I think I have a hero," Sera confessed. Then she motioned forward with her chin. "We've got a one-wheeler beyond the trees. But we definitely need to hurry. Pterus can't hold a copied state long."

Ahead, a vehicle had just pulled up. While its occupants poured out, Sera counted six harvest fauns among the lot. Like those she'd met behind the building, each slave was clearly a shadow of its former self. It was apparent that even the captive fauns' present, terrible situation could not possibly rouse them to flee.

As the last faun clopped forth, onto the road, all six began howling, shrieking. Sera watched, mortified, while the mossy mesh over each faun's horns began writhing, sprawling down until its face had been fully covered. Amid muffled gasps and convulsions, all six were becoming faceless, leaving little more than empty, reflective sockets where hallowed eyes had been visible.

Sera did her best to feign indifference. But as she reached the tree line, she turned back for one more look. While some of the harvest fauns were still contorted in agony, others had discovered new purpose: pursuing Sera and Golamon. "They're coming for us! RUN!" Abandoning their charades, the two dashed to the thicket.

Unfortunately, a new challenge soon came into focus: Pterus was decaying, morphing from Enry's likeness back to his native form. In this awkward, unsightly transition, the bumbling mutant was hitting every tree in their path. Sera and Golamon were soon forced to drag the deadringer's dwindling body through the remainder of the thicket.

Once they'd reached the other side, Golamon threw himself onto the front half of their waiting vehicle's sole seat and directed it take them to Corpsea. As it sped off, a frenzied mob of harvest fauns exploded from the trees.

"So much for my disguise," he huffed from the front of the vehicle. "Deguile!" While Sera maintained a hold on the ram's waist, his body reverted back to Nixie's far-more-tolerable form. With the change, she suddenly had room, Golamon's nauseating odor was gone, and she could see over Nixie's frame.

Sera exhaled and assessed the world before her. Since her dusk arrival, a million more colorful lights had bejeweled Old Town's intricate mosaic of storefronts. And yet the guild's once-majestic state had taken on a new light;

having witnessed its inner workings, Sera now saw Old Town as one big blur of neon transgressions.

Among the details whirring by, she spotted a second group of frenzied harvest fauns. "Look!" she remarked in horror. They too were enduring the unnerving transformation.

"Yeah, it's really sad," Nixie replied. "They're being commandeered."

"By whom? Your mother?"

Nixie let slip a nervous chuckle. "No, this is the work of the Sorcerer."

"It's hard to watch," Sera muttered. Then she gasped. "They're *sprinting* after us! But there's no way they can catch us, so why bother?"

"They're not going to catch us … yet. But they're also not going to stop."

Sera got chills. "Nixie, what sort of magick can do this?"

"Black magick."

"Black?"

"Yes." Nixie craned back as the vehicle barreled through the city. "There are three forms of primary craft: black, bone, and crimson. I once heard some poesy to explain them." Nixie's eyes faded while she scanned some distant memory.

Black is the night masking horrors unseen.
Black sullies sooth in the name of the Queen.

Black are the shadows that haunt the mind.
Black are the sinister spells that bind.

Black for deception, black for revenge,
Black to empower thy darkness within.

In our deepest depths, buried and broken,
Bone holds old answers, unwritten, unspoken.

Un-hexed, un-vexed by others' dark crafting,
The importance of portents, of fates everlasting.

Our past, our future, exhumed from the night,
Our path, our purpose, Bone's virtuous light.

Crimson pours forth in passion and haste.
Drink from its chalice if you don't mind the taste.

Ancient incantations unfit for the chaste.
Newborn incarnations, unnaturally based.

From frenzied first wail to frantic last breath,
Crimson's the craft to cure life and death.

Nixie's eyes returned to their usual, piercing intensity. "Primary magick is mostly exclusive to the Grand Sorcerer and his kin. But we do have some concoctions that come close. Secondary magick is where inventive craft has allowed the Coven to match the Grand Sorcerer in many ways—usually by extending on the endowments he left for us. They blur the line between science and magick."

After a moment of silence, Sera posed one of the many questions the exchange had inspired. "At what point is magick no longer magick?"

Nixie seemed tickled. "The answer comes down to your perspective, I suppose. To eeries, all of it—primary and secondary forms—are magick. To aeries, I'd say just primary craft is. And to the Grand Sorcerer—he might not consider any of it to be magick."

Magick is just science beyond understanding. Sera smiled at the outrageous notion. *But this doesn't change the effect magick has on me or my kin.*

Out of the corner of her eye, she spotted a few open-topped wagons. Each was bearing the Queen's Corps emblem. Dozens of aerie soldiers were

in pursuit. "Nixie, we have a prob—"

"Yes, we are being followed. *Those* would be my mother's minions."

"What are we going to do?!"

"Get to Corpsea ahead of 'em. We're getting close.... OH NO! HANG ON!"

Sera indeed had to hold on tight as Nixie forcibly took control of their one-wheeler. A pack of commandeered harvest fauns had just launched into the road, leaving no time for the girls' vehicle to safely respond. Under Nixie's control, it whipped left and right violently, and yet thanks to her maneuvering—or some onboard magic—the vehicle managed to stay upright.

A second later, they had cleared the deadly obstacle. Nixie sighed loudly. "They both know what we're up to."

Fortunately, the girls had arrived. Corpsea was a pitch-black void directly ahead of them. It was so devoid of detail, in fact, the only way Sera could tell a body of water was present was to study its perimeter—one marked by the lights of far-off settlements.

"Drop us at Pier Zeta!" Nixie commanded. The vehicle subtly adjusted its heading. Soon, Sera spotted the pier they were bound for. At its front, an old ram was busy mending a fish net. Behind him, a weathered shack lit the pier with its single light. As they pulled up, the ram turned to face them.

"I need a boat and two suits, Abe! I need 'em now!"

"Hello Nixie." Nonplussed, the tup stood frozen as he considered how to proceed. "You want one with paddles?"

"No, I need the boat with a motor. Seriously though, I need it right now. Charge me whatever. I just need to get on the water RIGHT THIS INSTANT, and then you need to hide! Please take this beast with you, but don't remove his goggles!"

"Yes, your Highness."

Nixie didn't wait for the ram to act. Instead, she threw Pterus' lead in his direction, grabbed Sera's hand, and raced to the end of the pier where a dinghy was docked. As they reached the boat, she whipped its rope free of the dock's cleat.

"Oh crap, the suits!" Just as Sera jumped into the boat, Nixie stopped short. "Sit tight!" she demanded. Then she raced back toward the old shack and disappeared inside. Farther back, their aerie pursuers were arriving, pull-

ing up sharply amid stirred clouds of rock dust. *Come on, come on, come on!* With every second ticking by, Sera's anxiety was mounting.

But just as she had written off any possibility of escape, Nixie dashed out of the shack and onto the pier. She was carrying two diving suits. A vast mob of transformed harvest fauns was mere paces behind her. "Start the engine!" she shouted while frantically gesturing a pulling motion with one arm.

Sera looked around for something to pull. She found a little handle on a small rope. It was hanging limply from a mechanical box on the side of the boat. Without time to consider alternatives, she yanked on the handle. *Grummmum.* Once again, she pulled. *GRUMUMUMUMM.* This time the roar was louder and longer, but still nothing happened. Nixie—with the crazed horde just behind her—was flout-out sprinting down the pier. Once more Sera yanked, giving the cord all her might. *GRUMBUMBUMBUBUMBUM bumbumbumbummmmm.*

I think it worked!

At the pier's end, Nixie threw her suits into the quick-departing boat.

Then she leapt from the pier to join the suits, causing a great wake as she splashed into the water at the edge of the dinghy. With the back half of her body still overboard, Nixie clambered to keep a hold of the boat. Sera pulled her companion inward with everything she had. Once Nixe was safe, the two collapsed backward.

As they pulled away, Sera watched the pier in awe. While the aerie soldiers were temporarily stalled, countless possessed harvest fauns were leaping from the tip of the pier just as Nixie had. Sera then understood what Nixie had meant when she'd said that their pursuers weren't going to catch them "yet."

"We're in this together now." Nixie handed Sera a suit before wrestling one on herself. As they suited up, she turned her attention to the front of the boat. "See out there, the middle of the black? That's where we're headed."

"How'll we know when we arrive?"

"There's a buoy there. I know where it is. I've done this many times." Nixie seemed to catch Sera's furrowed brow. "The past—it's important. My father founded the academy at the center of all this. There was a lot of knowledge lost when they flooded the crater. And what little this world knew of my father was lost as well, buried under a sea of cadavers.

"Eventually, I pieced together enough of the truth to start asking coherent questions. I learned about lines of magick lost, the Yantra, and some diabolical plots spearheaded by the Royal Coven—by a group that was supposed to be like family to me."

"Sounds all too familiar." Sera stared quietly into black, open night, feeling the sea's cool spray and whishing wind ease her taxed body and soothe her frazzled mind. *There's so much to learn. I wanted to understand my place in the cosmos, to know my significance. But the more I venture, the more I wander, the less I understand.*

In time, she turned to face Nixie. "I wish I saw the universe as you do. Care to share the secondary classes?"

"Sure." Nixie paused. "There are three forms of secondary craft: green, gold, and midnight." Her eyes may've been on Sera, but her mind was now a full league ahead as she plotted words that, like the girls' charter, would brave the darkness.

SORCE

Light bulbs and logs have afforded new access,
Not for those served, for those seeking to track us.

They wire our guilds, they wire our minds,
But this trade that is made affords power *in kind.*

Gracious "gifts" bearing tethers unseen,
Powerful pathways are governed by Green.

Gold is the new dawn and its joyous lark,
Gold is the synapse, the inkling, the spark.

You are your thoughts; you decide what you think,
But this "you" isn't *you,* it's now OmniSync.

One needn't a voice, it offers a chorus.
One needn't a choice when Gold can think for us.

Midnight is, at the end of the day,
The point of the power, the price that you pay.

A harrowed harvest huddles in sorrow,
Its marrow harnessed to pay for tomorrow.

A child defiled, a vial made vile,
Ours become hours under Midnight's guile.

Nixie ended with a sob as she lost a desperate internal fight to skirt some haunting sadness, a belief buried deep that she, as one of the beneficiaries of secondary craft, was somehow responsible for the Coven's actions.

For Sera, Nixie's visible struggle was more profound than her poetry. The girl's miserable delivery spoke to her, wrestling a similarly deep shame from Sera's guarded core; it was a guilt that she'd failed Constantine just as she had initially failed Gordy, that she should never have acquiesced as the girl was taken. Sera bit her quivering lip, imagining Constantine's last moments, before she, like Nixie, gave way to tears.

In time, the girls' crying faded. Sera wiped her face and looked up. To her surprise, Nixie had moved. She was now seated directly before Sera at the front of the boat, her flushed face very close to Sera's own. But gone was Nixie's sorrow. In its place was a look of sheer resolve—a look Sera knew all too well. Nixie grabbed Sera's hands. "You are *going* to succeed. I believe in you."

"Why? Because of the *time* I was born? You can't believe the prophecy, Nixie. You're too smart for that."

"This has nothing to do with the prophecy, … even if you, Miss Skohli-*don,* are a 'don.'" Nixie studied Sera before shrugging. "You know, a 'world leader?'" she added with air quotes.

"No, I believe in you because *you* got yourself here. It took great cunning and determination to get this far, but you did it. You got *here,*" Nixie tilted her head toward the now-visible buoy, "to your journey's end."

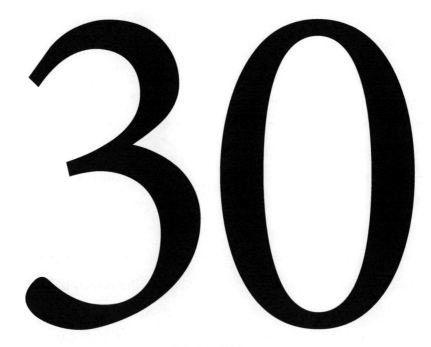

30

CORPSEA

Beneath the surface, Sera marveled at her suit's integrated goggles and breathing apparatus. She was also surprised by the power of its lamps. Wherever they shone, they dredged detail from the void. To her right, she found Nixie grippingthe buoy's tether: a rope that seemingly extended to the seafloor.

"We just follow this down," Nixie announced. "It'll take a few minutes. We're going descend to a depth few have ventured to in over a century —and even *fewer* have returned from. But don't worry, that regulator inside your mask will help you withstand the changing pressure."

Somehow, Nixie's voice was inside Sera's suit. Sera wondered whether she could answer normally or if some unknown incantation was needed. "Truth be told, I don't know what a regulator is or why I should care about pressure."

Sera sighed, still not sure whether Nixie could hear her. "There's so much I don't know. But the thing that worries me most—I have no clue what I'm supposed to do next. How are we supposed to locate the Yantra? And let's say I attempt to use it; how will I know whether I've succeeded?"

"I think you'll know," Nixie reassured. "We're being chased by the Sorcerer's minions as they serve my mother. That sort of interference should end once you've succeeded." Sera was reminded of the way stone Maeve's enchanted worms had instantly disappeared when she halved the authentic one. "What's less clear to me," Nixie continued, "is whether primary magick in its entirety will also cease to function."

After a few minutes' silent descent, Sera spotted the seafloor. The buoy's bottom rope had been tethered to a flagpole at what Sera surmised to be the main entrance to the old academy. Nixie wasted no time swimming in. "The Yantra—and its guardian—await us in the depths of this building, Sera. Well, actually, beneath the building."

"The Yantra's Guardian?"

"Yes, he's a—a fairy I suppose. I mean, that's what I'm told he looks like to your kind. To us, he's what we call a 'fury' (like a 'furious' beast). Whereas you will see some beautiful feathery figure, I'll be seeing the sort of thing that seeds nightmares. Furies are abominations. When the Coven figured out how to graft horns onto fauns with the aid of mycosis, they saw little reason to stop. So, they didn't; they expanded their work, grafting all sorts of unnatural things onto retired fauns—each to serve some specialized purpose. In the case of the Yantra's Guardian and the Coven's Heralds, the extra appendages were the wings of my father's pegasi.

"To make matters worse, the Grand Sorcerer supports these wicked acts, imbuing the victims with immortality so they can serve the Coven *forever*. Anyway, keep that in mind when you meet the Guardian. It can be easy to forget who you're really dealing with."

As she spoke, Nixie led the way to a main hall of sorts. The academy was stunning, even in its present, flooded state. Underwater plants had grown up along its many bookshelf-lined walls and stone pillars. Pulpy masses that once were books floated up from the floor as Sera and Nixie paddled by. "This place is a watery wonderland!"

"It used to be a dry one," Nixie noted. "This is Harlequin House, the only spot in the known universe where all six classes of magick were taught in one place. This is where my father enlightened generations of students."

Sera swam upward, reviewing the endless shelves of books. Soon, she noticed the world above. Inexplicably, the surface of the sea appeared to be extremely close. After a few more kicks, her head emerged from the water. Sera grabbed a bookshelf and unclipped her mask for a better look.

The top half of the main hall was dry. In this preserved state, most of its shelves were still lined with books and bottles. Up top, an intricate glass dome was keeping the sea at bay.

Nixie popped up beside Sera and removed her mask. After noticing Sera's bemused expression, she provided an explanation: "That's an air pocket. The glass ceiling here has managed to withstand the weight of the sea. We face a lot worse radiation on Mars, so we take glass and seals very seriously. I seem to recall Earth has weaker glass because of the type of sand you use to make it."

"So, this ceiling will hold forever?"

"No. Many of the others have caved."

"Well, I'm glad it's held out this long. This library is glorious. I really wish we had the time to explore!"

"Me too. But we don't. We really need to find the way down—" *BOHMM.*

A deep vibration filled the room. It was so jarring, in fact, that it felt as though the two were inside a rung bell. Sera turned to Nixie only to find her friend studying the glass dome intently. "I think—" *BOHMM. BOHMM.* "Masks on!" Nixie demanded.

As Sera anxiously clipped her mask into place, she caught the terrifying sound of glass cracking. By the time she could see through her mask, she was overwhelmed by calamity. Huge segments of the dome were crashing down, threatening to impale the girls. Water—and harvest fauns—were roaring down from the ruptured canopy. Harlequin House's once-calm, airtight world was rapidly disappearing.

Sera instinctively dove beneath the tumult. Once below the surface, she spotted Nixie racing down to the floor. "Where do we go?!"

"I don't know! There should've been a metal plate here, a seal at the center of the room. I typically— LOOK OUT!"

Sera spun around to find a cluster of possessed harvest fauns thrashing their bodies furiously as they closed in. One was so close she could practically touch the mossy shroud enveloping his head. Her heart was in her throat as she kicked to distance herself. But speed alone wouldn't suffice; there was only so far one could retreat. "PLEASE DO SOMETHING!" she pleaded.

Nixie, too, was frantically evading the harvest fauns. But her task was even harder; she was simultaneously shouting a string of spells to reopen the seal: "APERTUS! REVELARE! DEGUILE!"

With each spell—while simultaneously paddling—Nixie would swing her arms and hands about to perform various accompanying gestures.

"Deprecari!"

At once, a hole appeared in the stone floor beneath them. As it dilated, the water supporting Sera and Nixie rushed downward. There was no fighting it, no slowing. The academy's once-calm waters were violently swirling within an ever-widening whirlpool. Around and around, they whipped as the floor below gave way in giant, jagged pieces.

Nixie was the first to plummet. As Sera neared the same fate, she noticed the immense stone pieces giving way were squared off and evenly spaced. *Almost like teeth!* And then, a freefall.

For a second, the abyss was effectively a vacuum. There was no friction or detail, just empty space. As Sera made her way upright and managed a quick sideways glance, she realized that she —and the water plummeting with her— had entered a mineshaft. A spiral staircase was channeling an extension of the whirlpool from above, its water building even greater centrifugal force.

Unfortunately, the water did little to soften a devastating blow as Sera hit one of the edges of the staircase. The force of the impact was so great, the pain so excruciating, she nearly blacked out. But with the pain came the realization she might yet survive the fall. Rather than plummeting through the middle of the mineshaft, she was now caught in the torrent *spiraling* down.

"EVISCERA!" Nixie's voice rang out. … Then again. Each time, Sera would pass through an open stone portal a few seconds later. As they descended, Sera found herself struggling to make sense of what she was seeing. *The walls are changing.… There's a fleshy lining!*

Suddenly, she careened into an all-too-shallow body of water. Like a cliffside lunge to a shallow bay, the pool had done little to soften her impact.

For a few seconds, she lay motionless at the bottom of the pool. The hit she'd sustained had been too great, the resulting pain too intense—more than any body was built to endure. Deep down, Sera's subconscious knew giving up was out of the question, but her conscious mind knew not how to rise.

Then a hand, thrust down on her, seized Sera's suit and wrestled her up. Battered and dazed but back on her hooves, Sera found herself in Nixie's embrace. "Way to survive the fall! I've never come down anywhere near as fast. But we're in the right place."

Above, a rumbling signaled the end of the torrent as the closest portal resealed. "Well, that's good, I suppose," Nixie observed. "I mean, unless we actually *survive* what comes next, 'cause then, venturing back up alongside all those trapped abominations—that certainly won't be fun."

"What does come next?"

Nixie stepped aside, inviting Sera to review the cavernous space beyond. In the center, bathed in shimmery blue light, a magnificent, feathery figure stood, swaying and chanting. "Him."

31

THE YANTRA'S GUARDIAN

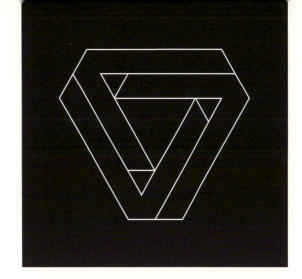

Dimensionally, the chamber was similar to the lowest level of the mineshaft Sera had ventured through on Earth. But there was no worm-wielding portal monster here. What the girl faced now was far more welcome: an angelic entity, seemingly unconcerned with the pool of water that had risen to its waist. The Guardian was repeating a single phrase over and over. Only as Sera neared the figure was she able make out the words:

"Stultum perspectus."

"Stultum perspectus."

"Stultum perspectus."

"He's incanting something you must not repeat," Nixie explained. "At least, I'm pretty sure you shouldn't. There are so many cadavers down here, now under this water—the remains of those who came before you. I imagine every one of them opted to repeat that spell."

A trap. Sera looked up to identify the source of their chamber's blue light. High above, a large, glowing crystal was levitating and slowly rotating. Its shape was unlike any Sera had seen before: a hollow triangle with sides that were folding into each other in a manner that seemed … impossible.

"There's no moving it, no touching it." Nixie explained. "The Yantra has always been there. It may no longer be entombed in stone, but it's forever fixed. I think there are two challenges:" Nixie raised one finger. "Getting to it." Then another. "And activating it. I've tried every imaginable spell to activate it. I suspect we have to reach it first."

Sera craned back. "What's the plan?"

"You tell me. This is where resourcefulness and intellect set you apart."

"I don't know." Sera laughed nervously. As she further approached the Guardian, she caught Nixie shutter. But in stark contrast to what Nixie was seeing, the Guardian's enchanted form was glorious. Like the Herald Sera had encountered on Soliday, he was tall, packed with soft feathers, and crowned with enormous, golden horns. He also seemed entirely unconcerned with the girls as he slowly swayed, staring up at the Yantra. Every five seconds, he incanted the same "Stultum Perspectus."

"I really don't want to see what you do if I get this wrong," Sera admitted to the figure before her. Then she turned to Nixie: "So, it's *always* the same?"

"Yes. I've been coming here for years. Always the same two words. Even the mole who showed me the ropes says it's always been the same. I have had nightmares I somehow recited them without realizing what I was doing."

Sera nodded. "Well, there's some significance to the spell. To free the Yantra, we need to respond to it, … or we need a way to safely recite it, … or it's a trick, another line of defense."

"Yes, all reasonable theories—but you can't afford to be wrong."

"I'm going to do some investigating." Sera joined OmniSync, requesting a view of her surroundings a day earlier. Sure enough, the fury was shown repeating the spell every five seconds.

A year before: the same.

A decade earlier: also the same.

A century prior: still the same.

Then she was reminded of Enry's prompt in the bowels of the Earth:

"Try your birthday on that thing." *Why not?* Sera retrieved the local log of her surroundings at the time she was born.

Then she logged out. "Whatever comes next, I want you to know you've restored my faith in our potential." Nixie looked bewildered. "Masks on!"

Then, just before Sera clipped her mask around her head, she shouted a spell only once before recited in the history of existence:

"Misericordia abortum!"

The seconds that followed were a blur. So much happened that it was difficult for Sera to comprehend it all.

For one thing, the Yantra plummeted from overhead, plunging into the shallow water below. The fact that it fell with such speed and heft surprised Sera. When it had been floating, she'd suspected it to be of the same magickal nature Ledbetter had explained as a "hologram." But a hologram it was not. The Yantra was really there, a massive crystal glowing brilliantly paces away.

For another, Sera finally had the Guardian's attention. In a flash, his plumage erupted from his body.

The fury that remained was the most terrifying thing she'd ever laid eyes on: a dark, mangled shadow of a being who was once a faun. The top of its head was filled with twisted horns. Its poor skin was covered in scars. It bore two wings that looked as though they belonged on a winged demon. And its eyes were hollow; Only the faintest glint of light reflected from deep within its head.

On top of it all, the chamber had started shaking, undulating.

Sera sprinted to the Yantra as the Guardian lunged to intercept her. She leapt sideways to escape his reach. Her maneuvering was made harder by the fact that the water around them had begun to slosh violently.

Sera plowed through the chaos. The water was rapidly rising. She feared she would soon be swept away, but she pressed on with the fury in tow. As she reached the Yantra, the entire chamber trembled, and its simmering waters gurgled. With one last lunge, Sera leapt to the crystal.

Instantly, the raging waters rushed upward with explosive force. Straight up all parties were thrust, smashing into the walls of the chamber and funneling through its ruptured threshold. Spiraling back up the shaft, bursting one portal after another, Sera was being rocketed from the depths of the planet at unfathomable speed.

As she was ejected from the top of the mine, Sera's view shocked her. *A tongue … and teeth?!* But there was no time to question such absurdities. She had been spewed forth, not into the open sea, but into the early morning sky. A league above the sea's surface, with Nixie's harrowed screams ringing in her ears, Sera's tumultuous ride transitioned from a terrifying upward thrust to an equally terrifying freefall.

Back to the sea she plummeted. And then … a devastating reckoning. Were it not for her special suit, the harsh impact that marked Sera's return to the Corpsea surely would have killed her. She was, at that moment, nothing more than a ragdoll. Once again, Sera was descending, this time sinking to the depths of the sea as she defiantly clung to the Yantra.

Suddenly, a huge, lengthy stone mass punched through the water next to her. As it barreled down, like a comet,

it formed whirlpools on all sides, sucking Sera and her Yantra deeper into the darkness. Below, the stony mass —which seemed to be articulated like a limb—hammered into the seabed, creating reverberations that shook Sera and threatened to pull the Yantra from her clutches. Among the sand and bubbles swirling, Sera was horrified to see bones and old garments.

Then, as abruptly as it had plummeted, the mass pulled up, sucking her back toward the surface in its mighty riptide. As the mass withdrew to the waters above, Sera was sure she saw the details of a gigantic hoof—one big enough to smash her in a single stomp. That's when she realized what she was contending with, *who* she was contending with.

But in the relative calm of that brief moment, Sera also realized that the Yantra was no longer in her clutches. "Nixie? Nixie, I need help!"

"I'm here, Sera. I got shot out into the sea. I'm close to the dock."

"Get to my deadringer. You've got to get the goggles off of him!"

"Already on it. Should reach him in a minute. Just—just don't die!"

Survival was proving most difficult. Again and again, giant stone hooves stomped into the sea, devastating the world below as a monster—one Sera imagined to be like stone Maeve, but even larger—attempted to crush her.

Through it all, Sera did her best to track the Yantra which had sunk to the seafloor. The problem was that each stomp kicked up more sand, sea junk, and skeletal remains, making the water cloudier and the Yantra harder to see.

But after a dozen such attempts, the last stomp didn't end like others. The stone hoof that rocketed past Sera exited sideways. Its return had been too soon, its motion no longer deliberate but instead haphazard and seemingly unplanned. *Nixie's unleashed Pterus!*

Sera's body swished violently as an eddy pulled her sideways. She knew she'd have to move quickly if she was going to whisk the Yantra to safety. Urgently, she paddled down to the seabed, fleeing the current while scanning for any hint of unnatural blue. Only after descending to a great depth did she locate it: a weak glow under a new dune of sand. *How can I dredge up that which weighs me down?*

Out of the corner of her eye, Sera spotted the academy's flagpole. While most of the once-magnificent Harlequin House lay in ruin, its flagpole had miraculously survived the day's destruction.

Sera reached the dune and clawed furiously at its sand to unearth the Yantra within. In every direction, stone legs punched through the water, creating calamitous reverberations and great, white plumes of bubbles.

At last, Sera pulled the Yantra from the sand and threw it over her head and one shoulder. With the Yantra hanging across her chest her like a giant, stone sash, she launched into an all-out, underwater sprint for the flagpole. Her movement was awkward. The task was exhausting. But somehow, despite the horrendous, deadly sprint, she managed to reach the pole.

Once there, Sera clambered up to reach the buoy's rope—the same rope she and Nixie had used an hour earlier. Climbing up was extremely difficult given the weight of the Yantra.

At the top of the flagpole, Sera frantically untied the buoy's rope and re-secured it to the Yantra. Free of its

weight, she found she could again move nimbly. Then she raced up the rope, bound for the dinghy she and Nixie had left behind.

Unfortunately, the closer she ventured, the more treacherous her climb was getting. The world above had become absolute chaos. As she reached the dinghy, she stared in awe at the surrounding spectacle. An enchanted stone ewe the size of a mountain was embroiled in an all-out battle with a replica of itself. Huge chunks of the two monstrosities rained down as the beings smashed into one another.

Sera threw herself into the boat that thankfully hadn't yet capsized. Waves crashed around her as she started reeling up the Yantra-tied rope, hand over fist. The rope seemed to go on forever. It was filling her boat and draining Sera of what miniscule energy she had left. In desperation, Sera cried a futile plea for the Yantra to emerge.

"You have it?!" Nixie's voice called out through Sera's discarded mask as it sloshed about in the dinghy.

"I do," Sera huffed as she continued hauling the heavy rope in. "Well, I just about have it back anyway."

"Good!" Nixie exclaimed. "I believe I know the spell. I'd have preferred we do this on the shore, with the benefit of time, but you have neither shore nor time. Assuming you have the Yantra, grab a hold of it, and say 'Caesareus.'"

"I'm working on it." Sera grunted. She had just spotted the radiant blue glow of the Yantra below. With each pull, she found new confidence that she might yet succeed.

But then something yanked back. Whatever it was, it pulled so hard that it nearly yanked Sera overboard. Panicked, the girl grabbed a loop of rope and wrapped it around the motor to keep from losing the substantial length she'd already dredged up.

Inch by hard-won inch, Sera continued to reel the Yantra in. With each pull, she wrapped newly resurfaced rope over the motor, securing incremental progress. As the Yantra entered view, Sera reached down to grab it.

To her horror, a dark, clawed hand reached up from the water. It grabbed a hold of her arm and pulled down mightily. She tried to cling to the boat, but it was no use. Sera was pulled, headfirst, into the sea.

Beneath the surface of the water, she suffered a brutal attack. A swirling darkness had closed in to deliver a barrage of blows. In seconds, it had left her suit and body in shreds. Worst of all, Sera was maskless, affording her no way to breathe. As she struggled desperately to survive, to escape, her attacker grabbed her ankles and wrapped the rope below around them. Then it swished back to watch her die.

Sera thrashed her body violently, struggling to resurface. She needed air or she would indeed perish.

As Sera's last breath left her body, she finally found a moment of peace. Before her, the Yantra's Guardian floated silently, staring back through dark, soulless eyes. Without air in her lungs, her body lost buoyancy, and all but her bound ankles sank down into the darkness.

Sera's vision faded as her mind took one last chance to remember others. She thought of Enry, a boy she loved but whom she'd never confessed her love to. She remembered Bram, a boy she would have traveled to the ends of the universe to protect. There were her mother and father who had battled

SORCE

heartrending loss to shield Sera from pain. She recalled Opa, Addie, and Thomas who'd nurtured Sera's pursuit of the truth when the world forbade it. There were Theo and Constantine: good souls robbed of their lives. And Nixie: an aerie who proved empathy knew no celestial bounds.

But the faun who stuck with Sera as her mind faded was one she couldn't picture: the unknown face of an unknown faun plucked from his home, enslaved on an alien planet, subjected to gruesome mutilations, and possessed to do an evil god's bidding. Sera mourned for the fury who had been forced to kill her.

With a thud, a sharp pain rocked Sera back to consciousness. Her head, now upside down as her body dangled by its ankles, had knocked into the Yantra below. *The Yantra.*

Sera could no longer see. Her lungs screamed for air. But it didn't matter, she knew what she must do, faculties be damned. At the edge of death, she thrust her hands down, grasped the crystal, and mouthed a single word:

"Caesareus."

32

THE ROYAL COVEN

From the old ram's second boat—the dingy without a motor—Nixie stopped paddling to look up. One of the raging titans above had inexplicably paused, mid-attack.

Both stone ewes had been badly damaged, but to stop so abruptly implied another ailment. Nixie studied the unanimated ewe. Pterus was smashing into her with everything he had, yet the monstrosity remained motionless.

Then, still oblivious to the unfettered assault against her, the stone titan redirected her attention downward. She knelt to inspect the surface of the sea. Cupping her gigantic hands together, she drew something up from just beneath the surface. Water rained down as she delicately raised her prize to her lips. She appeared to kiss the object. Or consume it.

Nixie was struggling to make sense of the actions. It seemed Pterus was too. Without stimulus, he'd stopped his attack. Nixie knew it was only a matter of time before the deadringer started shrinking—which meant he was at risk of drowning. *Okay,* she thought. *I'll get you too. But first, Sera.*

Behind Nixie, a battalion of aerie

soldiers were hurriedly unloading and helming newly delivered military pontoons. Nixie resumed her breakneck paddling. *Please be in the boat. Be in the boat!* Sera had stopped responding, so Nixie had taken matters—and oars—into her own hands.

But as she reached the dinghy in the middle of the sea—now with only a narrow lead on her pursuers—Nixie was distraught to find no sign of Sera. Glancing upward, she spotted only a single titan—surely the authentic one—still intently studying the object in her cupped hands.

Then Nixie noticed Pterus on the horizon: a modest lump barely peeking above the surface. There was no way she could make it to him before he shrank into the sea and drowned. All the same, she leapt from her oarpowered boat into the motorized one ready to make a mad dash.

Suddenly, the kneeling titan shifted again. Nixie stopped to watch in awe as the ewe scooped Pterus from the sea. Now he too was part of some precious concoction. With fingers the size of tree trunks, her mother's likeness finessed and plucked at the prizes in her hand.

Next, as though satisfied, she leaned forward, directly over Nixie, and gingerly deposited her prizes into the boat. The immense scale of her hand was hard to register. Along with the Yantra, three bodies were laid down at Nixie's hooves: Sera, Pterus, and the Yantra's Guardian. With the ewe watching over, Nixie reviewed her company.

The Guardian no longer carried a sinister air—but he was most certainly dead. Nixie was distraught to see the former fury's true, emaciated form. His sockets were still pronounced, but his eyes were now visible—and open. Through every angry vein and wrinkle, a hardened anguish in his fierce eyes told Nixie they had seen it all. His poor, scarred limbs told a thousand stories too. But most shocking: his defining wings were gone. Nixie was overcome at the sight of him.

To his side, Pterus too had been transformed. Inexplicably, the dead-ringer's sad, vestigial wings had been replaced with those of the fury. On an animal of his stature, they looked truly grand. *Pop.* Nixie laughed weakly as she was met with a copy of herself.

And to Pterus' left: Sera. Her body lay limply, propped up against the side of the boat. But Sera was conscious, seemingly at peace with their preposterous circumstances. "Did we do it?"

"I don't know," Nixie confessed. Then she looked back to the titan smiling down at her.

"A mother's love," Sera explained.

With her words, the monumental figure kneeling beside them crumbled. Chunks of her form crashed to the sea, tossing the dinghy about, and farther back, a wide perimeter of soldier-filled pontoons. Nixie was knocked off her hooves. From the floor of the boat, she turned to Sera and laughed. "Yes, I think we did it."

…

I know what I saw. We all saw it."

"Captain, are you questioning the High Priestess?"

"Absolutely not, sir. Not in a thousand years. I'm sure her Majesty recognized more in today's events than we can. I'm just sayin' that the giant, stone incarnation of Her Majesty willingly handed the Yantra, that pig-dragon, and the eerie witch back to the Princess, and then crumbled into the sea. Nothing about that looked like a deci-

SORCE

sive victory for her Majesty. It looked like willful surrender."

"Her Majesty has asserted that her daughter played no role in this conspiracy. How then, is it conceivable that a stone representation of the Queen would willfully place the apostate and the Yantra in a boat with her daughter? If I were you, Captain, I'd watch my words. Taken out of context, one might interpret them as heresy. I'm sure that's not how you intended them."

"Of course, that's right, Major.… You know, my eyes must have been playin' tricks on me. Surely some wicked craft on the part of the eerie witch."

From the back of the wagon transporting her, Sera wasn't supposed to hear anything spoken in the front of the vehicle. But Uncommon Sense had afforded her exceptional hearing. She was curious what her Queen's Corps captors would say of the spectacle at sea. It seemed they might not say much at all. *It doesn't matter. They can say —or not say—whatever they want. I did what I came here to do. The aeries lost their all-important ally today. With that blow, the balance of power will change.*

When the soldiers had stormed the girls' boat, there had been a moment of great tension when they confronted the conundrum that was Nixie. She was royalty. She was soon to be a member of the Coven. She could do no wrong. And yet, she had clearly abetted the vilest faun ever to set hoof on their planet. In the end, they opted to arrest her without describing their actions as such. Nixie was sternly asked to accompany them back to the Royal Temple. She was placed in a separate vehicle, apart from Sera and Pterus.

As Sera felt her wagon pull to a stop and heard the soldiers get out, she leaned forward to address her once again blindfolded companion. "Okay, buddy, it's game time."

Click. Creak. The rear door of the wagon was unlocked and unhitched. As it opened, two soldiers leaned in. On cue, Sera started screaming: "Get it away from me! Get it away! Why would you stow the Princess' beast in here?! It's going to eat me!"

One of the soldiers leaned into the wagon to grab Sera. The other cleared his throat. "Um, … if we bring 'em in together, we're just going to make the Princess look like an accomplice." He shook his head. "Discretely return the beast to the Princess, … with a stern warning. I'll watch the apostate." Sera nearly let slip a chortle as she continued feigning terror.

Once outside the wagon, she marveled at the strange world before her. A spectacular pyramid towered above, blocking the midday sun. Unlike the pyramid she'd seen in the Grimwoods, this immense structure was made of stone—and not your run-of-the-mill stone either: iridescent, black stone. The building appeared ancient. It was clearly sacred. But most of all, its effect was wickedly unnervingly.

All about, fountains and horrible sculptures of headless fauns decorated a vast square. A few military wagons were parked next to Sera's, near to the pyramid, while a perimeter of trees in the distance gave Sera the odd sense that she was back in the Grimwoods' central clearing.

As she studied her surroundings, her courier soldier returned from one of the other wagons. She was pleased to find he'd returned empty-handed, having dutifully done her bidding.

Hurriedly, he looped an arm under Sera's left pit and motioned for his comrade to do the same on her other side. Then, without a word of warning, the two dragged Sera forward, toward an oversized staircase at the base of the towering temple. Sera resisted with every ounce of her will as they wrestled her up the stone steps, but in the end, her hulking captors succeeded. A deep thud announced their entry as the temple's gargantuan, wooden doors were swung open.

At the far end of an expansive room littered with lit candles, a near-complete ring of seated parties awaited. Those present paid Sera little notice as their formal exchange carried on. But as Sera was dragged to the center of the ring, a closer examination of each witch's and warlock's eyes betrayed the effect: *all eyes are on me.*

"Miss Skohlidon," a warlock called out. Sera turned to face the party. It was Roald.

"Oh, hello, Roald." Sera stood tall and wiped the hair from her eyes. "Fancy seeing you here."

One of the ram's eyes twitched as he worked on his own witty response. "The new horns look good on you."

Sera was careful not to bat an eye as she returned another dry quip. "Yours would look good on my wall."

Behind Sera, someone cackled. "You weren't kidding. She *is* prickly!"

Sera swung around to face the witch. "You've turned my head into a thornbush. I'm packed with prickly parts."

"Yes, about them," another chimed in, "I'd say the alterations were … worth the effect." *Maeve.* Sera recognized the Queen's voice from her prior encounter. *Finally, in the flesh.* "But no need to thank me, child. I actually wanted to thank you. You've pressure-tested our system and shown us our failings. Your actions will pave the way to a stronger Coven.

"You've taught us that monitoring speech is inadequate; we must monitor thought. You've proven that fauns your age are more capable than we've credited; we'll be re-evaluating retirement age policies for inducted eeries. And you've highlighted weaknesses in our handling of the Yantra, so we'll be relocating it. I dare say, we're grate—"

"The Yantra's nothing more than a big rock at this point. You should bring it in here and turn it into an altar."

"You see, that's where you're wrong, Miss Skohlidon." The Queen Witch was getting flushed. "I realize you *think* you used the Yantra, but you had no idea what you were doing. The Grand Sorcerer is just fine."

"Is that why your stone incarnation abandoned battle, forfeited the Yantra, and crumbled to the sea? Seems an odd way to respond if my effort was a bust."

"Abandoned battle?" The Queen was growing red as she paused to consider her words. "Sera, your distorted perception is appalling!"

"Then don't distort my perception!"

At this, the High Priestess lurched forward. But just as quickly, she caught herself and returned to her seat.

"*YOU* are the reason our new crop of young fauns had to perish! *YOU* are to be credited with spurring new, more onerous monitoring and retirement policies! And *YOU* are to blame for the just-restocked Corpsea! Your parents tried to shelter you. OmniSync was tailored to focus your precocious mind on *safe* material. Even our woodland spirits were placed to keep you from danger. But no, there could be no helping the headstrong eerie witch.

At every fork in the road, you chose the darker path. AT EVERY TURN, YOU STRAYED *TOWARD* DANGER!"

Sera stared brazenly at the Queen and stepped forward. "I believe you know which … 'witch' … is which. I believe that appropriately scares you.

And that fear has made you desperate. It makes you vulnerable."

She took another step forward. "Here you are, high-and-mighty royalty, reduced to clawing through mineshafts, brawling with deadringers. You're desperate—and you should be."

THE ROYAL COVEN

The Queen was boiling over. Her face had gone crimson, veins in her temple were throbbing, and her hands were strangling the arms of her throne. "ENOUGH! I'm just astonished by you, by your pathologically distorted reality and your reckless confidence!

"It's time you see where this cavalier disregard for social order has led you." The Queen shooed a dismissal of Sera and turned to the waiting guards. "See this petulant brat to the dungeon. May Hades himself find some merit in her mettle or pleasure in breaking it."

33

THE BEGINNING

Oh, no no no no. The royal guards had just left. After dragging Sera to a sacrificial chamber laden with black mirrors and gaudy gold instruments, they had forcefully removed the cylinder from her head. She was certain her captors would soon be scanning the incriminating device, discovering how she'd smuggled Pterus to Nixie, that the latest faun harvest was actually aboard the Bostromo, and that Sera and Corporal Dade were in cahoots planning an imminent escape.

Compounding Sera's many stresses, nearly a full sol had passed since the ship's landing. If she were going to pull off an ambitious getaway, she had little time to break free from the dungeon. As she played out various escape scenarios, the High Priestess entered her cell. "Come to finish the job yourself?"

Maeve didn't bother responding. Instead, she smiled, raised her arms to form the sacred gesture and incanted "Deguile." In a blue flash, the ewe transformed, leaving Nixie in her wake.

Sera grinned nervously. "The more I get immersed in your world, the more unsettled I become. How do I know you're not actually the Queen Witch? Seems like a pretty good ploy to get me to lower my guard."

Nixie knelt and handed Sera a vial. "Would the Queen give you a helixir?"

"She handed me a Yantra, so … yes?"

"That wasn't my mother. That was the Grand Sorcerer. I don't know why he did it. I've been pondering that bit all day. But I'm convinced my mother had nothing to do with any of it—the stone beast, the handling of the Yantra, the Guardian, and Pterus. My mother wouldn't have done those things. She would have crushed you. Now she's extremely upset with me, madder than I've ever seen. And my support here is only going to make matters worse."

"What support might that be?"

"You're going to drink the helixir I just gave you, you're going to picture my mother and say the enchantment spell. Then you're going to take this '*dead ring*,'" Nixie handed Sera a large, jewel-studded ring, "and stride out of here like a queen not to be trifled with.

"I hope you're reunited with Enry, wherever it is you're headed. I *think* I know where that is, but I definitely don't want you to tell me."

"As soon as they see I'm missing—"

"They aren't going to notice." Nixie shrugged. "I'll be taking your place."

"Is that safe?! That seems so dangerous. Shouldn't you come with me?"

"I would, but we have no margin for error here. The Queen entered with Sera in this cell. She must leave with Sera *still* in this cell. Besides, what's a bit of interplanetary travel these days? I'll see you again."

Sera lunged forward and hugged her friend. "I'll be counting on it." Then she uncorked the vial and toasted Nixie. "Bottom's up."

The contents burned as they went down. Sera felt a wave of heat cascade through her as the concoction reached her stomach, her heart, and her entire circulatory system. After a few seconds, the heat dissipated. "Did I flash blue?"

"Not yet. Now do your thing."

Sera performed the sacred gesture and incanted the corresponding spell while picturing High Priestess Maeve: "Beguile."

At once, her internal heat returned with such intensity that she momentarily blacked out. As she regained her vision, blue smoke was indeed in the air. But Sera's perspective had changed.

She was standing taller, her head was heavier, and her blood felt sickly.

"You get used to it." Nixie offered a smile and handed Sera the ring she'd referenced. "That's Pterus, so we really do need to move quickly. Now it's my turn." Nixie performed the sacred gesture again and recited the same spell. After the transformation, Sera's likeness stood in Nixie's wake.

"This is seriously confusing for me," the real Sera confessed.

"Well, seeing *you* as my mother's disorienting for me too," Nixie admitted.

"So how do you do it? How is it you enchant without a helixir?" Sera asked.

"There are different types. The rarest ones can be used as often as you like and last a lifetime. My mother had me inoculated when I was little. It's helped keep me safe more than once, but it's also caused her endless grief."

"Well, here's to a little more grief." Sera slid the jewel-studded ring onto one of her aged fingers. Already, it had begun to quiver, an indication it would soon be decaying into Pterus' natural form. Then, with a tear in her eye, she waved goodbye to Nixie—to a clone of herself—and exited the dungeon.

…

At the space center, vast fleets of soldiers were assembled outside, ready to board the ship, as service teams hurried carts in and out of its bay.

Sera, who still looked like Maeve, had chosen to be dropped off as close as possible to the launch pad. In an uncomfortably high-profile arrival, she and Pterus stepped out of a Coven vehicle and, directly before the Queen's Corps, strode up the loading bay ramp.

As she reached the top of the ramp, Corporal Dade approached hesitantly. "Your Majesty."

"It's me," she replied with a wink.

"You're down to the wire. And your deadringer's looking quite … different."

Sera smiled and glanced down at her leashed and blindfolded friend. Even with the accessories, he no longer looked cute. Pterus looked absolutely fierce. "The wings suit him. I just didn't realize we would be parading before an entire battalion. Anyway, I think he's endured enough for one trip. So how did you and the kids fare?"

"We made out just fine. I managed to enlist help; a handful of eerie-sympathetic soldiers I've been keeping tabs on. They should help us seize control of the ship when the time's right. The kids were certainly apprehensive at first, but once Enry made it back—"

"He's here?" Maeve's expression lit up as Sera, in her likeness, performed a tiptoe dance before the Corporal.

The ram waited, his face dull, until Sera regained Maeve's regal composure. "So how long do we have?"

"We'll close the bay as soon as the battalion boards," the Corporal explained.

"Why board loyal soldiers that we'd then have to contend with in space?"

"You expect to just turn them away?"

"Yes."

"Just like that? You're just going to march out there 'n tell them to leave?"

"Watch me." Sera swung around and strode down the ramp. Without hesitation, she approached the massive gathering of troops. "Change of plans!" she shouted. "We need the ship for official Coven business today. You're dismissed." Then she pivoted back.

"Please close the ramp, Corporal."

"That's … not how things are done," the officer observed with a grimace. Sera smiled, shrugged, and turned to the bay's staircase. "Now, if you're looking for Enry, he's in the control room."

As she ascended, the ship's gargantuan loading ramp closed behind her. By the time Sera had reached the control room, the bay had been sealed. She found her friend gazing through the window. "Enry!"

"STAY BACK!"

"Oh," Sera laughed, "give me a sec." Then she performed the sacred gesture and incanted "Deguile." This time, the sensation that spread from her fingertips to her heart was cold, like a winter chill blasting through her veins. Again, Sera blacked out. But this time, as she regained her senses, she discovered a new warmth: Enry's embrace.

"How'd you get back?" she asked.

"Nixie left me a key. I suspected it to be a master key to the exam rooms, so I crept across the hall and tried it on the next room. It worked!

"Inside, I found a harvest faun awaiting some terrible fate. The two of us darted to the next room, found another and so on until we'd hit all the exam rooms. Anyway, it worked. As promised, a wagon was ready and waiting. We packed in and had it bring us here."

"I'm so impressed!" Sera gushed.

Enry gazed at the girl in his arms.

"I'm just happy to have played a part, to have supported the esteemed eerie witch." The boy's eyes momentarily landed on Sera's lips.

This time, before he could catch himself, before he could look away, she stretched up to accept him.

But after an interminable pause with her eyes closed, the gentle touch that followed came not from his lips. Sera felt the boy's fingers caress the length of her jaw. His hand rested under her chin as he then raised her head. Sera tingled feeling his electric touch.

As she opened her eyes, she found his chiseled, beautiful face waiting so very close to her own. Features she had secretly studied for years were now intimately close. Excitingly close.

Sera's heart and eyes fluttered. Then her worshipper pulled her close and kissed her with sparkling intensity.

…

For the ship's faun passengers, the return home was the inverse of their original voyage. Every rescued faun was treated to their own bed and regimen of meals, courtesy of an aerie soldier denied passage. Instead of days spent dreading the next surprise ab-

duction or forced surgical procedure, fauns young and old spent their time giddily considering post-landing plans.

When the big day finally came, the positive energy coursing through the Bostromo was more magnificent than its powerful landing rockets. The ship was bound for the only logical landing site: the center of the Grimwoods.

Alongside her friends, Sera waited anxiously for the loading bay to open. She'd actually come to miss the aroma of the Grimwoods' pine trees, how she longed to inhale its wholesome air, and how very ready she was for a return to Earth's secure, stabilizing gravity.

But as the ship's ramp rested on her home world's soil, a surprise nearly knocked Sera off her hooves. A welcome party of relics had been waiting —and they were accompanied by Opa and Enry's parents. Fenora rushed up to embrace Enry and Sera as Irving bellowed from the pack. "I knew it! I just *KNEW* it!"

Enry, smothered in Fenora's bosom, managed a muffled response: "How?"

"After returning your brother to your parents, Enry, we found your mother, Fenora, to be an excellent ally." Irving turned to Sera. "We've stayed in touch with the guild since you left.

"About a month ago, the Coven sent word that you had been caught attempting to use the Yantra. They made it clear you'd failed. Then they broadcasted your execution."

Sera pulled back from Fenora, wide-eyed, as she turned to Irving. "What EXACTLY did you see?"

"The Queen. They made it look like she herself killed you. Very convincing.

"So many were utterly distraught, Sera. In the guild. In the Core. Truly inconsolable. But this time, the Coven's shady tactics have backfired; they've turned you into a martyr. We don't know whether you found the Yantra, whether you activated it, but your quest *was* successful. You started something. Your cause has taken root."

Sera stood trembling, struggling to breathe as she confronted the notion that Nixie may have been executed in her stead.

Then Fenora pulled her inward.

The warm, swaddling embrace did help, soothing the girl's tortured mind.

Eventually, Sera peeled back to address the gathering. "I can't tell you how

moved I am to see you all. To be home."
She wiped her face. "I think it's impossible, actually. But if you'll indulge
me," she inhaled deeply, "I'd like to try."

Sera reviewed those before her. All
the familiar faces, the love and acceptance she felt. She wanted to connect
with each individual, to lock eyes with
particular parties as she spoke so that,
one by one, they would recognize the
admission aimed at them.

"Home isn't simply where I grew
up. It's anywhere that invites me to
truly be myself. I found my core in
yours, a league underground.

"Home has been recognizing I'm
part of a grander story—knowing that,
before it's all over, I'll add to that story.

"Home, I've observed, is security. It's
knowing you wholeheartedly believe
in me. Home is your enduring love.

"It's steeped in our waters. It blows
over our meadows. And it crackles in
our cabins. It's passed from elders to
grandchildren. It's in our—our—" Sera's
shoulders sank. "It's in our bones."

The world stood still as she faced
her friends, fresh tears spilling down.
She was searching for words, words
that had always come naturally, words

that now seemed a solar system away.

"HA-YOH!" Like a war cry, Phaedra's
shrill call gave voice to Sera's acute pain.

Then Opa bellowed a deep, rumbly
"OY-YAH!" that left no doubt he was
now a member of the Core.

Clop Clop. Enry stomped proudly at
Sera's side prompting all parties before
her to slap their chests in unison.

Sera closed her eyes and took a deep
breath as her world went silent.

Badumbadum. Badumbadum....
Badumbadum. Badumbadum....

There was another sound. Like a
drumbeat, its powerful rhythm drew
Sera inward to consider herself, her
strengths, her plight and purpose.

She was audacious and ambitious
because she understood the magick of
ingenuity. She was wise because she
always made space for the truth, no
matter how uncomfortable it might be.
And she was confident because she'd
allowed herself to acknowledge, without shame, what denial and rote acceptance had cost her kin, the price of fear.

Sera opened her eyes and exhaled.
We are strong. I am ready:

"The Coven mined our sacred lands.
They tapped our sacred minds.
They seized the day, they seized your son,
And claimed they were divine.
They mollified with magick
While dark deeds went unchecked.
But when we rose to face the mirror,
The mirror did not reflect.
Our neighbors made their magick,
Rigged a game that they could own.
Well, I, for one, am furious,
And I am not alone.
We stormed their sea, seized back our day,
Split Sorcerer from throne.
From this day forth, our magick's source
Is none other than

home."

Kira Night

is an independent artist based out of Minnesota. The beauty of nature, the complexities of the human soul, and the nuanced spaces between good and evil are some of the primary inspirations behind her work.

Charles Armstrong

prefers to see the world as a kid might. During the pandemic, while parenting three kids of his own, he organized the Joy Scouts, a skills and achievements program for his pod. To honor Pixar's Up, he authored a complete, unofficial Wilderness Explorer handbook. When Charles isn't being a kid, he works at Google.

THE STORY CONTINUES WITH BOOK TWO